Each mission held surprises

Few, if any, ran exactly as the plans were drawn—in quiet moments, prior to contact with the enemy. Whether you called it chaos theory or the human element, it all came down to the same thing: variables that could never be anticipated.

Mack Bolan had stayed alive this long because he planned ahead and still retained the flexibility required to change his plans, adapt to any given situation that arose. Some day, he knew, the switch would be too fast for him, his enemy too deadly accurate, and that would be the end.

But hopefully, it wouldn't be this night.

He understood that there was too much riding on his mission to Colombia, too many lives at risk if he should fail. His own fate was of less concern to Bolan than the job at hand, but he could hardly carry out that job if he was dead.

That wasn't part of the plan.

Don Pendleton's Mack

Bolan®

Colony of Evil

A GOLD EAGLE BOOK FROM

WORLDWIDE®

TORONTO • NEW YORK • LONDON
AMSTERDAM • PARIS • SYDNEY • HAMBURG
STOCKHOLM • ATHENS • TOKYO • MILAN
MADRID • WARSAW • BUDAPEST • AUCKLAND

Recycling programs
for this product may
not exist in your area.

First edition January 2009

ISBN-13: 978-0-373-61527-8
ISBN-10:   0-373-61527-2

Special thanks and acknowledgment to
Mike Newton for his contribution to this work.

COLONY OF EVIL

Printed in U.S.A.

At least two-thirds of our miseries spring from human stupidity, human malice and those great motivators and justifiers of malice and stupidity, idealism, dogmatism and proselytizing zeal on behalf of religious or political idols.

—Aldous Huxley,
Tomorrow and Tomorrow and Tomorrow

Fanatics never learn. They never change. Defeat in argument or battle doesn't faze them. Time has no impact on their beliefs or tactics. When they go too far, the only thing that works is cleansing fire.

—Mack Bolan

To Senator James Webb, for courage under fire in Vietnam and Washington, D.C.

PROLOGUE

Park Avenue, New York City

The man had proved untouchable; his wife was not. The man—the real target—employed security devices and armed guards, remained inside his consulate whenever possible, and generally lived as if his life was constantly at risk.

In that belief, he was correct.

The trackers had considered sniper rifles, car bombs, even rocket launchers, but they ultimately realized that an assault against the consulate itself would likely guarantee their own deaths, while their target had a good chance of emerging from the blitz unscathed. They found that prospect unacceptable, and so adjusted their approach.

The target's wife was reasonably pretty, undeniably vivacious, and would not allow herself to be penned up inside drab walls simply because her husband was afraid. She had been hoping, even praying, for the diplomatic posting to New York, and she was not about to waste a moment of her golden opportunity. There were too many stores, boutiques, salons, spas, theaters, cafés—the list was endless, and she meant to try them all before they were recalled to Tel Aviv.

That afternoon she needed jewelry, and she refused to have samples delivered to the consulate. Why suffer a parade of fawning salesmen when she could go out and visit them, have lunch, enjoy herself in the heart of Manhattan?

The trackers watched and waited, mingling with the sidewalk crowd. They were dressed down to fit the setting, pass for tourists, and the woman's driver didn't seem to notice them.

Her single bodyguard was first to leave the jeweler's shop, scanning the street before he beckoned to his charge. The woman followed, carrying a small black satin bag and chatting, distracting her protector when he should have been alert.

The trackers moved together, one drawing a pistol, firing at the bodyguard from point-blank range, then spinning toward the black Mercedes at the curb and bouncing three rounds off its windshield. If the driver chose to save himself, he had to stay inside the car.

The second tracker pulled a clear glass bottle from his pocket, twisted off the cap and hurled its contents at the woman's startled, screaming face. The tone of her screams changed immediately, from a note of panic to soul-searing agony.

The trackers fled and within heartbeats had been swallowed by the crowd.

Sonora, Mexico

THE BUS HAD BROKEN DOWN again, which meant the tour would be late arriving at the stop in Hermosillo. The hotel was not a problem, and the Mexican tradition of late dining meant they wouldn't starve, but food was not Eli Dayan's primary focus.

He was tired of traveling and wondered why he'd let his wife persuade him that a Mexican vacation was a good idea.

The kibbutz where they lived was in a desert, and he'd flown halfway around the world to see more desert through the tinted windows of a bus that suffered some mechanical disruption every day, like clockwork. He was tired of cactus, tired of rural villages that seemed to be constructed out of mud and cast-off refuse, tired of drinking beer because he couldn't trust the water.

His bowels were grumbling, and he reckoned that he was about to suffer the revenge of Montezuma. It would make the last five days of their grand tour a misery, and something told him that his wife would never forgive him.

The bus was slowing. Mouthing a silent curse, Dayan wondered what the excuse would be this time. A flat tire? Had the lazy driver failed to fill the diesel tank that morning?

"What is this? Why are we stopping?" Hilda, his wife, asked him.

"How should I know?"

"Well, find out!"

"They'll tell us, if it's anything important."

They were stopped now, and he heard the front doors open with a hiss. Two men in military jackets, wearing black ski masks, stood near the driver. Both held rifles Dayan recognized as folding-stock Kalashnikovs.

"What is it! What's this all about!" Hilda demanded.

"Shut your mouth, woman, before you get us killed!"

On of the gunmen spoke, his accent strange to Dayan's ears. "Your trip ends here," he said, smiling behind the horizontal slit that showed his lips. "If you know any prayers, this is the time to call upon your god."

Miami Beach, Florida

THE DAY HAD STARTED WELL for Ira Margulies. He'd closed the deal on Morrow Island, all two hundred million dollars of it, and his personal commission was a cool three million. His clients on both sides of the transaction were well pleased, and he could almost smell the leather seats in the new Maserati that he planned to buy.

Who said a man of fiftysomething was too old to play with toys?

His brief stop at the strip mall on Dade Boulevard did not involve his business. It was strictly personal. The storefront that he entered, darting from his car at curbside to the swinging door through scalding tropic heat, was one of half a dozen mail drops where he kept post boxes under different names.

Why not? It was entirely legal, and the correspondence he received, while not fit for wife or children to peruse, made his days—and nights—more pleasant. After long days at the office, he enjoyed a little something on the side, and in these days of killer viruses, the safest sex of all was solitary.

He was out again in less than sixty seconds, carrying a package and six envelopes in his left hand. He barely registered the movement on his left, until a man's voice asked him, "Ira? Is that you?"

Margulies turned, already trying to concoct an explanation, but he did not recognize the speaker. Frowning, he was on the verge of a reply when the stranger produced a pistol, smiled and shot him in the chest.

Already dead before he hit the pavement, Ira Margulies had no thought of embarrassment about the package and the envelopes strewed all around him, soaking up his blood.

CHAPTER ONE

Bogotá, Colombia

Mack Bolan's Avianca flight was ninety minutes late on touchdown at El Dorado International Airport. It hadn't been the pilot's fault, but rather issues of "security" that slowed them. Bolan supposed that meant drugs or terrorism, possibly a mix of both.

For close to thirty years, throughout Colombia, it had been difficult to separate cocaine from politics. The major drug cartels bought politicians, judges, prosecutors, cops, reporters, and killed off the ones who weren't for sale. They backed right-wing militias that pretended to oppose crime while annihilating socialists and "liberals," occasionally using mercenary death squads as their front men to attack the government itself.

Colombian police had coined the term *narcoterrorism*, but they rarely spoke it out loud. To do so invited censure, demotion and transfer, perhaps an untimely death.

Back in the States, Bolan read stories all the time claiming that cocaine trafficking was up or down, strictly suppressed or thriving at an all-time high. He took it all with several hefty grains of salt and got his information from a handful of selected sources he could trust.

The traffic was continuing, and U.S. Customs seized approximately ten percent of the incoming coke on a good day. That figure had been static since the 1980s, with a few small fluctuations. Nothing that had happened in the interim—from cartel wars and Panamanian invasions to the bloody death of Pablo Escobar—had altered the reality of narcopolitics.

Drugs paid too much, across the board, for any government to halt the traffic absolutely. Narcodollars funded terrorism and black ops conducted by sundry intelligence agencies, bankrolled political careers and made retirement comfy for respected statesmen, greased the wheels of international diplomacy and commerce.

The filth was everywhere, and Bolan wasn't Hercules.

But he could clean one stable at a time.

Or, maybe, burn it down.

His latest mission to Colombia involved cocaine, but only in a roundabout and somewhat convoluted way. His main target was equally malignant, but much older, an abiding evil beaten more than once on bloody battlefields around the world, which still refused to die.

As Evil always did.

In spite of its delays, his flight down from Miami had been pleasant—or at least as pleasant as a flight could be when he was traveling unarmed toward mortal danger, with no clear idea of who might know that he was coming, or of how they might prepare to meet him on arrival.

First, there was the matter of his contact on the ground. The man came recommended by the CIA and DEA, which could spell trouble. Bolan knew those agencies were frequently at odds, despite the "War on Terror" and their separate oaths to operate within the law. One side was pledged to halt narcot-ics traffic by all legal means; the other frequently played fast and loose in murky realms where drugs were just another form of currency.

The fact that both sides found his contact useful raised a caution flag for Bolan, but it wouldn't make him drop out of the game. He'd worked with various informers, spooks and double agents in his time, and had outlived the great majority of them.

A few he'd killed himself.

So he would give this one a chance, but keep a sharp eye on him, every step along the way. One false step, and their partnership would be dissolved.

In blood.

Their first stop in the capital would have to be a covert arms merchant, someone who could supply Bolan with the essen-tial tools of his profession. That, he guessed, would be no problem in a nation whose homicide rate topped all the charts. That meant guns in abundance, and Bolan would soon have what he needed.

His bankroll would cover a week of high living, assuming the job took that long and he lived to complete it. The cash was a tax-free donation, furnished that morning by one of Miami's premier *bolita* bankers who'd decided, strictly from his heart and the desire to keep it beating, that he wouldn't miss $250,000 all that much.

Right now, Bolan supposed, the macho gambler's goons were scouring Dade County and environs for the man who'd dared to rob him, but they wouldn't find a trace. Bolan had played that game too often to leave tracks his enemies could follow—if, in fact, they had the stones to look him up in Bo-gotá.

And they would have to hurry, even then, because he didn't

plan on spending much time in the capital. Some shopping, some discreet interrogation, and he would be on his way. His target was not found in Bogotá, in Cali or in Medellín.

That would've been too easy.

Bolan couldn't smell the jungle yet, riding in pressurized and air-conditioned semicomfort, but he'd smelled it many times before. Not only in Colombia, but on five continents where Evil went by different names, wore different faces, always seeking the same ends.

Evil sought power and control, the same things politicians spent their lives pursuing. Which was not to say all politicians were dishonest, prone to wicked compromises in pursuit of private gain. Bolan acknowledged that there might be various exceptions to the rule.

He simply hadn't met them yet.

And something told him that he wouldn't find one on this trip.

JORGE GUZMAN WAS SMART enough to check the monitors, but waiting in the crowded airport terminal still made him nervous. El Dorado International's main terminal sprawled over 581,000 square feet and received more than nine million passengers per year. Toss in the families and friends who came to see them off or to meet them on arrival, thronging shops and restaurants and travel agencies, and visiting the airport was like strolling through a crowded town on market day.

Which made it difficult, if not impossible, for Guzman to detect if anyone was watching him, perhaps waiting to slip a knife between his ribs or to press a silenced, small-caliber pistol tight against his spine before they pulled the trigger.

Guzman had no special reason to believe that anyone would try to kill him here, this evening. He had been cautious in preparing for his new assignment, as he always was, informing no one of the covert jobs that came his way, but he had enemies.

It was inevitable, for a man who led a covert life. Guzman had been a thief and then a smuggler from his youngest days, but for the past eight years he'd also served the cloak-and-dagger lords of Washington, who paid so well for information if it brought results.

Guzman had started small, naming street dealers and some minor smugglers with the U.S. Drug Enforcement Administration, first obtaining their assurance that his name would never be revealed to any native law-enforcement officer or prosecutor under any circumstances. Some of them were honest, to be sure, but Guzman saw them as a critically endangered species, with their numbers dwindling every day.

As time went by and he became more confident, Guzman had traded information on the larger drug cartels. It was a dicey game that guaranteed a slow and screaming death if he was found out by the men he had betrayed. From there, since drugs touched everything of consequence throughout Colombia, it was a relatively short step to cooperating with the Central Intelligence Agency on matters political, sometimes helping the famous Federal Bureau of Investigation find a fugitive from justice in America.

But Guzman's latest job was something new and different. In the past, he'd kept his eyes and ears open, asked some discreet questions and sold the information he obtained for top dollar. This time, he was supposed to serve as guide and translator, helping a gringo agent carry out his mission, which had not been well explained.

It smelled of danger, and Guzman had nearly told his contacts to find someone else, perhaps a mercenary, but the money they offered had changed his mind. He was a mercenary, after all, in his own way.

Because he was concerned about the greater risks of this particular assignment, Guzman had been doubly careful on his long drive to the airport, glancing at his rearview mirror every quarter mile or so, detouring incessantly to see if anyone stayed with him through his aimless twists and turns.

But no one had.

Still, he was nervous, sweating through his polo shirt, beneath the blazer that he wore for dual reasons. First, it made him look more formal, more respectable, than if he'd shown up in shirtsleeves. Second, it concealed the Brazilian IMBEL 9GC-MD1 semiautomatic pistol wedged beneath his belt, against the small of his back.

The pistol was a copy of the old Colt M1911A1 pistol carried by so many U.S. soldiers through the years, rechambered for 9 mm Parabellum rounds. The magazine held seventeen, with one more in the chamber. Guzman wore it cocked and locked, prepared to fire when he released the safety with his thumb, instead of wasting precious microseconds when they mattered, pulling back the hammer.

He had a second pistol in his car, beneath the driver's seat. It was another IMBEL knock-off, this one chambered in the original .45ACP caliber. Guzman had considered carrying both guns into the terminal, but it had seemed excessive and he worried that his trousers might fall down.

A canned voice, sounding terminally bored, announced the long-delayed arrival of the Avianca flight Guzman had been awaiting for the past two hours. Since he did not have a ticket or a boarding pass, he would not be allowed to meet his party at the gate—but then, the pistol he was carrying made it impossible for him to clear security, in any case.

He found a place to watch and wait, between a café and a bookstore, lounging casually against the cool tile of the wall behind him. When the passengers began to straggle past security—ignored because they were arriving, not departing on an aircraft—Guzman studied faces, body types, seeking the man he was supposed to meet.

He had no photograph to guide him; it was too hush-hush for that. Instead he had been given a description of the gringo: six feet tall, around two hundred pounds, dark hair, olive complexion, military bearing. In case that wasn't good enough, the man would have a folded copy of that morning's *USA Today* in his left hand.

He watched a dozen gringos pass the gates, all businessmen of one sort or another. Guzman wondered how many had been aboard the aircraft, and was pondering a way to get that information if his man did not appear, when suddenly he saw an Anglo matching the description, carrying the proper newspaper.

The brief description from his contact had been accurate, but fell short in one respect. It made no mention of the gringo's air of confidence, said nothing of the chill that his blue eyes imparted when they made contact.

Guzman pushed off the wall and moved to intercept the stranger he'd been waiting for. Above all else, he hoped the gringo would not botch his job, whatever it turned out to be.

Guzman devoutly hoped the stranger would not get him killed.

BOLAN HAD MADE HIS CONTACT at a glance. Unlike the slim Colombian, he *had* been furnished with a photo of the stranger who would assist him in completion of his task.

He wasn't looking for a backup shooter when the job got hairy, just a navigator, translator and source of useful information on specific aspects of the local scene. If the informant Jorge Guzman could perform those tasks without jeopardizing Bolan's mission or his life, they ought to get along just fine.

If not, well, there were many ways to trim deadwood.

The man was coming at him, putting on a smile that didn't touch his wary eyes. He stuck a hand out, making Bolan switch his carry-on from right to left, crumpling the newspaper that was his recognition sign.

"Señor Cooper?" Guzman said, using Bolan's current alias.

Bolan accepted the handshake and said, "That's me. Mr. Guzman?"

"At your disposal. Shall we go retrieve your bags?"

A flex of Bolan's biceps raised the carry-on. "You're looking at them," he replied.

This time, the local's smile seemed more sincere. "Most excellent," he said. "This way for Immigration, then, and Customs. Have you any items to declare?"

"I travel light," Bolan replied.

The Immigration officer asked Bolan how long he was staying in Colombia and where he planned to travel, took his answers at face value and applied the necessary stamps to "Matthew Cooper's" passport. Customs saw his one small bag and didn't bother pawing through his socks and shaving gear.

They moved along the busy concourse toward a distant exit, Guzman asking questions. Bolan rejected offers of a meal, a drink, a currency exchange—the latter based upon his knowledge that one U.S. dollar equaled 2,172 Colombian pesos. He would've needed several steamer trunks to haul around the local equivalent of $250,000, and all for what?

The people he'd be meeting soon would either deal in dollars, or they wouldn't deal at all.

Those who refused the bribe, received the bullet—or the bomb, the blade, the strangling garrote. Death came in many forms, but it was always ugly, violent and absolutely final.

"My car is in the visitors' garage," Guzman informed him. "This way, if you please."

Bolan observed his usual precautions as they moved along the concourse, watching for anyone who stared too long or looked away too suddenly, avoiding eye contact. He caught no one observing their reflections in shop windows, kneeling suddenly to tie a loose shoestring or search through pockets for some nonexistent missing item as they passed.

Of course, he didn't know the players here in Bogotá. Those who had tried to take him out the last time he was here were all long dead.

It would be easier when they got out of town, he thought. The open road made them more difficult to track, and once he reached the forest, started hiking toward his final target, it would be his game, played by his rules.

Or so he hoped, at least.

Each mission held surprises. Few, if any, ran exactly as the plans were drawn in quiet moments, prior to contact with the enemy. Whether you called it Chaos Theory or the human element, it all came down to the same thing: variables that could never be anticipated.

Even psychic powers wouldn't help, if they existed, since most people in a crisis situation acted without thinking, running off on tangents, never stopping to consider what might happen if they turned left instead of right, sped up or slowed, cried out or bit their tongues.

Bolan had stayed alive this long because he planned ahead *and* still retained the flexibility required to change his plans, adapt to any given situation that arose. Someday, he knew, the switch would be too fast for him, his enemy too deadly accurate, and that would be the end.

But, hopefully, it wouldn't be this night.

The sun was setting as they left the airport terminal, but most of the day's humidity remained to slap him in the face like a wet towel. Bolan followed his contact from the blessed air-conditioning, across a sidewalk and eight lanes of traffic painted on asphalt, to reach the visitors' garage. Inside, Guzman led him to an elevator, pushed the button, waited for the car and took them up to the fifth level.

"Over here, *señor.*"

Guzman led Bolan toward a Fiat compact, navy blue, which Bolan guessed was three or four years old. Inside it, Bolan pushed his seat back all the way, to make room for his legs.

"You need certain equipment, yes?" Guzman asked as he slid into the driver's seat.

"That's right."

"Is all arranged," Guzman replied, and put the car in gear.

"THEY'RE CLEARING THE GARAGE right now," Horst Krieger said, speaking into his handheld two-way radio. "Be ready when they pass you."

"Yes, sir!" came the response from Arne Rauschman in the second car. No further conversation was required.

"Get after them!" snapped Krieger to his driver, Juan Pacheco. "Not too close, but keep the car in sight."

"*Sí, señor,*" the driver said as he put the Volkswagen sedan in gear and rolled out in pursuit of Krieger's targets.

Krieger thought it was excessive, sending eight men to deal with the two strangers he had briefly glimpsed as they'd driven past, but he never contested orders from his commander. Such insubordination went against the grain for Krieger, and it was the quickest way that he could think of to get killed.

Besides, he thought as they pursued the Fiat compact, Rauschman's six-year-old Mercedes falling in behind the Volkswagen, if they faced any opposition from the targets, he could use the native hired muscle as cannon fodder, let them take the brunt of it, while he and Rauschman finished off the enemy.

The Fiat quite predictably took Avenida El Dorado from the airport into Bogotá. It was the city's broadest, fastest highway, crossing on an east-west axis through the heart of Colombia's capital.

It was early evening, with traffic at its peak, and Krieger worried that his driver might lose the Fiat through excessive caution.

"Faster!" he demanded "Close that gap! We're covered by the other traffic here. Stay after them!"

He waited for the standard *"Sí, señor,"* and frowned when it was not forthcoming. He would have to teach Pacheco some respect, but now was clearly not the time. The Volkswagen surged forward, gaining on the Fiat, while cars that held no interest for Krieger wove in and out of the lanes between them.

Krieger turned in his seat, feeling the bite of his shoulder harness, the gouge of his Walther P-88 digging into his side as he craned for a view of Rauschman's Mercedes. There it was, three cars back, holding steady.

At least, with a real soldier in each vehicle, the peasants he was forced to use as personnel would not give up and wander off somewhere for a siesta in the middle of the job. Krieger would see to that, and Rauschman could be trusted to control his crew, regardless of their innate failings.

Krieger couldn't really blame them, after all. The peasants had been born inferior, and there was nothing they could do to change that fact, no matter how hard they might try.

But they could follow orders, to a point. Drive cars. Point guns. Pull triggers. What else were they good for? Why else even let them live?

Horst Krieger would be pleased to kill the two men he was following, although he'd never met them in his life and knew nothing about them. One of them looked Aryan, or possibly

Italian, but the race alone meant nothing. There was also attitude, philosophy and politics to be considered.

All those who opposed the sacred cause must die.

Some sooner, as it happened, than the rest.

Speaking across his shoulder, Krieger told the two Colombians seated behind him, "Be ready, on my command."

He heard the harsh click-clack of automatic weapons being cocked, and felt compelled to add, "Don't fire until I say, and then be certain of your target."

"No civilians," one of them responded. *"Sí, señor."*

"I don't care shit about civilians," Krieger answered. "But if one of you shoots *me,* I swear, that I'll strangle you with your own guts before I die."

The backseat shooters took him seriously, as they should have. Krieger meant precisely what he said.

Rauschman's two gunners in the second car would have their weapons primed by now, as well, although the order had to come from Krieger, and he hadn't found his kill zone yet. It might be best if they could pass the target vehicle on Calle 26, he thought, but then he wondered if it would be wiser to delay and follow them onto a smaller and less-crowded surface street.

Something to think about.

"You're losing him!" Krieger barked, and the Volkswagen gained speed. Still no response from Juan Pacheco at the wheel.

That bit of insubordination would be more expensive than the driver realized. When they were finished with the job and safely back at headquarters, he had a date with Krieger and a hand-crank generator that was guaranteed to keep him on his toes.

Or writhing on the floor in agony.

The prospect made Horst Krieger smile, though on his finely sculpted face, the simple act of smiling had the aspect of a grimace. No one facing that expression would find any mirth in it, or anything at all to put their minds at ease.

"You see the signal?"

Up ahead, the Fiat's amber left-turn signal light was flashing, as the driver veered across two lanes of traffic. He did not wait for the cars behind him to slow and make room in their lanes, but simply charged across in front of them, as if the signal would protect him from collisions.

Krieger's wheelman cursed in Spanish and roared off in pursuit of their intended victims. Angry horns blared after them, but Pacheco paid them no heed.

Krieger considered warning Rauschman, but a backward glance told him that the Mercedes was already changing lanes, accelerating into the pursuit. Rauschman would not presume to pass Krieger's VW, but neither would he let the marks escape.

"Stay after them!" Krieger snarled. "Your life is forfeit if they get away."

"WE HAVE A TAIL," Bolan said, turning to confirm what he'd already seen in his side mirror. Two cars, several lengths behind them, had swerved rapidly to match Guzman's lane change.

"Maybe coincidence," Guzman said as his dark eyes flickered back and forth between his rearview mirror and the crowded lanes in front of him.

"Maybe," Bolan replied, but he wasn't buying it. The nearest off-ramp was a mile or more ahead of them. Commuters would already know their exits. Tourists new to Bogotá would have their noses buried in guidebooks or street maps, and the odds that two of them would suddenly change lanes together without need were minuscule.

"You wouldn't have a gun, by any chance?" Bolan asked. "Just to tide me over, through our little shopping trip."

"Of course, *señor,*" his guide replied, and reached beneath his driver's seat, drawing a pistol from some hidey-hole and handing it to Bolan.

Bolan recognized the IMBEL 45GC-MD1. He checked the chamber, found a round already loaded, pulled the magazine and counted fourteen more.

It could be worse.

Most .45s had straight-line magazines, and thus surrendered five to seven rounds on average to the staggered-box design employed by most 9 mm handguns. IMBEL had contrived a way to keep the old Colt's knock-down power while increasing its capacity and sacrificing none of the prototype's rugged endurance.

Bolan wished he might've had a good assault rifle instead, or at the very least a few spare magazines, but he was armed, and so felt vastly better than he had a heartbeat earlier.

"Two cars, you think?" Guzman asked.

Bolan looked again, in time to see a third change lanes, some thirty yards behind the second chase car. "Two, at least," Bolan replied. "There might be three."

"I took every precaution!" Guzman said defensively. "I swear, I was not followed."

It was no time to start an argument. "Maybe they knew where you were going," Bolan replied.

"How? I told no one!"

Grasping at straws, Bolan suggested, "We can check the car for GPS transmitters later. Right now, think of somewhere to take them without risking any bystanders."

"There's no such place in Bogotá, *señor!*"

"Calm down and reconsider. Last time I passed through town, there was a warehouse district, there were parks the decent people stayed away from after dark, commercial areas where everyone punched out at six o'clock."

"Well...*sí.* Of course, we have such places."

"Find one," Bolan suggested. "And don't let those chase cars pull alongside while we're rolling, if you have a choice."

"Would you prefer a warehouse or—"

"It's your town," Bolan cut him off. "I don't care if you flip a coin. Just do it now."

His tone spurred Guzman to a choice, although the driver kept it to himself. No matter. Bolan likely wouldn't recognize street names, much less specific addresses, if Guzman offered him a running commentary all the way.

Bolan wanted results, and he would judge his guide's choice by the outcome of the firefight that now seemed a certainty.

Headlights behind the Volkswagen sedan showed Bolan four men in the vehicle. He couldn't see their backlit faces, and would not have recognized them anyway, unless they'd been featured in the photo lineup he'd viewed before leaving Miami. Still, he knew the enemy by sight, by smell, by intuition.

Even if the dark Mercedes and the smaller car behind it, which had changed lanes last, were wholly innocent, Bolan still had four shooters on his tail, almost before he'd scuffed shoe leather on their native soil. That was a poor start to his game, by any standard, and he had to deal with them as soon as possible.

If he could capture one alive, for questioning, so much the better. But he wasn't counting on that kind of break, and wouldn't pull his punches when the bloodletting began.

"All right, I know a place," Guzman announced. "We take the first road on our left, ahead."

"Suits me," Bolan replied. "Sooner's better than later."

"You think that they will try to kill us?"

"They're not the welcoming committee," Bolan said. "Whether they want us dead or spilling everything we know, it doesn't work for me."

"There will be shooting, then?"

"I'd say you could bet money on it."

"Very well."

Guzman took one hand off the steering wheel, leaned forward and retrieved a pistol from his waistband, at the back. It was another IMBEL, possibly a twin to Bolan's .45, although he couldn't tell without a closer look. Guzman already had it cocked and locked. He left the safety on and wedged the gun beneath his right leg and the cushion of the driver's seat.

"We're ready now, I think," he said.

"We're getting there," Bolan replied. "We need our place, first."

"Soon," Guzman assured him, speaking through a worried look that didn't show much confidence. "Three miles, I think. If we are still alive."

CHAPTER TWO

"It's your ass if they get away!" Horst Krieger snapped at Juan Pacheco.

"Sí, señor."

"But not too close!"

"Okay."

It didn't matter if his orders were confusing. Krieger thought the driver understood their need to keep the target vehicle in sight, without alarming their intended victims and precipitating a high-speed chase through the heart of Bogotá that would attract police.

Another backward glance showed Krieger that his backup car, with Arne Rauschman navigating, had followed them down the off-ramp from Avenida El Dorado. Krieger was surprised to see a third car exiting, as well—or fourth, if he counted his target—but he dismissed the fact as mere coincidence.

Some eight million people lived in Bogotá. Many more commuted to jobs in the city from outlying towns, and Krieger supposed that thousands arrived at the airport each day, for business or pleasure. It was no surprise, no cause for concern, that four cars should exit the city's main highway at any given point.

"Where are they going?" Krieger asked, and instantly regretted it.

"I couldn't say, *señor,*" Pacheco answered.

Was the bastard smirking at him? Krieger felt a sudden urge to smash his driver's face, but knew such self-indulgence would derail his mission.

He drew the Walther pistol from its holster, holding it loosely in his right hand, stroking the smooth polished slide with his left. A simple action, but he felt some of the pent-up tension draining from him, as if it was transferred to the weapon in his hand.

The better to unleash hell on his enemies, when it was time.

Krieger had not bothered to memorize the streets of Bogotá, but he knew his way around the city. He could name the twenty "localities" of the great city's Capital District and find them on a map, if need be. He knew all the major landmarks, plus the home addresses of those who mattered in his world. As for the rest, Krieger could read a map or tell his driver where to take him.

But uncertainty displeased him, and whatever happened to displease Horst Krieger also made him angry.

He was angry now.

He couldn't tell if those he followed knew that he was trailing them, or if the exit off of Calle 26 had been their destination in the first place. And, in either case, he didn't know where they were going at the moment, whether to a private residence, a restaurant or other public place, perhaps some rendezvous with other enemies, of whom Krieger was unaware.

The latter prospect worried Krieger most. He was prepared to stop and kill his targets anywhere that proved convenient, both in terms of an efficient execution and a clean escape. However, if he led his team into a trap, the eight of them might be outnumbered and outgunned.

Another backward glance showed Rauschman in the second car, holding position a half block behind the Volkswagen. Another car trailed Rauschman's, hanging back a block or so, but Krieger couldn't say with any certainty that it was the same car he'd seen departing Avenida El Dorado.

Ahead, his quarry made a left turn, drove two blocks, then turned off to his right. Krieger's Volkswagen followed, leading the Mercedes-Benz. Unless the bastard at the wheel was drunk or stupid, he had to know by now that he was being followed.

Still, there came no burst of speed, no sudden zigzag steering into alleys or running against the traffic on one-way streets. If the target did know he was marked, he appeared not to care.

"I think he goes to Puenta Aranda, *señor,*" Pacheco said.

"You think?"

"We're almost there."

And Krieger realized that he was right. Ahead, he recognized the fringe of Bogotá's industrial corridor, where factories produced much of the city's—and the nation's—textiles, chemicals, metal products and processed foods.

It was not a residential district, though Krieger supposed people lived there, as everywhere else in the city. There would be squatters, street people and beggars, the scum of the earth. Conversely, Krieger knew that some of the factories operated around the clock, which meant potential witnesses to anything that happened there, regardless of the time.

Too bad it wasn't Christmas or Easter, the two days each year when the church-enslaved peasants were granted relief. On either of those "holy" days, Krieger could have killed a hundred men in plain sight, with no one the wiser until they returned the next morning.

This night, he would have to take care.

"Move in closer," he ordered. "They must know we're here, anyway."

Palming the two-way radio, he told Rauschman, "Be ready when I move. I'll choose the spot, then box them in."

"Yes, sir," came the laconic answer.

"There!" he told Pacheco, pointing. "Can you overtake them and—"

Without the slightest warning, Krieger's prey suddenly bolted, tires squealing into a reckless left-hand turn, and sped into the darkened gap between two factories.

"Goddamn it! After them!"

BOLAN WAS BRACED and ready when he saw the opening he wanted, aimed an index finger to the left, and told Guzman, "In there! Hit it!"

Guzman was good behind the wheel. Not NASCAR-good, perhaps, but so far he had followed orders like a pro and handled his machine with total competency. Even on the unexpected left-hand turn, he kept all four tires on the road and lost only a little rubber to acceleration, in the stretch.

Great factories loomed over them on either side, their smoke stacks belching toxic filth into the sky. Bolan had no idea what kind of products either plant produced. It had no relevance to his survival in the next few minutes, so he put it out of mind.

"We're looking for a place to stand and fight," he told Guzman. "Some cover and some combat stretch."

"What is this *stretch?*"

"I mean some room to move. So we're not pinned, boxed in."

"Of course."

Bolan had leafed through Guzman's dossier, the one provided by the DEA, but it had said nothing about his fighting ability. He carried guns, but so did many other people who had no idea what it was like to kill a man or even draw a piece in self-defense. He might freeze up, or waste all of his ammunition in the first few seconds, without hitting anyone.

Bolan would have to wait and see.

"There is a slaughterhouse ahead," Guzman informed him. "On the railroad line. Beside it is a tannery. I think they may be what you're looking for, *señor.*"

"Let's take a look," Bolan replied. "And call me Matt, since we're about to get bloody together."

"Bloody?" Guzman asked.

"Figure of speech."

"Ah." Guzman didn't sound convinced.

Two sets of headlights trailed the Fiat through its final turn. No, make that three. The final car in line was playing catch-up, running just a bit behind.

"Sooner is better," Bolan told Guzman.

As if in answer to his words, a muzzle-flash erupted from the passenger's side of the leading chase car. The initial burst was hasty, not well aimed, but Bolan knew they would improve with practice.

"Are they shooting at us?" Guzman asked, sounding surprised.

"Affirmative. We're running out of time."

"Hang on!"

With only that as warning, Guzman cranked hard on the Fiat's wheel and put them through a rubber-squealing left-hand turn. At first, Bolan thought he was taking them into some kind of parking lot, but then he saw lights far ahead and realized it was a narrow access road between the leather plant and yet another factory, much like its neighbor in the darkness, when its lighted windows were the only things that showed.

Somewhere behind him, Bolan thought that he heard the hopeless cries of cattle being herded into slaughter pens. It seemed appropriate, but did nothing to lighten Bolan's mood.

"We still need—"

Guzman interrupted him without a spoken word, spinning the wheel again, feet busy with the gas pedal, the clutch, the brake. He took them through a long bootlegger's turn, tires crying out in protest as they whipped through a 180-degree rotation and wound up facing toward their pursuers.

"Is there 'stretch' enough?" Guzman asked.

Bolan glanced to either side, saw waste ground stretching off into the night. The hulks of cast-off vehicles and large machines waiting for someone to remove them sat like gargoyles, casting shadows darker than the night itself.

"We'll find out in a second," Bolan said. "Give them your brights and find some cover."

Leaping from the vehicle, Bolan ran to his right and crouched behind a generator easily as tall as he was, eight or ten feet long. Approaching headlights framed the Fiat, glinting off its chrome, but the pursuers would've lost Bolan as soon as he was off the pavement.

As for Guzman…

Bolan heard the crack of a 9 mm Parabellum pistol, saw the muzzle-flash from Guzman's side of the Fiat. Downrange, there came the sound of glass breaking, and one of the onrushing headlights suddenly blacked out.

Not bad, if that was Guzman's aim, but would he do as well with human targets that returned fire, with intent to kill?

Bolan supposed he'd find out any moment, now, and in the meantime he was moving, looking for a vantage point that would surprise his enemies while still allowing him substantial cover.

He assumed that some of them, at least, had seen him breaking toward their left, his right. He couldn't help that, but he didn't have to make it easy for them, either, popping up where they'd expect a frightened man to stand and fight.

Fear was a part of what he felt. No soldier who was sane ever completely lost that feeling when the bullets started flying, but he'd never given in to fear, let it control or paralyze him.

Fear, if properly controlled, made soldiers smart, kept them from being reckless when it did no good. The mastery of fear prevented them from freezing up, permitted them to risk their lives selectively, when it was time to do or die.

Like now.

"HE'S TURNING! Watch it!"

Krieger realized that he was shouting at Pacheco, but the driver didn't seem to hear or understand him. How could the pathetic creature not see what was happening two hundred yards in front of him?

After its left-hand turn down another dark and narrow access road between two factories, the target vehicle had first accelerated, then spun through a racing turn that left its headlights pointing toward Krieger's two-car caravan. At first, he thought the crazy bastard was about to charge head-on, but then he realized the other car had stopped. Its headlights blazed to high beams, briefly blinding him, as doors flew open on both sides.

"They're getting out! Watch— There! And there!

He pointed, but Pacheco and the idiots seated behind him didn't seem to understand. Pacheco held the wheel steady, but he was slowing as he approached the stationary vehicle they had followed from the airport.

"Christ! Will you be careful?"

Even as he spoke, a shot rang out and Krieger raised an arm to shield his face. The bullet drilled his windshield, clipped the rearview mirror from its post, but missed all four of those who occupied the Volkswagen.

"Get out, damn you!" he snapped at no one in particular, and flung his own door open, using it for cover as he rolled out of the car.

It wasn't perfect, granted. Anyone who took his time and aimed could probably hit Krieger in the feet or lower legs—even a ricochet could cripple him—but all he needed was a little time to find himself a better vantage point.

He could've fired the Walther blindly, made a run for it, but Krieger hated wasting any of the pistol's sixteen rounds. He had two extra magazines but hadn't come prepared for any kind of siege and wanted every shot to count.

Both of his riflemen were firing now, short bursts from their CZ2000 Czech assault rifles. They had the carbine version, eighteen inches overall with wire butts folded, each packing a drum magazine with seventy-five 5.56 mm NATO rounds. The little guns resembled sawed-off AK-47s, but in modern times had been retooled to readily accept box magazines from the American M-16 rifle, as well as their own standard loads.

The CZ2000 fired at a cyclic rate of 800 rounds per minute, but Krieger and Rauschman had drilled the *mestizos* on conserving ammunition, firing aimed and measured bursts in spite of any panic they might feel. So far, it seemed they were remembering their lessons, taking turns as they popped up behind the Volkswagen and stitched holes in the Fiat.

Krieger saw his chance and made his move, sprinting into the midnight darkness of a field directly to his right. He'd seen enough in the periphery of headlights to determine that the field was presently a dumping ground for out-of-date or broken-down equipment. Krieger reckoned he could use the obstacles for cover.

As he crept along through dusty darkness, eardrums echoing to gunfire, Krieger took stock of his advantages. He had eight men, himself included, against two. As far as he could tell, his weapons were superior to those his enemies possessed. He should be able to destroy them without difficulty.

Now, the disadvantages, which every canny soldier had to

keep in mind. Krieger was unfamiliar with the battleground, and he could see no better in the darkness than his adversaries could. Night-vision goggles would've helped, but how was he to know that they'd be needed?

Another deficit: his men, with one exception—Arne Rauschman—were *mestizos*, capable of murder but indifferent as soldiers. They obeyed Krieger and his superiors from greed, fear, or a combination of the two. Still, if their nerve broke and their tiny peasant minds were gripped by fear, they might desert him.

Not if I can kill them first, he thought, then focused once again on his hasty Plan B.

Plan A had been to trail the targets, find a place to kill them without drawing any real attention to his team and do the job efficiently. Now that the basic scheme was shot to hell, he needed an alternative that wasn't based entirely on the prowess of his personnel.

Plan B had Krieger circling around behind his targets, looking for an angle of attack while Rauschman and the six *mestizos* kept them busy. Now that he considered it, already on the move, it might have been a better scheme with Rauschman circling to the left, a pincers movement, but that hadn't come to Krieger in his haste.

Besides, he needed someone with the peasants, to make sure they didn't drop their guns and run away.

More shooting, as he edged around the rusty housing of a bulky cast-off air-conditioner. He marveled at the things some people threw away, while others in the country lived in cardboard shanties or had no roof overhead.

Gripping his pistol in both hands, he was about to edge around the far end of the obstacle when more headlights lit up the scene behind him. Turning, half-expecting the police or some kind of security patrol, Krieger saw a fourth civilian car, convertible, slide to a halt some thirty yards behind Rauschman's Mercedes.

Who in hell...?

But Krieger's mind rebelled at what he saw next.

A young woman, pretty at a glance, leaped from the convertible without resort to doors.

Clutching a pistol in her hand.

BOLAN ALSO OBSERVED the fourth car's entry to the battle zone and saw its lights go out as someone vaulted from the driver's seat. He had no clear view of the new arrival, but it seemed to be a single person, no great wave of reinforcements for his enemy.

Whoever they were.

Bolan had his IMBEL autoloader cocked and ready as he circled to his left around the bulky generator. It was shielding him from hostile fire, but it also prevented him from taking any active part in the firefight. To join the battle, he had to put himself at risk.

Same old, same old.

Erratic gunfire—pistol shots, full-auto bursts, a shotgun blast—and he wondered whether Guzman had already fled the scene on foot. Bolan could hardly blame him, if he had, but he still hoped his guide and translator was made of stronger stuff than that.

Leaving the generator's cover, moving toward what seemed to be an air-conditioner, he glimpsed the fourth car's driver rising from the murk behind his vehicle and squeezing off to shots in rapid-fire.

Another pistol, aiming...where?

It almost seemed as if the new arrival fired toward the pursuit cars, rather than toward Guzman's vehicle. Bolan dismissed it as an optical illusion, knowing Guzman had no allies here this night, except Bolan himself.

He started forward, cleared another corner, and immediately saw one of the hostiles standing ten or fifteen feet in front of him. Blond hair, as far as he could tell, and military bearing, minus a defensive crouch.

Take him alive for questioning, Bolan thought, but instantly dismissed the notion as too risky. He had nine guns against himself and Guzman. Playing games with any of his adversaries at the moment was an invitation to disaster.

Bolan raised his IMBEL .45 and shot the stranger in his back, high up between the shoulder blades. It wasn't "fair" by Hollywood standards, but Bolan wasn't in a movie and he couldn't do another take if anything went wrong.

At that range, if the .45 slug stayed intact, he was expecting lethal damage to the spine and heart. If it fragmented, jagged chunks might also pierce the lungs and the aorta.

Either way, it was a kill.

His target dropped facedown into the dust, quivered for something like a second, then lay still. Bolan approached him cautiously, regardless, thankful that the dead man's comrades couldn't see him for the bulk of old equipment strewed between them.

Bolan rolled the body over, saw the ragged exit wound and looked no further.

One down, eight to go.

How long before police arrived? He guessed that it was noisy in the factories surrounding him, but someone would be passing by or working near an open window, maybe pacing off the grounds on night patrol. Even in Bogotá, where murders were a dime a dozen, someone would report a pitched battle in progress.

But until the cops showed up, he had a chance to win it and escape.

A sudden escalation in the nearby gunfire startled Bolan. First, he feared the hunters had grown weary of their siege and had decided it was time to rush the Fiat, throwing everything they had into the charge. As Bolan moved to get a clear view of the action, though, he found something entirely different happening.

Two of the hostile shooters—make it three, now—had stopped firing at the Fiat and had turned to face the opposite direction. Bolan checked the access road, saw nothing but the last car to arrive—and then he understood.

The driver of the sleek convertible wasn't a member of the hunting party: he was something else entirely, and he *had* been firing at the chase cars, rather than at Guzman.

Why? Who was it?

Bolan couldn't answer either of those questions in the middle of a gunfight, but he recognized a universal truth.

The enemy of my enemy is my friend.

The strange diversion gave him hope and opportunity.

The Executioner had never wasted either in his life.

JORGE GUZMAN WAS FIGHTING for his life, and he was hopelessly confused. He couldn't figure out how anyone had tracked him to the airport, but it wouldn't matter if the gunmen killed him in this filthy place, with rank pollution blotting out the stars above.

He also didn't understand why a strange woman in a car he didn't recognize had joined the fight, apparently on his side. It defied all reason, made Guzman question whether he was hallucinating, until one of his opponents stopped a bullet from the woman's gun and crumpled to the ground.

Don't think about it! Guzman told himself. Just stay alive!

That was no small task, in itself, with eight men—seven,

now—intent on blasting him with automatic weapons, pistols and at least one shotgun. Even in his near panic, Guzman could recognize the sounds of different weapons, picturing what each in turn would do to him if he was hit.

Flesh torn, bones shattered, blood jetting from wounds to drain him dry in minutes flat. Maybe he'd suffer every agonizing second of it, or a bullet to the brain might grant him swift release.

Guzman peeked out, around the Fiat's left-rear fender, and fired two shots toward the nearest of the enemies who'd pinned him down. He guessed the shots were wasted, since the two men he'd been hoping to deter immediately answered him with rapid fire.

Bastards!

As far as Guzman knew, he hadn't even wounded one of them, although he'd been the first to fire a shot. God knew it hadn't helped him, but at least he'd had a fleeting moment when he almost felt courageous, capable of anything.

Now that the grim truth of his situation was apparent, he could only wonder who the woman was, and what had happened to the tall American.

It seemed impossible that Matt Cooper had simply run away and left Guzman to fight alone. He had to have had some strategy, but so far—

Even with the other din, Guzman picked out a gunshot from one side, off in the dark field to his right. Cooper had run in that direction when the Fiat came to rest, not long ago in real-world time, although it felt like hours with the bullets snapping past Guzman.

He wondered if his car would ever run again, after the hits that it had taken and was taking, even now. He doubted it. Cars were such fragile things, despite their bulk and high price tags. A single loose wire ruined everything, and now his little ride was taking bullets like a target in a shooting gallery, most of them through the hood and grille.

Stranded, he thought, then almost laughed out loud.

What did it matter if his car was broken down when Guzman died? Where did he plan on driving, with his brains blown out?

That image made him angry, spurred his need to fight and leave the other bastards bloody, hurting, when he fell at last. Blazing away from cover, Guzman emptied his pistol's magazine and actually thought he'd seen one of his targets fall before the weapon's slide locked open on an empty chamber and he fumbled to reload.

He slapped his next-to-last clip into the receiver, knowing that it might as well have been the very last, since he would never have a chance to take the third one from his pocket. Once he rose, exposed himself, and charged the hostile guns, his life span would be timed in nanoseconds.

Still, the Latin concept of machismo said he had to do something, take some action that did not involve hiding and waiting for the enemy to root him out. If he had to die this night, at least it would be as a man and not a cringing worm.

Guzman lunged to his feet, snarling through clenched teeth as he felt the air ripple with bullets zipping past him. One of them would find him soon, but in the meantime he was firing, choosing targets, giving each in turn the double-tap that a policeman friend had taught him at the firing range. Advancing without hope that he would see another sunrise.

And, incredibly, his enemies fell back from Guzman's wrath, reeling as his rounds sought their flesh and blood. It didn't quell the hostile fire, but at the very least it spoiled their aim, sent some of the incoming bullets high and wide.

Amazing!

Guzman bellowed at them now, his rage echoing to the

sounds of gunfire. He was vaguely conscious of new weapons firing on his left and right, joining their voices to his IMBEL's hammering reports, and while he knew one of them had to be Cooper's pistol, one of them the unknown woman's, Guzman felt as if he had the battlefield all to himself, charging his enemies with more courage than common sense.

The bullet, when it found him, had the impact of a giant mailed fist, slamming viciously into the side of Guzman's skull. He staggered, felt the earth slip out from underneath his feet, then saw it rush to meet him in a wave of darkness as he fell.

BOLAN SAW GUZMAN DROP but couldn't help him at the moment. Only finishing their other adversaries would allow him to examine, and perhaps to treat, his contact's wounds. Meanwhile, he also had to figure out who else had joined the fight, and why a total stranger would risk death to help him.

Nothing made sense yet, in the chaotic moment, and he couldn't stop to mull it over while five or six gunmen were trying to kill him.

Bolan circled toward the Benz through darkness, ready with the IMBEL .45 for anyone who challenged him. His first clear shot, after the blonde he'd left behind him in the junkyard, was a short and swarthy shooter with some kind of AK-looking weapon, firing from a fat drum magazine.

The gunner didn't see him coming, likely never knew what hit him when a single round from Bolan's autoloader drilled his skull behind the right ear, dropping him as if he was a puppet with its strings cut.

Forward from the crumpled corpse, between the dark Mercedes and the Volkswagen, three shooters bobbed and weaved, rising to fire at Guzman's Fiat, crouching again for someone else's turn. Two of them had the same short rifles as the man

Bolan had killed a heartbeat earlier; the third carried a sleek pump-action shotgun with extended magazine.

Bolan came in behind them, wasted no time on a warning, caught one of them turning to investigate the sound of his last shot. He drilled that shooter through the left eye, swung a few feet to his left and gave the survivor a double-tap before the target realized that anything was wrong.

The shotgunner was turning, quicker than the others, ratcheting his weapon's slide-action. Bolan wasn't sure that he could beat the other man's reflexes, but it didn't matter.

From Bolan's left, a gunshot sounded, and the side of his adversary's head appeared to vaporize. The dead man standing looked surprised, but if the killing shot had caused him any pain, it didn't register in his expression. He stood rock-still for a few heartbeats, then folded at the knees and toppled over backward, sprawling on the pavement.

Bolan had already swiveled toward the source of that last shot, the IMBEL automatic following his gaze. The woman who had saved his life—he saw her clearly now, and there could be no question of her femininity—held up an open hand, as if to block his shot, then nodded toward the other gunmen who were still blasting at Guzman's car.

Split-second life-or-death decisions were a combat soldier's stock-in-trade. Bolan made his and nodded, turning from the woman who could just as easily have killed him then, returning his whole focus to their common enemy.

Bolan had no idea where she had come from, who she was, or why she'd risk her life to help him in the middle of a firefight, but those questions had to wait. There would be time enough for talk if both of them survived the next few minutes.

Part of Bolan's mind, condemned to deal with practicalities, wondered if he'd need Guzman to translate his conversation with the woman. And if Guzman died, how in the hell would they communicate?

Focusing once again on here and now, Bolan moved up toward the Volkswagen, with the woman flanking on his left. As far as he could see, two gunmen still remained. One was a short *mestizo* like most of the others, while the second was a dirty-blond white boy, stamped from the same mold as the one Bolan had left behind him, in the waste ground.

Bolan took the shooter nearest to him, offered no alerts or other chivalrous preliminaries as he found his mark and drilled the rifleman between his shoulder blades. The gunner went down firing, stitching holes across the trunk of the Volkswagen, while his Nordic-looking partner ducked and covered.

Rising from his crouch, the sole survivor caught sight of the woman first, and raised his pistol to confront her. She was faster, snapping off three rounds in rapid fire, stamped a pattern on her target's chest and slammed him to the ground.

Bolan advanced with caution, made sure that the dead were all they seemed to be, then took another risk and let the woman have a clear shot at his back, while he ran to examine Jorge Guzman's wounds.

Guzman was grappling back to consciousness as Bolan reached him, tried to raise his pistol, but he didn't have the strength to stop Bolan from taking it away. Blood bathed the left side of his face and stained the collar of his shirt.

"Wha-What? Am I… Are we…?"

Bolan examined him and said, "You've got a nasty graze above your left ear, but the bone's not showing. Scalp wounds bleed a lot. It doesn't mean you're dying."

"Not…dead?"

"Not even close," Bolan replied. "You may need stitches, though."

"Hospital…no…report…."

"I can take care of him," a new voice said from Bolan's left. He glanced up at the woman as she nodded toward Guzman. "I've stitched up worse than that, believe me."

Bolan helped Guzman to his shaky feet and held him upright, left hand on the other man's right arm. It left his gun hand free as he turned toward the woman, saying, "Maybe we should start with names."

"Of course," she said. "I'm Gabriella Cohen, and I work for the Mossad. We share, I think, a common goal."

CHAPTER THREE

Two days earlier, Northern Virginia

The Blue Ridge Mountains looked entirely different from the air than they appeared to earthbound motorists and hikers. Bolan was reminded of that fact each time he flew to Stony Man Farm.

Airborne, he always tried to picture how the area had looked before the first human arrived, despoiling it with axes, saws and plows, road graders and the rest. Sometimes Bolan thought he was close, but then the pristine image always wavered, faded and was gone.

Maybe next time, he thought.

The Hughes 500 helicopter was a four-seater, but Bolan and the pilot had it to themselves.

On any graduated scale of secrecy, the Farm and its activities would rank above "Top Secret," somewhere off the chart. From day one, Stony Man's assignment—seeking justice by extraordinary, often extralegal means—had been one of the deepest, darkest secrets of the U.S. government. Beside it, aliens at Roswell and the stealth experiments performed at

Nevada's Area 51 paled into insignificance. Aside from on-site personnel and agents in the field, only a handful of Americans knew Stony Man existed.

Fewer still knew the extent of what it did, had done and might do in the future.

At its birth, the concept had been simple: organize a unit that, when necessary, in the last extremity, would set the U.S. Constitution and established laws aside to deal with urgent threats and/or to punish those whose skill at gliding through the system made them constant threats to civilized society at large.

Some might have called it vigilante justice; others, sheer necessity. In either case, it worked because the operation wasn't public, wasn't influenced by politics, and didn't choose its targets based on race or creed or any factor other than their danger to humanity. Sometimes, Bolan thought it was more like dumping toxic waste.

"Ten minutes," the pilot said, as if Bolan didn't know exactly where they were, tracking the course of Skyline Drive, a thousand feet above the treetops. Cars passing below them looked like toys, the scattered hikers more like ants. If any of the hardy souls on foot looked up or waved at Bolan's chopper, his eyes couldn't pick them out.

Bolan had been wrapping up a job in Canada when Hal Brognola called and asked him for a meeting at the Farm. Quebec was heating up, with biker gangs running arms across the border from New York. Some of the hardware, swiped from U.S. shipments headed overseas, traveled from Buffalo by ship, on the St. Lawrence River, while the rest was trucked across the border at Fort Covington. Don Vincent Gaglioni, Buffalo's pale version of The Godfather, procured the guns and pocketed the cash.

It had to stop, but agents of the ATF and FBI were getting nowhere with their separate, often competitive investigations.

By the time Bolan was sent to clean it up, they'd lost two veteran informants and an agent who was riding with his top stool pigeon when the turncoat's car exploded in a parking lot.

Bolan had sunk two of the Gaglioni Family's cargo ships with limpet mines, shot up a convoy moving overland, then trailed Don Gaglioni to a sit-down with the gang leaders outside Drummondville, Quebec. The meeting had been tense to start with, but they'd never had a chance to settle their dispute. Bolan's unscheduled intervention, with an Mk 19 full-auto grenade launcher had spoiled the bash for all concerned.

It had been like old times, for just a minute there, but Bolan didn't set much store in strolls down Memory Lane. Especially when the path was littered with rubble and corpses.

There was enough of that in his future, he knew, without trying to resurrect the Bad Old Days of his one-man war against the Mafia. A little object lesson now and then was fine, but there could be no turning back the clock.

Which brought him to the job at hand—whatever it might be. Brognola hadn't called him for a birthday party or a housewarming. There would be dirty work ahead, the kind Bolan did best, and he was ready for it.

Which was not to say that he enjoyed it.

In Bolan's mind, the day a killer started to enjoy his killing trade, the time had come for him to find another line of work. Only a psychopath loved killing, and the best thing anyone could do for such an individual was to put him down before he caused more misery.

Soldiers were trained to kill, the same way surgeons learned to cut and plumbers learned to weld. The difference, of course, was that a warrior mended nothing, built nothing. In battle, warriors killed, albeit sometimes for a cause so great that only blood could sanctify it. Some opponents were impervious to grand diplomacy, or even backroom bribes.

In some cases, only brute force would do.

But those were not the situations to be celebrated, in a sane and stable world. Peace was the goal, the end to which all means were theoretically applied.

Back in the sixties, bumper stickers ridiculed the war in Vietnam by asking whether it was possible to kill for peace. The answer—then, as now—was "Yes."

Sometimes a soldier had no choice.

And sometimes, he was bound to choose.

"We're here," the pilot said as Bolan saw the farmhouse up ahead. Below, a tractor churned across a field, its driver muttering into a two-way radio. There would be other watchers Bolan couldn't see, tracking the chopper toward the helipad. Fingers on triggers, just in case.

They reached the pad and hovered, then began to settle down. Bolan looked through the bubble windscreen at familiar faces on the deck, none of them smiling yet.

It wasn't home, but it would do.

Until they sent him off to war again.

"GLAD YOU COULD MAKE IT," Hal Brognola said, while pumping Bolan's hand. "So, how's the Great White North?"

"Still there," Bolan replied as he released his old friend's hand.

Beside Brognola, Barbara Price surveyed Bolan with cool detachment, civil but entirely business-like. The things they did in private, now and then, might not be absolutely secret from Brognola or the Stony Man team, but Barbara shunned public displays. She was the perfect operations chief: intelligent, professional and absolutely ruthless when she had to be.

"You want some time to chill? Maybe a drink? A walk around the place?" Brognola asked.

"We may as well get to it," Bolan said.

Clearly relieved, Brognola said, "Okay. Let's hit the War Room, then."

Bolan trailed the big Fed and Price into the rambling farmhouse that was Stony Man's cosmetic centerpiece and active headquarters. From the outside, unless you climbed atop the roof and counted dish antennae, the place looked normal, precisely what a stranger would expect to see on a Virginia farm.

Not that a stranger, trespassing, would ever make it to the house alive.

Inside, it was a very different story, comfort vying with utility of every square inch of the house. It featured living quarters, kitchen, dining room—the usual, in short—but also had communications and computer rooms, though major functions were in the Annex, an arsenal second to none outside of any full-size military base, and other features that the standard home, rural or urban, couldn't claim.

The basement War Room was a case in point. Accessible by stairs or elevator, it contained a conference table seating twenty, maps and charts for every part of Mother Earth, and audio-visual gear that would do Disney Studios proud.

How many times had Bolan sat inside that room to hear details of a mission that would send him halfway around the world, perhaps to meet his death?

Too many, right.

But it would never be enough, until the predators got wise and left the weaker members of the human herd alone.

Aaron Kurtzman met them on the threshold of the War Room, crunched Bolan's hand in his fist, then spun his wheelchair to lead them inside. As Stony Man's tech master, Kurtzman commonly attended mission briefings and controlled whatever AV elements Brognola's presentation might require.

Brognola took his usual seat at the head of the table, his

back to a large wallscreen. Price sat to the big Fed's right, Bolan on his left, while Kurtzman chose a spot midway along the table's left-hand side. A keyboard waited for him on the tabletop, plugged into some concealed receptacle.

"Okay," Brognola said, "before we start, I don't know if you've had a chance to keep up with the news these past few days."

"Not much," Bolan said. "Scraps from radio, while I was driving. Headlines showing from the newspaper dispensers."

"Fair enough. We're in the middle of a flap that has the White House nervous, not to mention certain friends abroad. Starting three days ago, on Thursday, we've experienced a series of attacks on Jews, here in the States and down in Mexico. It has the White House in an uproar, for assorted reasons, and we've got our marching orders."

Bolan knew the protocol for Stony Man briefings. Brognola went by a script of sorts, and liked to keep his ducks all in a row.

"Who were the victims?" Bolan asked.

The big Fed tipped a nod to Kurtzman and the overheads dimmed just enough to simulate twilight. Behind Brognola's back, a photo of a smiling couple dressed for formal partying filled up the screen.

"That's Aderet Venjamin on the left," Brognola said, without glancing around. "His wife's Naomi. For the past five years, Venjamin has been assigned to the Israeli consulate in New York City."

"Someone hit him?" Bolan asked. It was the logical assumption.

"Nope. The wife."

Bolan's surprise was indicated by a raised eyebrow.

"On Thursday morning," Brognola pressed on, "she went out shopping on Park Avenue. One bodyguard, one driver, both ex-military. As she left a jeweler's, two men on the sidewalk shot the guard, threw nitric acid in her face and fled on foot. No clear description of the perps, no vehicle observed."

"Survivors?" Bolan asked.

"The lady's still alive," Hal said, "if you can call it living. Left eye gone, partially blinded in the right. Skin grafts may help a little, but she'll never look like that again." He jerked a thumb in the direction of the screen behind him.

"Anyone claim credit for it?" Bolan asked.

"We're not sure."

"Meaning?"

"Two days prior to the attack, the consulate received a note, postmarked Bogotá. It took nine days to be delivered. No one in the postal service can explain exactly why."

Another nod to Kurtzman, and the happy-couple photo was replaced by a plain sheet of paper. Roughly centered on it was a typed message: "See now, how ugly are the Jews who suck our blood."

"That's it?" Bolan asked. "I'd imagine the Israeli consulate gets bags of poison-pen notes every day."

"You'd win that bet," Brognola said. "I checked it out. Apparently they average fifteen pounds of hate mail daily, double that around well-known religious holidays."

"So what sets this apart? The timing or the 'ugly' reference?"

"The postmark, actually," Brognola replied. "But that's hindsight. Stay with me for a minute, here."

A nod, another change of photos. Now the carcass of a tour bus filled the screen. Fire damage showed around the frames of shattered windows. Bolan picked out bullet holes along the one side he could see. The bus's logo, what was left of it, read *Tourismo Grand de Sonora*.

"This went down about an hour after the Park Avenue attack," Brognola said. "A busload of Israeli tourists traveling around Sonora, as I'm sure you gathered from the sign. They were en route to Hermosillo, from some kind of mission, when a group of masked men stopped the bus and started shooting. Passersby, they left alone."

"They wanted witnesses," Bolan observed.

"Apparently."

"Survivors on the bus?"

"Not one."

"You're linking this to acid on Park Avenue, because…?"

"Of this," Brognola said, and Kurtzman keyed the next slide. Once again, it showed a common piece of stationery with a one-line message: "Jews suck the lifeblood of nations."

"So?"

"I couldn't see it, either," Brognola replied, "but the Mossad and FBI agree that both notes were prepared on the same manual typewriter. It's a vintage German model, specifically an Erika Naumann Model 6, last manufactured between 1938 and early 1945."

"You're kidding, right?"

"I wish. It just gets worse."

This time the picture changed without a signal from Brognola. On the screen, a body sprawled in blood and sunshine, with pastel storefronts and palm trees in the background. Bolan couldn't see the dead man's face.

Small favors.

"Ira Margulies," Brognola said. "One of the top fifteen or twenty richest people in Miami Beach. He was a force to reckon with in banking, real estate, what have you—until Friday morning, when a shooter took him down."

"Where was the note?" asked Bolan.

"Tucked under his left elbow, away from the blood flow," Brognola said.

And as he spoke, another note filled up the hanging screen.

It read, "The Jews are not the people who are blamed for nothing."

Bolan frowned and asked, "Why does that sound familiar?"

Price fielded that one, telling him, "It's similar, but not identical, to a note left at one of Jack the Ripper's London crime scenes back in 1888. The original note misspelled 'Jews,' and a couple of other words are slightly different. For plagiarism, it's a sloppy job."

"You said, from 1888?"

She nodded, adding, "But it's quoted in every book and article written about the Ripper since then. How many hundreds are there, all over the world? We think it stuck in someone's mind. They're playing games."

"Same typewriter?"

"Affirmative," Brognola said.

"But only one note sent by mail," Bolan observed.

"We think," Brognola said, "that they were leery of a drop-off at the consulate."

"One source for all three notes," Bolan confirmed. "One mind behind the crimes."

It was the big Fed's turn to nod. "And on the rare occasions when he mails a note—"

"It comes from Bogotá," Bolan finished the thought.

"Or somewhere in Colombia, at least. We think the author's tied in to a Nazi clique established in the country during 1948 or '49. Are you familiar with a place known as Colonia Victoria?"

"Victory Colony?" Bolan translated with his meager Spanish. "It's not ringing any bells."

"No reason why it should, really," Brognola said. "It gets some bad publicity every ten years or so, but mostly it's a hush-hush operation. The Colombians don't like to talk about it, with their public image in the crapper as it is. The German immigrants and their descendants in the colony, well, it's in their best interest if they don't get too much ink or TV time."

"How so?" Bolan asked.

"The colony was founded by war criminals, for starters," Brognola replied. He slid a dossier across to Bolan, an inch-thick manila folder with a CD-ROM on top. "You'll find the major players there. Or what we know of them, at least. Nutshell, they've got substantial acreage in coca and they deal with the Aznar cartel. Some say they use native slave labor, harvesting the crop, refining it. The local police take their bribes and look the other way."

"So, Nazi narcotraffickers?"

"Tip of the iceberg," Brognola said. "Through the years, there've been reports that the resident führer—one Hans Dietrich, formerly an SS captain under Eichmann—runs some kind of cult. We've had reports of child-molesting and polygamy, you name it. As I said, the local cops are deaf and blind. On one or two occasions, when investigators made the trip from Bogotá, they claimed the place checked out okay. Whatever that means, when you think about the status quo down there."

"Somebody's getting greased," Bolan suggested.

"Six or seven ways from Sunday," Brognola agreed. "Bribes are a given. On the flip side, the Israelis and a few left-wing reporters have tried sneaking in, over the years. Most of them disappear without a trace. One, as I understand it, wound up eaten by a jaguar or a crocodile, something like that."

Old Nazis raising new ones in the jungle. And an antique German typewriter.

"It's thin," Bolan said, "if that postmark's all you've got."

"Did I say that?" Brognola's grin was just this side of sly.

"Okay, I'm listening."

"When Margulies got hit, down in Miami Beach, somebody got the shooter's license tag. Of course, it was a rental car."

"Dead end," Bolan said.

"But they keep a photocopy of the client's driver's license," the big Fed stated.

Another image on the screen. It was a blow-up of an Alabama driver's license, with a color photograph of one George Allen Carter and a home address in Birmingham. The photo's subject was a crew-cut man of twenty-four, if you believed the license stats.

"Phony?" Bolan surmised.

"As the proverbial three-dollar bill. Except for the mug shot."

"How did you trace it?"

"CIA," Brognola said. "Computers are a miracle, you know? Put in a face, and if it's ever shown up in a friendly nation's dossier, *voilà!*"

"I'm guessing that he doesn't come from Alabama," Bolan said.

"Not even close. He kept his old initials, though. Meet Georg—no *e* on that one—Abel Kaltenbrunner. Born and raised, as far as anyone can tell, inside Colonia Victoria."

"He got away." It didn't come out as a question.

"Sure he did. Clean as a whistle, with a passport in some other name. We'll run it down, one of these days, and it will be another phony, long since shredded."

"Well, then," Bolan said. "It looks like I'll be going to Colombia."

BOLAN'S ROOM was at the northeast corner of the second floor. He occupied the small room's only chair, a laptop humming on the table before him, with documents spread out around it. Everything he saw and read convinced him that someone before him should have undertaken this assignment long ago.

The founder of Colonia Victoria, Hans Gunter Dietrich, had been charged with genocidal actions at the Nuremberg tribunal, after World War II, but he'd slipped through the net, using the old ODESSA network, slipping out of Germany through Franco's fascist Spain to Argentina, then to Paraguay, and finally Colombia. After the allies hanged a handful of his cronies and imprisoned several hundred more, the Nazis who escaped were basically forgotten by the world at large, except for the Israelis and a few die-hard Resistance veterans in France. Many who went to jail were sprung ahead of schedule, "rehabilitated" and recruited to the service of their former enemies, as Britain and America began their long cold war with Russia.

Names like Bormann, Eichmann, Mengele, and Barbie—Klaus, that is, who never had a doll cast in his honor—still cropped up from time to time, as they were sighted here and there around the world, sometimes kidnapped or executed by Mossad hit teams. But thousands got away and never spent a night in custody for their horrific crimes.

Hans Dietrich was a perfect case in point.

Fleeing the Reich before V-E Day, fortified with looted gold, artwork and God alone knew what else, he'd bribed politicians when they still came cheap, bought sweeping tracts of land that no one wanted, and had built himself a kingdom, welcoming his fellow fugitives from justice, acting as a law unto himself within his fiefdom, ruling those who had acquired the habit of obedience in Germany and knew no other way to live.

Dietrich had been a young man then, midtwenties when Hitler's Thousand-Year Reich had collapsed after twelve years of pure Hell on Earth. He would be pushing ninety now, unless you bought the argument advanced by certain theorists on the Internet, that he had died and been replaced by a successor, clone or robot—take your pick.

Colonia Victoria had grown with time. More Nazis joined

the fold, by one means or another. How many were born inside the colony, over the past six decades? No one knew. Some sources claimed as many as three thousand had left homes in other countries where their racial hatred was unwelcome, and had sworn allegiance to Herr Dietrich in Colombia. They straggled in from Europe, North America, South Africa, the Balkans—aging fascists, skinhead punks, veterans of cliques and Klans and fascist parties few people would even recognize by name.

Colonia Victoria was aptly named, Bolan decided. While it wasn't huge, by any means—one hundred square miles, give or take an acre—Dietrich ruled a territory nearly twice the size of Liechtenstein. Most of his land was cloaked in montane forests, ideal for the coca crop that guaranteed his little realm would never want for cash.

That had to be a victory of sorts, in anybody's book.

Some of the immigrants to Dietrich's colony, upon reflection, had decided that Colonia Victoria was not their cup of tea. Those who returned from Nazi Never Land told grim, disturbing tales of what went on inside the colony. Hal's list had barely scratched the surface with reports of slavery, polygamy, weird rites and child abuse. Some also spoke of human sacrifice to pagan gods, blood-drinking and executions without trial.

According to the information Brognola supplied, Colombian authorities had made three separate investigations of the colony, based on complaints from former residents. Meaning *white* residents, since tales spread by the forest-dwelling aboriginals were generally ignored by everyone except a couple of devoted missionaries living in the bush. After the missionaries disappeared, such stories passed unnoticed by the denizens of "civilized" society.

The first investigation had been launched in 1955. A couple from West Germany, Gunter and Ilse Stern, spent two years at Colonia Victoria, then left, complaining to Colombian authorities that Hans Dietrich reserved unto himself the right to "sample" wives and daughters, to ensure their fitness for the task of breeding little Aryans. A prosecutor visited the colony with two detectives, spent the night and then reported that he found no evidence of any impropriety. The fact that he immediately bought a brand-new Cadillac convertible was certainly a mere coincidence.

The next official look-see came in 1970, when a teenager named Rolf Schumacher surfaced in Mocoa, forty miles northwest of Dietrich's colony. He'd been delirious from fever, ultimately lost one leg to hemorrhage from a snakebite, and took weeks to tell his halting story in disjointed bits and pieces. Bottom line: Schumacher claimed that Dietrich and his SS-style Home Guard had killed Rolf's parents and two brothers when the family opposed Dietrich's selection of their teen daughters for his breeding program. Rolf had managed to escape, eluded trackers in the forest, but had worse luck when it came to Mother Nature.

Once again, investigators made the trek to Dietrich's hideaway. This time they spent three nights and came back empty-handed. Their report, which had been classified on grounds of "national security, then photocopied by a contract agent of the CIA and sent to Langley, found no evidence of any "organized eugenics program," sexual abuse of minors or restraint of any resident against his-or-her will. In fact, the bureaucrats found nothing to suggest that any Schumachers had ever joined the colony.

The third and last official peek inside Dietrich's domain occurred in 1995. On that occasion, a Mossad agent informed the DAS—Colombia's Administrative Department of Security, equivalent to the FBI—that Dietrich was allied with certain drug cartels and with a global network of Muslim extremists. DAS Deputy Director Joaquin Menendez had promised a thorough investigation, but nothing seemed to happen. Except, that is, a car-bombing in Cali that killed the complaining Mossad agent seven weeks later. Israel had not protested, since the agent's presence in Colombia was technically illegal, but a CIA informant claimed that two low-level DAS agents were subsequently executed by Mossad, for the bombing.

Menendez, meanwhile, kept his post at DAS headquarters and compiled a record Hans Dietrich himself might have admired. In May 2000, acting on information supplied by Menendez, soldiers of the Colombian Army's Third Brigade ambushed and killed ten members of an elite police narcotics unit trained by the DEA. In its two years of existence, the unit had captured 205 cocaine smugglers, including several who were sent to the United States for trial. The massacre—or "tragic accident," as local newspapers described it—had occurred, Menendez said, because one of his most reliable informants had mistaken the police for leftist rebels. The list went on.

Menendez, in the photos Brognola provided, scowled behind a set of bushy eyebrows and a thick mustache. His eyes were dark brown, nearly black, and in the shots provided seemed devoid of all humanity.

As for the Sword of Allah, documents procured from the Mossad alleged that one of the group's top planners, Nasser Khalil, spent an average four months per year at Colonia Victoria, flying in to Dietrich's private airstrip without interference from the DAS or anybody else. Khalil was sought by Israel, France and Italy for acts of terrorism planned and carried out against them, while the CIA had placed a bounty on his head, on general principles. He was suspected of collaborating with al Qaeda and Hamas on various attacks over the past ten years, but he had never been arrested or detained for questioning by any of the governments pursuing him.

If Bolan had an opportunity to meet him…

Gentle rapping at his door distracted Bolan from the files in front of him. He rose and crossed the room, opened the door, and felt himself relax at sight of Price's smile.

"I wasn't sure if you'd want company," she said.

"Always," he told her, stepping back to clear the doorway.

"You've got a lot to read and memorize."

"I'm nearly done."

"Any surprises?"

"Anytime I see the old Hitlerian mystique crop up again, I guess a part of me's surprised," he said. "My father fought those guys, you know? It's hard to fathom anyone believing in the Master Race and all that crap, after so many years."

"Some people never learn," she said.

"I guess they need another lesson, then."

"You'll be careful, right? Colombia's no place to let your guard down for a nanosecond."

"Hey," he said, "careful's my middle name."

"Your middle name is Sam, and careful is the farthest thing from what you are," she answered.

"Well…"

"I mean it, Mack. Nazis, the DAS and drug cartels, the Sword of Allah. Toss them all together, and you don't have many friends down there."

"There's always Jorge Guzman," Bolan said.

"I say it again, be careful. Just because he draws a paycheck from the DEA and the CIA, it doesn't mean he's clean. You know the kinds of characters they deal with. Watch yourself, is all I'm saying."

Bolan said, "I always do. But at the moment…"

"What?"

"I'm busy watching you."

"Smooth talker."

"I'm a little out of practice," he admitted.

"I hope so."

She wore a jumpsuit with a zipper down the front, running from chest to somewhere south of modesty. As Bolan watched, she gripped the tab and lowered a fraction of an inch, teasing.

"I was about to have a shower," Bolan said.

She smiled. "I thought you'd never ask."

CHAPTER FOUR

Bogotá

They left the shooting scene in Gabriella Cohen's car, with Guzman slumped in the backseat, holding a scarf against his bloody temple.

"That's pure silk, you know," Cohen said as she drove through downtown Bogotá toward some point she had yet to clarify. "I'll never get the blood out."

"I'll buy you a new one," Bolan told her. "First, though, could you tell me where we're going?"

"What? Didn't I tell you that already?"

"No," Bolan replied. "I'd have remembered it."

"Sorry. I thought your friend could use some patching up, a little quiet time. I have a small house in the Teusaquillo district, just a few miles farther on. The neighbors mind their own business."

"I hope so."

"I'd be more at risk than you, if they did not."

"You think so?"

"Well…perhaps not more, but just the same. The DAS

hates foreign spies. Can you imagine? And from Israel, oh my God! Due process is a fairy tale they heard when they were children, then forgot."

"You're pretty far afield," Bolan replied.

She flashed a winning smile. "I like to, um…how do you say it in America—go where the action is?"

"That's how we say it," he agreed. "I wouldn't think there'd be much action for Mossad in Bogotá."

Another smile. "Not like tonight, you mean?"

"Don't get me wrong," he said. "I'm glad you happened by—"

"You make assumptions now," she interrupted him. "You think I'm simply driving past old factories and hear gunshots, then tell myself, 'I simply must go join the fight, and maybe find a handsome man'?"

Bolan ignored her sarcasm and said, "Well, if it wasn't a coincidence, you should explain yourself. If you were trailing us—"

"Not you," she cut him off again. "The men who tried to kill you. I've been watching them for three weeks. Now, because of you and my softheartedness, they're dead. My time is wasted."

"You were tracking them?"

"Why are you so surprised? We do watch out for Nazis, young or old. Some still owe debts from their participation in the Shoa. Others must be stopped before history can repeat itself."

Bolan had no quarrel with eliminating fascists, but he asked her, "What's the Shoa?"

"You, perhaps, call it the Holocaust. In Israel, we say Shoa. It is Hebrew for *'catastrophe.'* In Yiddish, it is *Churb'n.* Yom ha-Shoa is our Holocaust Remembrance Day, in April. We do not forget."

"Nobody should," Bolan replied.

"Our interest in Colombia, therefore, is not mysterious. The Nazis here, including very old ones from the Reich, are well established and protected. They grow richer by the day from sale of drugs and push the enemies of Israel toward extremist action that results in loss of life."

"Especially in the last few days?" Bolan asked, playing out a hunch.

No smile this time as Cohen quickly glanced at him, then pulled her eyes back to the road in front of them. "I'm not sure what you mean," she answered rather stiffly.

Bolan showed another card. "Acid in New York City. Murder in Miami Beach and Mexico. Somebody with an antique typewriter who wants the credit for his work but doesn't have the guts to sign his name. Ring any bells?"

They covered two blocks before Cohen spoke again. "Those aren't the only cases," she replied, checking her rearview mirror as if someone might be crouching at her shoulder, eavesdropping.

"Where else?" Bolan asked.

"In Madrid and Athens. Two murders, a week apart. One victim was a secretary from our consulate, stabbed in a marketplace with people all around. Of course, no one saw anything. The other was a diplomat's young daughter. An apparent hit-and-run, the rental car abandoned. Greek police considered it an accident until—"

"The note arrived?"

"Yes."

"Same typewriter and postmark?"

"Erika Naumann Model 6," she said, with small chips on the *A* and *W*. They also need to clean the *O* and *Q*. And, yes, the letters both were mailed from Bogotá."

"Somebody showing off, but still feeling secure," Bolan observed.

"Someone who may be legally untouchable," Cohen said, "but not by other means."

It was unusual to hear the aim stated so plainly, by a foreign agent whom he'd barely met. Still, Israel made no bones about the fact that it reached out around the world to punish terrorists and those who murdered Jews. From Adolf Eichmann to the architects of Munich's cruel Olympic massacre, Mossad had kidnapped or eliminated mortal enemies of Israel. One unit, active during the seventies, had been nicknamed the Wrath of God. And it had lived up to its name.

"I've shocked you now," she said.

"Surprised," Bolan corrected her. "And by your candor, not the thought."

"Then may I ask what brings you to Colombia, and why the Nazis want you dead before you have a chance to change clothes from your flight?"

He took another leap of faith. "I'd say we're in the same line, coming at it from a slightly different angle."

"You, of course, desire to keep such nasty business out of the United States."

"Of course, there's that," he granted.

"And what else?"

"I won't pretend to know all that your people suffered," Bolan said, "although, I've seen enough man-made catastrophes to have at least a general idea. Israelis aren't the only ones who'd like to nip these bastards in the bud."

"Too late for that," she said. "The old men I referred to have been living here, and living well, for fifty years."

"I found that out for the first time, this week," Bolan replied. "Your people must've known it—what? For years?"

"Decades," she said. "It shames me to admit it, but we fight the battles that demand immediate attention. Eichmann was a symbol. Everybody knew his name and what he'd done. As for the rest, we had our Arab neighbors to contend with. No one gave much thought to aging Germans squatting in a jungle, halfway around the world."

"One of your agents took a shot in 1995," Bolan replied.

"You're well informed. Then you must know what happened afterward."

"The bombing and retaliation, right."

"Of course. But I'm referring to the cover-up by leaders of the DAS, perhaps Colombia's own president, himself. Who do you trust here, Mr. Cooper?"

He had given her the cover name, and now said, "Make it 'Matt.' And trust is earned where I come from."

"You've met this one before?" she asked, nodding toward Guzman, huddled in the rear.

"I checked his references," Bolan replied. "He hasn't let me down, so far."

"How did Herr Krieger and his men know you were coming to Colombia?"

"Who's Krieger?" Bolan asked, buying some time to think about her question.

"Krieger, Horst Andreas," she replied, as if reading the label on a file. "Until this evening, he was one of old man Dietrich's young elite. But now you've killed him, I believe. At least, *I* didn't, and he would have shot us both if he was still alive."

"Blond guy, midtwenties, maybe six feet tall?"

"The classic Aryan," Cohen said.

"You've seen the last of him."

"Good riddance. I am satisfied to have eliminated Arne Rauschman and at least two of their mercenaries. It's amazing, isn't it? How people they despise as less than human *still* work for the Nazis, seek to curry favor with them? Truly, wonders never cease."

"About this house of yours…"

She turned into a quiet residential street and then into a driveway two doors from the corner.

"As you say," she said. "We're here."

GUZMAN WAS SILENT, for the most part, while she cleaned his wound with alcohol. It had to have burned like fury, but he clenched his teeth and swallowed any sounds of pain that tried to struggle free. Granted, there was a little moan when she applied the iodine, but nothing that should shame a man concerned about his macho image.

"That's the worst of it," she said. "I'll stitch it now. Unfortunately, I have nothing for a local anesthetic."

"Any whiskey? Rum? Tequila?" Guzman asked.

"Sorry. I have some wine."

The wounded man looked glum. He shook his head. "No wine."

The tall American watched as Cohen removed a curved needle from her first-aid kit and began to thread it. She had used it on herself once, closing up a razor slash in Paris, and she never traveled far without the means to clean and patch most wounds that did not call for major surgery.

"You've done this kind of thing before," Bolan observed.

"It's good to be prepared for an emergency," she said.

"And use a Jericho sidearm. It sounded like the .40 caliber."

"The .41 Action Express, in fact."

"You like an edge," he said.

"Whenever I can get one."

"Still, it isn't much for going up against an army."

"You're prepared to try it with an IMBEL .45," she hastened to remind him.

"I was on my way to do some shopping when we got sidetracked."

"That's inconvenient. Can you still keep the appointment?"

Bolan glanced at his companion, Jorge Guzman, who responded with a cautious nod and said, "I will make the arrangements."

"Maybe we should just surprise him," Bolan said. "I'd hate to find another welcoming committee waiting on the doorstep."

Guzman flared. "You think I told them where to find us? If you doubt me—"

"Chill out," Bolan warned. "If I thought you were doubling on me, you'd be lying back there at the factory."

"What, then?" Guzman asked, slightly mollified.

"There are too many leaks around this town. Make that, around this country. We don't telegraph our moves from this point on. No tip-offs to our plan for friend or foe. We'll drop in for the hardware when your dealer least expects it, and he won't know where we're going when we leave."

Finished threading the needle, Cohen dipped it into alcohol and turned toward Guzman. He observed the needle, nodded grimly, and she went to work, distracting Guzman and herself with words.

"Krieger and Rauschman met you at the airport," she reminded Bolan. "That means they were either following your friend here, or they knew beforehand when you would be landing."

"I'd prefer the first choice," Bolan said.

"Of course. In that case, they may not know who you are, or why you're here in Bogotá. You'd have a chance—although a slim one—to surprise them, yet."

"That's still the plan," Bolan replied.

"Americans are always optimistic."

"Not Americans, in general," he said. "I set a goal and do my best to reach it, after planning for the worst contingencies that I can think of."

"Is it sometimes wiser not to try?" she asked.

"If you believe that," Bolan challenged, "why aren't you at home in Tel Aviv?"

"I go where I am sent," she said. "And I was not sent here to storm Colonia Victoria."

"You think I was?"

She shrugged, aware of Bolan watching her. Not only following the movements of her hands.

"I'm not a mind reader, of course," she said. "But you impress me as a soldier, not a spy. I don't think you were sent to simply build a dossier on Dietrich and his cronies."

"No," he said. "Were you?"

"I am supposed to gather evidence that can be used to blow his cover, as you say. Perhaps to shame the government that shelters him. Myself, I'm not convinced it will be an effective strategy. Colombians appear to have great tolerance for such embarrassment, and very little shame."

"You went beyond your brief tonight," Bolan observed.

"In a good cause, I hope."

"So, when we're finished here," he said, "Jorge and I will get out of your hair."

"You plan to walk?"

"Well, maybe you could drop us at a rental agency," Bolan said, smiling ruefully.

"Maybe," she told him, "I can do better than that."

"SLOW DOWN," the man in black advised his driver. "They're already nervous, and you know they're trigger-happy at the best of times."

The driver slowed their black Mercedes to a crawl, passing between the rows of factories that smoked and fumed around the clock. Downrange, six cars with flashing lights on top surrounded three more vehicles, their headlights highlighting the damage suffered by those other cars. Armed men in quasi-military uniforms scurried around the scene, peering at bodies scattered on the ground.

"I see him," said the driver as they neared the scene of orchestrated chaos.

"Yes," the man in black replied. "I wondered if he'd come out at this hour, himself."

"Maybe he hasn't been home yet," the driver said with a smirk. "You've seen his mistress, eh?"

"The new one? I'm surprised her parents don't impose a curfew."

"Would they dare?" the driver asked.

"You have a point. Stop here. Stay with the car. If anything goes wrong, get out at any cost and warn him."

"Herr Hauptmann—"

"I order it!"

"Yes, sir!"

Of course, something already had gone wrong. If Krieger had completed his assignment as commanded, Otto Jaeger would be sleeping at the moment, maybe dreaming of his wives at home. Instead, he had to deal with corpses in the middle of the night and listen to Joaquin Menendez complain.

With one hand on the Walther P-5 compact pistol in his coat pocket, Jaeger approached the scowling DAS chief. There was no reason to think that he would need the gun tonight, but given the dramatic mood swings Menendez was famous for, it couldn't hurt to be prepared.

Perhaps he's crazy, Jaeger thought.

And said, "Good morning, Herr Director. It's unfortunate that your subordinates disturbed you for a matter of this sort."

"Unfortunate, you say? With eight men dead."

Krieger's whole team? It seemed impossible, but would explain why no one had called Jaeger to report their failure. There was no one left.

Jaeger was cautious in replying to Menendez. He might easily have said that eight dead meant a sluggish night for Bogotá, but he preferred not to antagonize Menendez. It was dangerous and unproductive.

"Only eight?" he asked instead.

"You were expecting more?"

"I had expected none at all," Jaeger replied with perfect honesty. Krieger was good enough—had been—to simply make his targets disappear, unless there were examples to be made.

This night, it seemed, Krieger and Rauschman, with their native help, *were* the examples.

"May I view the bodies?" Jaeger asked Menendez.

The Colombian considered it, then dipped his chin in the affirmative. "Touch nothing."

"That's a promise."

Jaeger left the DAS director, turning toward the shot-up vehicles. He needed to replace the Volkswagen and the Mercedes. Both of them were badly damaged, and it left him short of rolling stock in Bogotá. He had another Benz on hand, besides the one that had delivered him to this grim scene, and half a dozen motorcycles. Not enough for fifty men by any means.

Now forty-eight, he thought as he approached the nearest corpse.

The third car, facing toward the others, was a cheap Fiat, run-down even before it ran into a hail of bullets and expired. The relative positions of the cars told Jaeger that the Fiat's driver had been taken by surprise, or else pursued here, where he turned to fight. The latter seemed more likely, but Jaeger supposed he'd never really know.

Jaeger found Rauschman sprawled between the Benz and the VW, lying on his back. A slug had entered through his left eye, taking out the right-rear portion of his skull. He looked surprised and vaguely guilty.

So you should, Jaeger thought. You have disappointed everyone.

Was there a Hell for failures? Jaeger didn't know, and at the moment didn't really care.

He checked the other corpses, walking all around the scene, crunching the spent brass underfoot. There were no bodies by the Fiat, no apparent blood, suggesting that his men had missed their targets, or at least had failed to wound them mortally.

"Where is the eighth?" he asked a DAS captain who'd followed him around the cars, watching his every move. "Herr Menendez said eight were killed, but there are only seven here."

The captain grunted at him, turned and pointed to a nearby field littered with pieces of equipment someone had discarded but had never hauled away. Now Jaeger saw a solitary officer standing beside what seemed to be a mound of earth or pile of dirty rags dumped on the ground.

He left the captain, walked over to Krieger's dusty corpse and crouched beside it.

"You need light?" the DAS man asked.

"It helps."

A flashlight beam lanced through the shadows, making Krieger's hair seem almost white. He lay facedown, blood soaking through his jacket where a slug had pierced his back, most likely shattering some vertebrae before it found the heart or lungs within.

"So, you were taken by surprise," he said in German. "You deserve no less."

He rose, walked back to where Menendez waited for him, hands in pockets, with the same scowl on his face. The bushy eyebrows and mustache made him almost a cartoon character, but laughing at that face could be the last thing Jaeger ever did.

"They're ours," he told Menendez.

"All of them?"

"Something went wrong."

"What were they doing here?"

A lie could ruin everything. Menendez took their money. He was bought and paid for—to a point.

"The Fiat's driver is an enemy. He asks too many questions, pokes his nose in where it isn't wanted."

"Name?"

"Jorge Guzman."

"I've never heard of him," Menendez said.

"No reason why you should have."

"He's some kind of soldier, this one?"

"No. I don't think so."

"But he has killed eight men."

"I can't explain it," Jaeger answered. "I can only clean it up."

Menendez thought about it, then replied, "The shifts change in these factories at midnight. All this must be removed by then, and made to disappear."

"No problem," Jaeger said, without checking his watch. "You may expect a bonus, Herr Director."

"So I do," Menendez said, turning away.

Dismissed, Jaeger retreated to his Benz, already fishing in another pocket for his cell phone. There was work to do, and swiftly, to conceal the relics of a massacre.

Colonia Victoria

HANS DIETRICH LIKED his schnapps flavored with peppermint. It made his breath smell fresh, while the delicious alcohol worked on his aging brain. He never drank enough to make him drunk, these days, but did his best to keep a rosy glow firmly in place.

This night, it took more schnapps than usual.

Dietrich was troubled. Not yet worried, which implied a

major threat, but certainly concerned. The news of questions being asked in Bogotá had prompted Dietrich to investigate, and what he'd learned had left him curious, confused.

Angry.

The man asking the questions was a peasant but not without connections. Subtle probing had revealed that Jorge Guzman was a minor criminal who supplemented his illicit income by informing on selected persons to American narcotics officers, perhaps even the CIA. That made him dangerous, although his interest in Dietrich had, thus far, delivered little in the way of new or useful information.

Dietrich knew that his community was not truly a secret. Far too many people shared the knowledge—and the wealth—of Colonia Victoria to guarantee complete security. There had been stories in the leftist media, complaints and subsequent investigations. Certainly, there had to be dossiers in Bogotá, in Washington, in London and in Tel Aviv.

But he was left alone, for the most part, and that was all Hans Dietrich asked of life.

That, and a chance to strike against his enemies when opportunity arose.

It was a problem, therefore, when Guzman started asking questions, seeking information that was none of his concern. When Otto Jaeger had reported it, Dietrich felt confident in ordering the usual response.

Discover who the rat was working for.

And, failing that, simply eliminate the rat.

Now, somehow, it had gone awry. Instead of one dead rat, Dietrich had two dead soldiers and six hired guns wasted. He was not concerned about the peasant labor, but Horst Krieger had been like a son to him.

In fact, considering Dietrich's liaison's with the young

man's mother, twenty-odd years back, there was a chance that Krieger might have *been* his son.

No matter.

Everyone within Colonia Victoria—the Aryans, at least— were Dietrich's children. He had been their patriarch for half a century, dictating every aspect of their lives between the cradle and the grave. He knew, at some level, that most of those now dwelling in the colony were bound to outlive him, but death still seemed remote, despite his age.

This night, though, he admitted to himself that it felt closer.

There were enemies around him, always, but the massacre in Bogotá was something new. There had been losses, certainly. Some accidents, a fatal illness now and then, some executions in the colony. Two of his people murdered by the Jews in 1995, after they killed the damned Israeli spy.

But never, since he set foot in Colombia, had Dietrich's men been cut down in such numbers. Never had he faced an enemy who killed so ruthlessly, efficiently, without apparent motive.

So, the bastards hated him. Of course they did. As millions hated Hitler for attempting to awaken them and teach them how to fight, to save themselves. Prophets were always vilified and persecuted. History had taught him that, if nothing else.

Jaeger had orders to continue the investigation, find the peasant Guzman and determine who directed him, who might have aided him in killing Krieger, Rauschman and the rest. Knowledge was power, and until those answers were within his grasp, Hans Dietrich knew that he was at a disadvantage.

It was not a feeling he enjoyed.

A leader of the Master Race was meant to lead, not hide while enemies worked day and night against him. Granted, it was different here than it had been in Germany, during the grand old days, but he was not without influence. If Menendez and the DAS could not help him, Dietrich would speak to someone higher in authority.

Someone who owed him much, in cash and gratitude.

His influence, combined with that of certain wealthy friends, could shake the state to its foundations if required to do so.

But, he thought, it would not be required. Serving his interest also served the interests of the men who had aligned themselves with him for profit, through the years. Men who allowed Colonia Victoria to thrive, when they could just as easily have crushed it. Having made that choice, like Faust, they had to live with it.

Hans Dietrich, imagining himself as Lucifer, the puppeteer. His reach was long, his grip still powerful.

Which made his doubts more troubling, yet.

Perhaps another glass of schnapps would calm the churning in his stomach.

Just one more, to help him sleep.

"WHAT DID YOU HAVE in mind?" Bolan asked.

"I've been working on this case longer than you have," Ghen answered, "and I think you will agree that we, Mossad, have first claim on the target. Everywhere, from Europe to New York and Mexico, they are Israeli diplomats and citizens who have been murdered, maimed and terrorized."

"Except Miami Beach," Bolan reminded her.

"Of course. Poor Mr. Margulies. But still, a Jew with family in Israel. Did you know that?"

Bolan frowned and told her honestly, "They must have missed that in my briefing."

"Now, you see. Israel has more against Hans Dietrich and his little monsters than America can ever claim. It is quite obvious."

She had a point.

"So, you're suggesting that I call my boss and tell him to forget the whole thing? That you've got it covered?" he said.

"Did I say that, Matt?"

"Not directly, but—"

"I am proposing we collaborate," she said. "Pool our resources for the common good."

"Right now," he told her, "my 'resources' are a pistol borrowed from Jorge. Washington won't be sending the Marines to help us out. I'm it, for this job."

"And from what I've seen," she said, "you're more than adequate."

"Gee, thanks."

She laughed and finished tying off the last suture at Guzman's temple. "There, all done," she said, "except for one more swab of alcohol and then a bandage."

As she finished, she said, "I don't mean to insult you, truly. But you *were* a bit outnumbered when I came along tonight."

"I noticed that." He turned to Guzman, asking, "Are you sure nobody trailed you to the airport?"

Guzman flinched as Cohen applied more alcohol, then said, "I did as I've been trained. Watched all the mirrors, made wrong turns, drove two and three times around certain blocks. If I was followed from my home, they were invisible."

"Okay, then," Bolan said. "That leaves two options. They were either tipped to find us at the airport—which could mean some kind of leak at my end, in the worst scenario—or they'd attached some kind of tracker to your car."

"Which will be useless to them now," Cohen said.

"Good point. If there's some kind of homer in the Fiat," Bolan said, "we'll let them sit and wait forever at the impound lot."

"It won't take long for them to realize what's happened," Cohen replied. "I am convinced that Dietrich has well-placed connections to the DAS and other law-enforcement agencies."

"I've heard the same thing," Bolan granted. "We'll assume that any badges who come knocking are the enemy."

"And deal with them accordingly," she said.

"I don't shoot innocent cops," he told her.

"Normally, I wouldn't, either," she replied, "but in this case—"

"Not even then," he answered. "It's a rule I live by. It's not open to debate."

She studied Bolan for a moment, then said, "In that case, we must make every effort to avoid them."

"That's a plan," he said.

"So, we're agreed?" she asked.

"On what?"

"What have we been discussing, Matt? Collaboration, for the common good."

Bolan considered it. Brognola didn't try to micromanage action in the field, knowing that it was better left to soldiers on the scene, who knew exactly what was happening at any given moment. There was no rule banning him from a collaboration with Mossad—in fact, he had joined forces with selected members of the agency on more than one occasion in the past.

And what about this time?

He knew that Gabriella Cohen was smart, fit, fully capable. She'd definitely helped him out with Dietrich's hit team, even though he wasn't ready to concede that he'd have lost the fight without her intervention.

What would be the down side of the plan that she proposed? She might object to Bolan taking on the leadership position, but there was an easy way to fix that. If she balked at being part of Bolan's team, then they could say goodbye and part as friends.

"If we do this together," he replied, "I have to go with my

instincts, my training. I've been in this game a long time, and they've served me well. If there's a disagreement over tactics that we can't resolve, we have to split."

"Agreed."

"Beyond that," he continued, "all of us are equals, pulling his—or her—own weight."

"Don't worry," Cohen responded with a smile. "If you begin to hold me back, I'll cut you loose."

"Sounds fair."

Her hand was warm, dry, strong when Bolan clasped it.

Jorge Guzman watched them and interrupted, asking, "So, is this suddenly a war? Am I a soldier now, instead of a simple seller of information?"

"There's nothing sudden about this war. It's been going on for over fifty years," Bolan said.

"For us," Cohen said, "it is as old as history."

"I fought tonight," Guzman said, "to defend myself. I have no training as a soldier. I am not prepared."

"You did all right until you showed yourself and let them shoot you," Bolan told him. "But I know where you're coming from. You want to bail, I'll ask for a replacement to interpret and—"

"I speak Spanish," Cohen said. "Also German and Arabic. It pays to understand the enemy."

"No Russian?" Bolan asked.

"Only enough to order meals and get directions to a bathroom. Sorry."

"Such a disappointment," Bolan told her, smiling to himself. "All right, Jorge, if you—"

Guzman cut Bolan off. "I did not say I want to leave. But you say we are all equals. I wanted you to know that is not true."

"Just keep your head down," Bolan said. "You ought to be okay."

Unless they kill you, Bolan thought, and kept it to himself. Guzman had nearly lost his life already. Obviously, he was clear about the risks involved.

"We're good, then, as you say?" Cohen asked.

"Not quite," Bolan replied. "I need to do some shopping first, give Jorge back his pistol when I get some hardware of my own."

"And then?" she asked.

"Before we hit the road, I'm hoping that you'll introduce me to Herr Dietrich's man in Bogotá."

CHAPTER FIVE

El Dorado International Airport

It was a risk, but doubling back was ultimately Bolan's only choice. He needed wheels, and couldn't stick with Cohen's two-door convertible. In his experience, people were far more likely to remember a convertible, and ragtops wouldn't slow a bullet down or spoil a sniper's aim. Four-doors, likewise, beat two-doors when it came to loading gear or passengers, as well as hasty entrances or exits.

So, he needed wheels. After a dozen phone calls, Bolan understood that he would only find a late-night rental at the airport, where he'd started out that evening.

And back they went, with Cohen driving. She put the top up first, to inconvenience any lookouts they might pass along the way, and kept her gun wedged between her right thigh and the driver's seat.

"It would be safer just to steal a car," she'd told him at the house, before agreeing to his plan.

"Then steal an extra set of plates and make the switch," he'd said. "And after that, keep hoping neither theft's reported to police or to the DAS. A rental's cleaner."

"Not if someone's waiting for you at the counter," she'd replied.

"Nobody knows I'm coming," he'd reminded her. "You made the call and asked about their hours, didn't give a name, made no appointment. There's no problem yet, unless your line is tapped."

"It's clean," she'd promised him. "I sweep it twice a day. But if they're waiting for you at the airport—"

"On the chance I might decide to turn around and fly back home so soon?" he'd said. "In that case, they'll be watching airline ticket counters and departure gates, not the car-rental companies. And they'll be looking for two men, from earlier, not a devoted, loving couple."

"Hey," she'd told him with a crooked smile, "don't press your luck."

Now, as they reached the airport and prepared to make the move, each of them understood the plan. Bolan was watching out for hostiles, from the shotgun seat, while Guzman sat in back, a baseball cap turned partly sideways in a kind of hip-hop fashion to conceal most of the bandage at his temple.

Cohen stopped at the curb in front of the domestic terminal, got out and walked around behind the car. Bolan was there ahead of her. While Guzman climbed out of the backseat, trying to act casual, Cohen opened the trunk to reveal two suitcases.

Both were empty, props for their performance, but the uniformed police standing nearby couldn't know that. They only saw a man and woman get out of a car, retrieve their bags, then bid farewell to their chauffeur. Some might have thought the driver looked a little odd, his cap askew, but they'd have thought him lucky when the pretty woman kissed his cheek.

And that was all. Bolan and Cohen passed through wide doors into the terminal, while Guzman drove away. His orders were to keep a sharp eye on his rearview mirror, on the airport's roads and sidewalks, watching for watchers as he circled, killing time. It should take twenty minutes, give or take, for Bolan to acquire a rental car, then Guzman could swing by and meet them as they claimed their wheels.

Inside the terminal, Bolan and Cohen bypassed the airline ticket counters and their lines of waiting would-be passengers. She talked nonstop to him in Spanish, Bolan nodding thoughtfully and saying *"sí"* from time to time, when Cohen shot him a glance. It wasn't an award-winning performance, granted, but between them, with their tans, her Spanish and their obvious intent on reaching a specific destination, Bolan thought they could've passed for locals.

He was armed this time, since they would not be passing through security to board a plane. Instead, they steered clear of the corridor that fed departure gates and followed signs directing them to baggage claims and transportation.

Every major airport in the world delivered bags to moving carousels, with easy access to an exit on a street. Nearby, in almost every terminal, are banks of posters advertising various hotels—and cubicles where passengers can rent a car to use during their stay.

Flights land at El Dorado International throughout the night. And Bolan, therefore, didn't have to worry about standing out when he arrived to rent a car at 1:05 a.m. The bored clerk in the rental booth he chose would not remember him, although he might recall the low-cut blouse that Cohen had worn as a distraction.

If the first booth didn't have a four-door, Bolan was prepared to try the other companies in turn, until he found one. The cover story, if he felt inclined to offer one, involved hauling coworkers to and from a business conference in relative comfort.

As luck would have it, he didn't need the cover. The rental agency had two four-doors available, a compact and a mid-size. Bolan took the midsize, showed his New York driver's license in the Cooper name, signed for the standard insurance and handed over "Cooper's" platinum American Express card. The clerk ran it through and received immediate confirmation.

One more notch on the Stony Man budget.

Bolan took his copy of the rental agreement, with a set of car keys, and received directions to the pickup lot. Leaving the terminal, they saw Guzman drive past, pretending not to notice them. The pair crossed six lanes of traffic to the rental parking lot, keeping watch for a trap, but none was waiting.

Their vehicle was a four-door hatchback Mazda 6, painted a kind of silver color that would pass for gray in most lights. Bolan liked the nondescript appearance, nothing flashy to draw glances or impress itself on someone's memory.

Leaving the pickup lot, they met Guzman again and Bolan led him to a nearby restaurant, where Cohen switched cars and Bolan placed the empty bags in her convertible. They would return to her house, drop her car and bags, then follow Guzman's lead to find the local armorer.

If they were ambushed there, Bolan knew Guzman was to blame, and he would settle that debt with his dying breath, if need be.

On the other hand, if all went well, Hans Dietrich's Nazis would be in for yet another grim surprise.

Bolan was looking forward to it.

One step on the payback trail that would, if he had anything to say about it, bring their evil fiefdom crashing down.

"HOW MANY LEFT?" Otto Jaeger asked.

"Three," Karl Einhardt said. "We're doing well."

"You think so?" Jaeger challenged.

Einhardt stiffened. "Sir, I meant with the disposal. Certainly, I don't think—"

"I know what you meant," Jaeger said, interrupting the apology. "We've lost two good men, Karl. Wheat thrown out with the chaff."

"Yes, sir."

Still, they *were* lucky that Mr. Dietrich's investments happened to include a metal-working factory in Bogotá. The manager had opened up without complaint when Jaeger called, and showed them how to operate the various machines. He waited in his office now, reading a dog-eared paperback, while Jaeger, Einhardt and their men did all the dirty work. When they were finished, Mr. Manager would check to see that everything was clean, secure and normal in appearance.

Simple. Lucky.

But it got on Jaeger's nerves, watching as Einhardt and his soldiers fed one corpse after another into a blast furnace. He had helped them empty pockets, sorting out the metal objects— watches, pocketknives, brass knuckles, coins—that could be saved. The rest, all flesh and bone and fabric, would be going up a smokestack, bleeding out into the stained sky over Bogotá.

Jaeger had no last words for Krieger or Rauschman. They couldn't hear him anyway, whether their souls were in Valhalla or there was no afterlife at all. Jaeger thought nothing of such things, more interested in making what he could of his remaining days and nights on Earth.

For him, that meant obeying orders, never failing to perform his duty to Mr. Dietrich and their holy cause. He might not live to see the Fourth Reich rise to rule the world, but when it happened, those who reaped the benefits would speak his name with reverence, would know him as a hero of the struggle that had lasted more than half a century.

Jaeger lit a cigarette as Einhardt's two assistants dragged

one of the hired guns toward the furnace by his ankles. They, the living, had been sweating since the work began, their faces reddened on the sides presented to the open furnace hatch.

There was a platform to assist them in their labor, six feet long and heated to the point where eggs and bacon could be grilled upon its shiny surface. Einhardt's men lifted each corpse in turn, to place it on the platform, then applied gloved palms to tip it, sliding the ungainly cargo down into the hungry flames.

"That's the last one, sir," Einhardt told him.

"All right. You take the bag of leftovers," Jaeger said, nodding toward the burlap bag containing metal objects looted from their dead. "Send someone for the manager, and let's get out of here."

"Yes, sir. We're staying at the compound, I suppose."

"Until we settle this," Jaeger confirmed. "Until we have our vengeance and some good news to report."

"Guzman won't slip away from us a second time, Mr. Jaeger."

"He didn't *slip* away this time," Jaeger replied, his tone knife-edged. "He stood and fought and kicked our asses. It's a fact we can't deny, but I demand an explanation."

"You shall have it, sir!"

"I don't want promises," Jaeger stated. "Show me results!"

"Yes, sir!"

Jaeger acknowledged Einhardt's heel-clicking salute, his own right arm raised just enough to make it count, without a full-dress spectacle. Einhardt turned on his heel, picked up the jangling bag and marched off to retrieve the manager.

Jaeger moved toward the exit, craving cleaner air.

THE HARDWARE DEALER OPERATED from a pawn shop in the Barrio Unidos district, near El Lago Park. Jorge Guzman directed Bolan west on Avenida 80, into the Siete de Agosto neighborhood until they found the place.

They hadn't called ahead, but Guzman claimed the dealer lived above his shop, a matter of security and economics all rolled into one. Bolan saw lights upstairs as they arrived and motored past.

Bolan took his time, scanning the street. He had expected them nearly four hours earlier. He would've given up by now, and might be angry at the snub, but injured feelings were not Bolan's main concern. A businessman would set anger aside for money.

On the other hand, if he had sold them out, there might still be a trap in place.

How long would the police—or Dietrich's men, for that matter—sit waiting on a public street, when their intended targets didn't show? Four hours seemed excessive, given the slaughter in Puenta Aranda that evening. Bolan guessed that any watchers, whether cops or killers would have bailed by now, assuming that the set was blown.

But still, he wanted to be sure.

He drove slowly around the block, scanning storefronts and darkened, recessed doorways, checking upstairs windows that could serve as snipers' nests. At last, when he was reasonably satisfied that no one lay in wait for them, he found a parking space outside the shop and pulled up to the curb.

Guzman using his cell phone, called from the shop's doorstep, and Cohen listened as he asked the dealer to come down. Her nod told Bolan that their guide had played it straight.

Which didn't mean there was no risk involved.

Bolan could time the dealer on his trip downstairs, but how long did it take to speed-dial the police or Dietrich's storm troopers and tell them what was happening? Five seconds? Ten?

In any case, they might emerge from shopping to be ambushed on the street, but Bolan had no other options short of locating a military arms depot and stealing what he needed for the job ahead. He'd try it this way, first, and keep his fingers crossed.

A long six minutes after Guzman phoned upstairs, they saw lights in a back room of the shop and someone's lanky silhouette advancing toward the front. Bolan was ready for a fast-draw with the IMBEL .45, and Cohen had one hand inside her floppy purse, no doubt clutching the Jericho 941.

The dealer was all smiles as he opened the door, dismissing Guzman's courteous apologies over the hour and their missed appointment, switching into English easily.

"It's nothing, I assure you. I won't sleep for hours, yet." He introduced himself to Bolan and to Cohen in turns. "I am Emil Barbosa. Come inside, my friends. Please, follow me."

Barbosa double-locked the door behind them, then retreated to the back room where a weak light burned. It was a standard office, nothing out of place. The dealer passed his tidy desk, opened another door and stepped into a lavatory barely large enough to hold the toilet on its east wall and a small sink on the south.

Barbosa wasn't showing off his plumbing, though. Turning to the north wall, he fiddled briefly with a towel rack, and the wall swung outward, yawning into darkness. Half a heartbeat later, when he threw a switch, fluorescent lights revealed a stairway leading downward to a basement storage room.

"My hideaway," the dealer told them with a little smile and shrug.

He led the way downstairs, Guzman behind him, Bolan third, with Cohen bringing up the rear. Bolan imagined that he heard the bare suggestion of a gasp escape her lips as they beheld the dealer's wares.

Three walls supported racks of weapons: rifles, shotguns, submachine guns, RPGs. The fourth, reserved for pistols, had at least a hundred handguns dangling from steel pegs by their trigger guards, a cornucopia of automatics and revolvers, with a few small SMGs—Ingrams and mini-Uzis—added for variety.

The middle of the showroom floor was heaped with crates of military ordnance, arranged so that potential buyers had three aisles available for browsing. At the south end of the room, farthest from the stairs, Bolan saw heavy weapons squatting on their tripods. He identified a Russian AGS-17 automatic grenade launcher, an American M2HB .50-caliber machine gun, an Austrian Steyr 51.2mm IWS 2000 anti-matériel rifle and a vintage M-224 60mm mortar from the States.

So many guns, so little room inside his Mazda 6.

Bolan began with his favorite assault rifle, the ever-trustworthy Steyr AUG, with factory-standard optical sights and a dozen extra see-through plastic magazines. For backup, just in case, he chose a Spectre SMG, the Italian design with a unique 50-round staggered box magazine, fourteen inches overall with its folding stock retracted.

Barbosa didn't have a Beretta 93-R to replace Bolan's borrowed IMBEL .45, so he chose a SIG P-226 with 20-round box magazines. When he had dry-fired it and loaded up, slipped on the fast-draw shoulder rig he'd picked to wear, Bolan returned the IMBEL to Guzman and asked his translator if he wanted to choose another gun.

Guzman considered it, then shook his head. "I know these two," he said. "The rest of this, I am more dangerous to you and to myself."

"Your call."

He turned to Cohen and found her checking out a mini-Uzi with a fat, foot-long suppressor mounted on its muzzle. From the way she handled it, she clearly had experience with the Israeli SMG, which, naturally, came as no surprise.

"You want to take that with you?" Bolan asked. And when she frowned, added, "My treat."

"You are too generous," she said.

"Push comes to shove," Bolan replied, "I think I'll get my money's worth."

"How much?" she asked.

Before Barbosa had a chance to speak, Bolan added, "For all of this, with, say, a thousand rounds for each?"

"Four weapons, the suppressor, seven thousand rounds of ammunition… Shall we say, um, eighteen thousand U.S. dollars?"

Bolan could've argued, but he had the gambler's bankroll. "Sounds all right to me," he said. "But we'll need duffel bags to carry these."

"Of course, *señor*. Four bags, I think, and make the holster for your pistol my gift, eh?"

Bolan turned toward the armory's south wall. "Okay," he said. "There's only one more thing I need."

"WHAT WILL YOU DO WITH this?" Cohen asked as Bolan placed his fifth and sixth fat duffel bags into the Mazda's trunk.

One bag was awkward, all sharp corners poking through the fabric, weighing a fraction over forty pounds. The final bag was heavier, some fifty pounds, and Bolan handled it with utmost care.

"From what you told me of the target," he replied, "I may not have a chance to get inside. With this, I can reach out and touch someone."

"It is a bit much, don't you think?"

Closing the trunk, he answered with a question of his own.

"You said no one but Dietrich's Nazis or their flunkies in the compound, right?"

"Sometimes they bring in whores," she said. "Tonight, I don't think they'll be in the party mood."

"In that case," Bolan said, "I think 'a bit much' is exactly right."

"But if you miss…"

"I won't."

The target, she had told him, was located in the Usaquén district, northeast of downtown Bogotá. To get there, Guzman guided Bolan through Chapinero, Bogotá's most important banking district—and, by some odd coincidence, the heart of the city's gay community.

They passed the Theatron, Bogotá's largest and most flamboyant gay disco, following the flow of traffic northward into Usaquén. This was Old Bogotá, including the Zona Colonial, built up around the Santa Barbara mission founded in 1665.

Bolan's interest lay farther east, in the Lijacá neighborhood, where Hans Dietrich had planted a five-acre outpost of Colonia Dignidad, encircled by eight-foot walls topped by razor wire, broken glass set in concrete and closed-circuit television cameras.

"You see?" Cohen said as he drove past the wrought iron gates and spotted two men just inside, both armed with automatic rifles. "If you had a trained assault team, possibly, it could be done. If you would do it on your own, please leave the car keys—and, perhaps, a copy of your will."

He smiled at that and said, "You're right. I won't be going in. I still have something for them, though."

"You're serious?"

"Believe it."

On his second circuit of the property, he drove into a vacant lot behind the Nazi compound, parked the Mazda and popped the trunk. His two companions followed as he got out of the car, removed two heavy duffels from the trunk and walked into the middle of the field.

"You'll need to keep an eye on traffic," Bolan told them. "Give a shout if a patrol car happens by."

"Don't worry," Cohen replied. "You'll hear me."

Mortars were uncomplicated weapons—basically a baseplate and a firing tube, adjustable for varied altitude. The 60 mm M-224 model he had chosen was familiar from his Special Forces days, but essentially they were all the same. Mortars were muzzle-loading weapons, with a firing mechanism at the bottom of the tube. Each round was dropped by hand, then lofted through an arc selected by the gunner, firing over hills and other obstacles.

Like puny eight-foot walls.

The M-224 had a maximum range of 1,500 meters—about 4,900 feet—but Bolan's firing point was less than 150 yards from the heart of Dietrich's compound. Accordingly, he cranked the mortar's bipod to an angle of some eighty-five degrees for starters.

If the first round fell short, that was fine. At least he knew it wouldn't sail on past his mark and land in someone's living room two blocks away.

"Ready?" he asked his two companions as he pulled the first of ten high-explosive rounds from the second duffel bag.

"As ready as I'll ever be," Cohen said.

Guzman was silent, nodding.

"Right, then. Here we go."

OTTO JAEGER NEEDED schnapps. His flask was empty, and he barely felt the buzz of alcohol at work inside his brain. Before he made the call that he was dreading, he would fortify himself.

Another sip or two. What could it hurt?

He found the bottle he was looking for, removed its cap and palmed a glass. Already, he could taste it, feel the burn inside him as it lit a fire to drive away the chill of death.

Jaeger deserved it. He was—

The explosion literally made him jump. He dropped the bottle and his glass, both shattering around his feet on impact, drenching Jaeger's shoes and socks. He didn't even feel it, wheeling toward the doorway, running in a crouch out of the study and along the hallway.

A second blast. This one significantly closer to the house. Jaeger heard windows shatter, smelled dust sifting downward from the ceiling overhead.

He fumbled for his pistol, having no idea how it would help him, who he meant to shoot. A gun in hand made him feel better, somehow. At the moment, that was all that counted.

What *was* it?

Not grenades. The blasts were much too loud for any hand grenade he'd ever heard of.

The house was damaged now. Jaeger could almost feel it tilting as he charged along the hallway, past the formal dining room into the parlor. Dust and smoke was everywhere, his soldiers milling in confusion.

Jaeger cursed and shouted orders at them, but they didn't seem to hear him. Some of them looked stunned. One sat cross-legged on the floor, holding his scalp in place with bloody fingers.

Jaeger was in the doorway, one foot on the front porch, when the room behind him detonated. Shrapnel, or perhaps the jagged bits of shattered furniture, ripped through his back and buttocks, wrenched a scream from Jaeger's lips as he was airborne, tumbling helplessly through space.

He landed on his back and screamed again, but weakly. With a force of will that cost him everything, he struggled to all fours and faced the house.

It was in flames, beyond salvation, sagging in the middle where its roof was shattered, walls swayed inward toward the funeral pyre.

Jaeger lurched backward, away from the terrible heat, but his arms and legs failed him. Crumpling, he felt another detonation, and another, rip through the shambles of his former home-away-from-home.

The last explosion punched the front wall outward, flaming bricks and mortar tumbling toward him, giving Jaeger barely time to scream.

CHAPTER SIX

Amazonas Region, Colombia

According to Guzman, Florencia was the nearest city of any real size to Colonia Victoria. It was the capital of Caquetá, Colombia's third-largest "department" or state, which sprawled over 88,965 square kilometers, most of heavily forested mountains.

Bolan passed on the suggestion of a charter flight for three reasons. First, he understood that most private pilots supporting themselves with short hauls had links to the various drug cartels and were likely covert DAS informants on the side. Second, in the present circumstances, he opposed the notion of a total stranger dropping them somewhere he'd never been, when they might find a firing squad assembled at their destination. Finally, they would need wheels to get beyond Florencia, and Bolan didn't want to leave a paper trail by renting yet another car, unless his other options were exhausted.

So, they drove.

Two hundred miles of mostly rural highway lay between Bogotá and Florencia. The journey would take them across three "departments," or states, with at least one stop for fuel plus others as required.

From Bogotá, in Cundinamarca, Bolan drove south along the Cordillera Oriental—the eastern face of the Andes range, its peaks still relatively tame before they marched down into Ecuador and then Peru. They took turns driving, pushing into Meta at the geographic center of Colombia.

"We won't be driving to the colony itself, I take it," Cohen said after some ninety minutes on the road.

"They'll have an access road," Bolan replied. "But no, we won't be driving in."

Before leaving the capital that morning, they'd gone shopping for outfits and boots more suitable to jungle hiking than their normal street clothes. Those items shared the Mazda's trunk with most of the team's military hardware, leaving only sidearms and the mini-Uzi readily accessible in an emergency.

Bolan was not expecting one. Some of his enemies in Bogotá were dead, the others badly shaken, and those shock waves would reach all the way to Hans Dietrich's Colonia Victoria.

It wouldn't feel like victory this morning.

So far, Bolan had no reason to believe his targets knew where he came from, or who he was. There was no question of their tumbling to his born identity, but on the down side, it would not require a hacker genius to discover that one Matthew Cooper had arrived on Avianca's shuttle from Miami, just before the feces hit the fan.

And after that…

If they were tracking Guzman, they would soon have "Cooper's" name—another reason why Bolan opposed renting a second car, when every agency demanded credit cards and driver's licenses. Beyond the Cooper front, however, he was smoke.

Of course, they'd find the rental agency where Bolan had

obtained the Mazda 6, but he was hoping it would take at least a little while. With any luck, they'd waste more time and manpower hunting the rental's license number through the streets of Bogotá, scouring public garages and hotels, driving in endless circles around parking malls.

But where else would they look?

As if reading his mind, Cohen asked Bolan, "Do you think they will be watching for us in Florencia?"

"I hope not," Bolan said, "but we won't know until we get there."

He was hoping for some lead time, for some luck to follow them at least until they had to leave the car behind. If they were spotted in Florencia, whether they had to fight or not, it meant that Dietrich knew where they were going, and his jungle fortress promised to be tough enough without a red alert in place when they arrived.

"It's been a few years since I passed survival training," Cohen said. "Of course, they trained us in the desert, but I promise not to slow you."

"I'm not concerned about it," Bolan said.

Why should he be? They'd already agreed that anyone who couldn't keep up with the team would be cut loose. And whether either of his two companions recognized the fact or not, Bolan was serious on that score. Once they started hiking, there would be no place for stragglers, weaklings, quitters.

"I agree it's bad if we are noticed in Florencia," Guzman announced from the backseat. "But they may still be waiting at Colonia Victoria."

"I don't mind preparation," Bolan answered. "But I don't like handing it to Dietrich on a silver platter."

It was only logical that Dietrich would increase security around his private fiefdom once he got the news from Bogotá by radio or telephone or e-mail—whatever the twenty-first century's Nazis were using these days. Bolan was counting on increased patrols, more lookouts watching the perimeter, and he could deal with that.

Or so he hoped.

The killer would be if their target knew exactly when and where they were arriving in his bailiwick. If someone, somehow, had discovered and betrayed their plan.

In that case, there would only be two suspects, both of them now riding with him in the Mazda 6. For Bolan's part, he hadn't briefed Brognola on his latest moves, nor had he cleared the southward thrust with Stony Man. His backup team at home knew he was going to Colonia Victoria sometime, somehow, before he left Colombia, but they could not have ratted Bolan out to save their souls.

If someone screwed him, it would be Guzman or Cohen. And while the latter prospect was attractive, taken in a different vein, Bolan would show no mercy to a traitor in the field. If Bolan reached Colonia Victoria alone, at least he'd know his one-man strike force was trustworthy and efficient.

"I can drive now, if you like," Cohen said.

"Suits me," the Executioner replied, and pulled his Mazda over toward the shoulder of the mountain road.

Bogotá

JORGE GUZMAN LIVED in the Ciudad Kennedy district of Bogotá, west of downtown. The district had been known as Ciudad Techo until 1963, when sentimental politicians renamed it in honor of America's martyred president. John Kennedy had toured Bogotá in 1961, promoting his Alliance for Progress in Latin America, and many locals still cherished the memory.

It was ironic, Wilhelm Kaufman thought, that JFK was safe

in Bogotá, with all its violence even in the sixties, but he'd had his brains blown out in Texas.

Like the peasant Kaufman had come to kill.

He didn't know why it had taken this long to discover Guzman's home address, nor did he care. Kaufman was not a strategist, beyond the details of whatever execution he might be assigned, and he would not share in the punishment of the investigators who had failed to locate Guzman's roost before this day.

He wondered if the bastard would be home, or if he'd had the basic common sense to run away somewhere and hide. Kaufman hoped not. It would be good for him if he could kill the man who'd caused his leader so much trouble overnight. Better if he could kill the second one, as well.

He knew Guzman had gone to meet someone at El Dorado International. From that point onward, everything was muddled, starting with the slaughter of Horst Krieger's hunting party and continuing through the bizarre assault on Otto Jaeger's stronghold hours later.

Who used mortars in the middle of a teeming city? Could some lunatic purchase a mortar and its high-explosive rounds, as if he was out shopping for the next week's groceries?

Apparently.

Kaufman had orders to interrogate Guzman and anybody found with him, if it was feasible. Of course, it wouldn't be. If he or they proved dumb enough to stay at Guzman's home, it was a certainty that they'd be armed and ready to defend themselves.

In fact, Kaufman was counting on it.

He had no scruples concerning torture. Warriors of the Master Race could not afford such childish weaknesses. But Kaufman was enraged by what had happened to his comrades, and he wanted blood to wash the bitter taste out of his mouth.

He beamed a silent thought to Jorge Guzman, whom he'd never seen. *Be stupid,* he urged silently. *Be at home.*

Under the circumstances, Kaufman would have liked to lead an eight- or ten-man team, but soldiers were in short supply that morning. Eight had been cut down in Puenta Aranda, six more killed and fifteen wounded in the wild mortar barrage at Jaeger's place. Kaufman was lucky to have three men with him—Aryans, not hired guns—after all the bloody chaos of the previous night.

Hans Becker had the BMW, while Johan Volker occupied the backseat, with an automatic rifle in his lap. At Guzman's they would all be going in. It was a breach of protocol, which said that no car should be left without a driver in a combat situation, but Kaufman was damned if he would enter Guzman's place with only one man covering his back.

It wasn't fear, of course.

Just common sense.

They turned off Avenida 68 and wound through residential streets until they found Guzman's apartment house. He didn't own a home, likely could not afford one if he'd wanted to. Apartments meant potential witnesses, and since Kaufman was not supposed to kill them all, some caution was required.

"Park over there," he ordered Becker, pointing to an empty stretch of curb across the street.

Becker swerved toward the parking space, nosed in against the flow of traffic on the two-way street, and killed the BMW's engine. All three men took time to double-check their weapons, then concealed them under jackets as they climbed out of the car.

It was a short walk to the entrance of Guzman's apartment house. From there, they climbed a flight of steps to reach the second floor and moved along a musty-smelling hallway to the door of Guzman's flat.

Kaufman was not about to knock and give the bastard time to reach a weapon. With a single kick, he smashed the door's cheap lock and lunged across the threshold, with his men behind him.

And he knew at once that they had missed their prey.

The flat was clearly vacant, but they still went through the motions, checking every room, peering beneath the bed, probing the closets, even looking underneath the bathroom and the kitchen sinks.

Mouthing a curse, Kaufman turned to his men, his grim face daring either one of them to speak.

"Start over," he commanded. "Tear this place apart. Find something, *anything* to tell us where they've gone."

His own job, meanwhile, was the hardest.

It was his task to report another failure, which would bring another tongue-lashing, at best.

And at the worst?

He didn't even want to think about it as he palmed his cell phone and began to dial.

Florencia, Caquetá Department

TO GABRIELLA COHEN, their next stop was simply one more Third World city that her nation's enemies had tainted with their madness. She remembered certain basic facts—founded by missionaries in 1902, with something like 140,000 year-round residents—but they were not important to her.

She was simply passing through.

There were no full-time Nazis living in Florencia, as far as Cohen knew. But the cocaine trade flourished there, as everywhere throughout Colombia, and Dietrich's fascists had enduring ties to that illicit industry. They might be *anywhere,* in fact, which kept her on alert as Jorge Guzman drove them into town, Matt Cooper lounging in the backseat for a change.

Guzman followed the street signs, rolling through the heart

of town past an eclectic mix of shops, amusements, offices and restaurants. Some of the shops aspired to greatness, offering designer clothing, golf clubs or expensive-looking jewelry. Others, often positioned side-by-side with those who strove to be their betters, catered to a rural clientele with basic tools, supplies and garments advertised for durability rather than style.

"We need to eat," Bolan said from the rear, "and we should top off the fuel tank. Find someplace that looks decent, off the main drag, with convenient parking if you can."

Ten minutes later they were sitting in a restaurant called Casa del Sol, perusing menus while a waitress fetched their coffee order. Cooper didn't seem as out of place as Cohen had imagined, with his bronzed complexion and dark hair. As long as he kept conversation to a minimum, the nearby diners might mistake him for a local.

Their coffee was delivered, and they ordered what might be their last real meal until the mission was completed. Thinking of her bowels, and of being left behind if she retarded progress on their journey, Cohen ordered well-done steak and baked potato, passing on the soup and salad. Cooper followed her example, while Guzman ordered a native dish with shrimp and chicken over rice.

They held their conversation to a minimum while waiting for their food, then dug in with a will when it arrived. Cooper ate like a soldier, putting food away with grim efficiency, as if he might be interrupted anytime by some new crisis. Cohen did not try to match her pace, but neither did she copy Guzman's leisurely approach to dining, sipping coffee after every second or third bite.

When they were finished and the plates were cleared away, Cooper paid the bill in cash and led them back in the direction of the metered parking lot where they had left the Mazda 6. It still had time remaining on the meter when they reached it, money wasted as they piled into the car and drove away.

Guzman was at the wheel again, this time with Cooper in the seat beside him, Cohen in the rear. She hadn't argued when the tall American had claimed the shotgun seat, guessing his motive when their eyes met briefly.

Cooper trusted Guzman to a point, likely because someone in the United States had vouched for him, and Guzman had done his part, apparently, in their first clash with Dietrich's Nazis. Whether he'd killed one was debatable, by now unprovable, but Cohen had observed him firing in their general direction and had stitched his bullet wound.

If that was all a sham, she gave Herr Dietrich points for planning it. But would he trust Guzman or any other native with so delicate a mission?

Cohen couldn't say, but Cooper clearly meant to watch Guzman as they approached the point where they had to leave their vehicle, change clothes and then continue overland on foot. If Guzman had some kind of double cross in mind, if he had tricked them somehow, Cohen knew the big American would kill him when the trap was sprung.

Unless I kill him first, she thought, her face deadpan despite the homicidal images filling her mind.

The trick would be split-second timing, picking out some piece of evidence that proved Guzman's betrayal, then reacting with a point-blank shot into his skull before the ambushers could riddle her with bullets.

Cohen reckoned she would draw her pistol as they neared their destination. Have it ready, just in case. If time was too short, she could simply shoot him through the driver's seat, keep firing until hostile rounds snuffed out her life.

Another fifteen minutes put Florencia behind them, as they motored on to the southeast. Their destination lay within Caquetá, near the Amazonas borderline, and while it was accessible by four-wheel drive, they would be walking in.

She didn't relish that, but understood the logic of it. Anyone expecting them would focus on the road, perhaps on aerial approaches, before staking out the forest. Dietrich would likely mount patrols, but they would not know who to look for or the route danger selected as it came to visit them.

Watching the countryside unroll around them, Cohen hoped that she would not be forced to kill Guzman. She hoped Cooper's air of confidence was justified, and that he wasn't simply one more arrogant American who still believed that God was always on his side.

She knew that wasn't true.

Despite her parents' faith, their efforts to respect the Torah's teaching on all subjects, Cohen often wondered whether God had any interest in choosing sides. She'd seen so many dreadful things befall good people in her lifetime, that she wondered if He even cared.

No matter, she thought as Guzman drove them farther southward. *I still care enough for both of us.*

Colonia Victoria

HANS DIETRICH STOOD before a full-length mirror, studying his own reflection in the glass. He would be ninety on his next birthday, in August, but he looked considerably younger. Ten years? Twenty? Twenty-five?

His full head of hair was snow-white, like his bristling mustache and the thick brows that capped his blue eyes. He still pursued a vigorous routine, at least for one his age, and made a point of copulating with his several wives as often as he could. Dietrich believed they all were satisfied with his performance, but as long as *he* enjoyed it and made every effort to extend his bloodline, that was all that really mattered.

Regular sex aside, Dietrich attributed his personal longevity to Adolf Hitler. Since his thirties, he had followed the Führer's example by abstaining from tobacco and pursuing a strict vegetarian diet. Dietrich did not demand the same of his people, but set an example for others to follow and lectured the colony's children twice yearly on subjects related to health.

His problem, at the moment, had nothing to do with wrinkles on his face or the impact of gravity on his once-sculpted body. No one lived forever. Did he have another ten years left within him?

Hopefully.

Unless he fell prey to his enemies.

And they were drawing closer to him, even now. Dietrich could feel it, reinforced by all the bad news pouring in from Bogotá. Who dared to shell his property and people with a mortar, in the very capital itself? Why couldn't Commandant Menendez and his DAS locate the scum responsible?

Because they're gone, he thought. *They're coming after me.*

A muffled rapping on his study door almost made Dietrich jump. He turned immediately from the mirror and called out, *"Hereingekommen!"*

The door opened, revealing Nasser Khalil. He glanced around the room, then said, "May I presume that means, *'come in'*?"

"Of course, my friend. Come in, by all means."

Khalil shut the door behind him, gently, almost as if worried that the noise might wake someone. Dietrich admired the Arab's grace and his economy of motion, not to mention his abiding hatred for the Jews. Sometimes he thought it was a shame that Khalil had been born an inferior, and not an Aryan.

"Forgive me for disturbing you, Herr Dietrich."

"Not at all. May I assist you in some way?"

By which he meant, Perhaps it's time for you to leave.

Two weeks with half a dozen Arabs living at the colony seemed quite enough to Dietrich, but it would be foolish to expel them when their great conspiracy was bearing such delicious fruit.

"Herr Dietrich, you're aware that I and my companions have satellite-communication access via telephone."

"Of course. Is something wrong with the reception?"

"On the contrary," Khalil replied. "It's perfect, but the news from Bogotá is…shall we say, alarming?"

"Ah." Dietrich felt anger coiling in his stomach. He controlled it with a will. "I've only learned the latest and the worst of it, myself. I planned to brief you fully over supper, but I see that you have questions now."

"Indeed. From the reports received so far, it seems your personnel in Bogotá have suffered major losses."

"An investigation is proceeding as we speak," Dietrich said. "I prefer to trust my own men, rather than the media, which, as you know, is dominated by the Jews."

"And if the sad reports are true, what does it mean? What are your plans?"

"Much like yourself, I live and operate within a world of enemies," Dietrich replied. "My first suspicion falls upon Mossad, but with the incidents coming so close behind our own forays in the United States and Europe, someone else may be to blame. When I determine the identities of those responsible—"

"But in the meantime," Khalil interrupted him, rudely, unthinkably, "what shall be done?"

"I take it you're concerned for our security, within the colony?"

Khalil shrugged casually, almost elegantly. "If these unknown enemies can strike with mortars in the heart of Bogotá," he said, "perhaps they also have artillery or aircraft. Will they shell or bomb us here, perhaps while we are sleeping in our beds?"

My beds, Dietrich thought as he forced a vaguely condescending smile. "You need have no concerns on that account," he said. "I have patrols out in the forest, sentries on the only road and ample weapons to repel airborne assault, if it should come to that. Which, may I say with all respect, seems rather fanciful."

"You guarantee our safety, then?"

"Beyond a doubt," Dietrich replied. "Would you enjoy a glass of schnapps?"

He knew better, of course. Strict Muslims drank no alcohol.

"No, thank you," Khalil answered stiffly. "I shall leave you to your meditation."

"And we'll meet again at supper," Dietrich said, escorting Khalil to the door.

I hope we're serving pork, he thought, and pictured Khalil with an apple in his mouth.

San José del Guaviare

NALDO AZNAR WAS RELAXING on a chaise longue beside his heart-shaped swimming pool when Ismael Calderon appeared beside him, blotting out the sun.

"Stand somewhere else," Aznar commanded. "I need all the UV I can get."

He'd read an article last week, replete with footnotes citing scientific studies, that contended that exposure to the sun did not, in fact, cause skin cancer. The very opposite was true, according to the authors who were doctors of some sort, each one a Ph.D. Citing statistics from the tropic regions of the world, they claimed that more exposure to sunlight, combined with the ingestion of specific herbs, increased virility and lengthened lives.

Aznar was sold. His chef had been instructed to obtain the herbs in question and incorporate them into every meal. Aznar, meanwhile, was soaking up the rays and testing the hypothesis at every given opportunity, with prostitutes who passed through his estate in relays. He expected two more on the stroke of four o'clock, and did not wish to be disturbed.

"Naldo," Calderon said, "it's Dietrich on the telephone."

Aznar stretched out a hand, heavy with gold and diamonds, to receive the cordless phone from his lieutenant. Putting on a smile that didn't reach his eyes, he spoke into the mouthpiece.

"Hans, amigo. It's a pleasure."

"Not for me, to call at such a time," Dietrich replied.

"What's wrong, my friend?"

There was a moment's hesitation on the line before Dietrich replied. "You haven't heard the news from Bogotá, I take it?"

Aznar felt a worm of tension start to wriggle in his stomach. "News, Hans? No. There was a film on satellite, you know. Bruce Willis. I don't like the propaganda on the news channels. What's happened?"

"Where do I begin?" Dietrich asked, then he launched into his tale as if he'd never asked the question. Aznar listened to the grim and somewhat muddled story of surveillance at an airport, followed by a shooting, then the demolition of Dietrich's estate in Bogotá. It left him wondering if the old Nazi's mind had come unhinged.

"Artillery, you say?"

"No, no! A mortar! The police found it outside the walls. The bastards sat there, if you can believe it, lobbing shells into my house!"

In fact, Aznar was having trouble with the story, but it was an easy thing to check, once he got off the phone. Meanwhile, he needed to calm Dietrich down before the old man did something bizarre and jeopardized their whole network.

"I will investigate at once," he said, using a tone that he believed to be both reassuring and authoritative. "In the meantime, do your men in Bogotá need help? Perhaps some reinforcements? Anything at all?"

"I've spoken to our friend at DAS," Dietrich replied, "but if you have some men to spare, I'm searching for the animals responsible."

"Of course. You know their names?"

"Just one. Jorge Guzman. As for the other, he arrived last night from the United States. Miami. Traveling as Matthew Cooper."

"You mean to say *two men* did all of this?"

"There must be more," Dietrich said. "I'm convinced of it. But these two are the only ones with names, so far. Guzman, I understand, is known among the criminal fraternity for smuggling contraband. He's known to the police and DAS but has not been to prison."

"When my people find him," Aznar promised, "he will wish he had."

"Before he dies," Dietrich said, "we must find out who he's working for."

"We have our ways," said Aznar. "As, I'm sure, do you."

"Good hunting, then," the aged German said. "I'll stay in touch."

"Yes, do."

Aznar called Calderon back and issued rapid-fire commands to mobilize his men in Bogotá. He didn't like being involved in Dietrich's business, but they shared too many interests for Aznar to simply stand aside and watch the German's outfit crumble without trying to assist him.

Dietrich was unstable, likely always had been, but he was a man of influence, whose mountain acreage in Caquetá provided a reliable supply of coca leaves and a base for Aznar's illicit refineries. Losing Colonia Victoria would not put Aznar out of business, but it would wound him.

Besides, he didn't like the thought of petty criminals and foreigners meddling in business that concerned him, interfering in his life, his world.

Dietrich would ultimately blame the Jews, of course. Aznar preferred to wait and find out for himself who was responsible.

And when he knew their names, knew where to find them, he would show no mercy.

Solano, Caquetá Department

BOLAN HAD GIVEN UP on trying to absorb the intricacies of Colombian geography and government. He understood that there were regions, broken up into departments, each with various municipalities that might be towns or largest areas, like counties in the States. Jorge Guzman had spent three-quarters of an hour trying to explain it, while they traveled, but it ultimately made no difference.

The last stop on their driving journey was a town called San José del Curillo. Judging by its appearance, Bolan guessed that it had to have two or three thousand inhabitants, reinforced on market days and local celebrations by the occupants of various outlying farms. It occupied high ground, with narrow winding streets, and held the forest at bay with an effort.

Although it was a frontier town of sorts, San José del Curillo did not have the wide-open feel of some places Bolan had seen on previous visits to Colombia. He saw no armed men loitering about the streets, no scars of gunfire on the reasonably clean facades of downtown shops and offices. The police had an office on the town square, but no uniforms were visible as Bolan drove through town from east to west and out the other side.

They had considered hiring someone to conceal and guard

the Mazda, then rejected the idea. The bottom line: they couldn't know which locals might be trustworthy, and anyone who played straight with them ran a risk of being killed—or worse.

Bolan preferred to take his chances and conceal the car himself, find someplace off the beaten track and hide it well enough that passing motorists—or even dedicated searchers—might not notice it. There was a chance he might return to find it stripped or stolen, naturally, but he could always find another ride.

And if, by chance, he didn't make it back, he wouldn't care what happened to the Mazda.

Bolan drove two miles past the eastern limits of San José del Curillo, then slowed and started looking for a likely place to hide the car. Ten minutes later, he turned off the two-lane highway, following an unpaved access road that petered out into a tangled wall of forest greenery after a hundred yards or so.

Perfect.

He stopped the car, got out and fetched his trail gear from the trunk. Guzman and Cohen followed his example, choosing separate trees to hide behind while stripping off their street clothes, changing into camouflage and hiking boots.

They soon returned and stashed their normal clothes, then armed themselves and buckled on their belts or bandoliers of surplus ammunition, with canteens, first-aid kits, flashlights and assorted other gear. Each of them carried rations for two days, the kind of foil-wrapped fare known to American military personnel as MREs—Meals, Ready to Eat.

When only street clothes and some empty duffel bags were left inside the Mazda, Bolan got behind the wheel and drove it slowly forward, nosing ever deeper into ferns and underbrush and clinging vines that dangled from the larger trees like stage props from a Tarzan movie. When the forest had completely closed around him, he crawled out with difficulty, wormed his way along the Mazda's flank, then spent five minutes rearranging flora he had crushed, until the car was more or less invisible.

It wasn't perfect, but it was the best that he could do. If Dietrich's hunters came along and found the car, so be it. Bolan would have reached Colonia Victoria by then.

"How far from here?" Bolan asked Guzman as he joined the others and retrieved his pack.

"Another five miles to the outskirts of the colony," Guzman replied. "Perhaps five more to reach the compound where most of the people live."

Ten miles, at least, and it was already midafternoon.

"We can decide when it gets dark, whether we camp or push on to the compound," Bolan said. "Right now, let's use the daylight we have left."

Using a compact GPS device, he struck off on a course that paralleled the forest highway without keeping it in sight. Sentries detailed to watch the two-lane blacktop would not see them, but he knew there could be roving foot patrols at large. After they reached Colonia Victoria, they'd also have to watch for traps, alarms and all kinds of surveillance gear.

All manageable, Bolan thought, as long as everyone stayed focused, stayed alert and stayed alive.

Before they reached the boundary of Colonia Victoria, the forest was their adversary. Although neutral in their puny human scheming, nature was an unforgiving host that seldom offered second chances. One misstep, a crippling accident, and someone would be left behind.

The mission took priority. It always had.

Bolan knew that. He knew that Cohen knew it, from her service with Mossad. He hoped their guide was on the same page, disabused of any notion that he was embarking on a grand adventure with a happy ending guaranteed.

Were endings ever happy, in the real world?

Someone, whose name Bolan couldn't recall, had once said that a happy ending simply meant the story wasn't finished yet.

Translation: nobody got out of life alive.

But while he still had time and strength remaining, Bolan meant to do his best, settling for nothing less.

And when he'd given all he had…to hell with it.

CHAPTER SEVEN

DAS Headquarters, Bogotá

Joaquin Menendez seldom smiled. From childhood, when he was a scrawny boy with alcoholic parents and few prospects, he had trained himself to mask emotions and present a grim, suspicious countenance to others, to the world at large. As he had grown, left school to join the army, and discovered that his true talent was treachery, smiles were superfluous, a sign of weakness.

On the rare occasions when he *did* smile, the expression was a mask, concealing his true feelings and intentions. A pleasant countenance disguised the storm of rage within. An offered hand distracted from the dagger clutched behind his back.

Menendez understood that he had realized his full potential, reached the pinnacle of his achievement in Colombia. He'd never be the president or any other kind of figurehead elected by the masses who mistook some politician's campaign promises for gospel truth. He would not rise above his present station and, in fact, remained at full alert each day to keep from being toppled by his enemies.

Or, in the present case, from being sabotaged by so-called friends.

Hans Dietrich was a problem. First, he was a German who had never bothered to become a citizen of his adopted nation. Second, he was infamous—or rather, had been, before age persuaded the Israelis that he wasn't worth a bullet or a kidnapping. And third, for all his quirks, he ranked among the twenty-five or thirty richest people in Colombia, which meant that he had influence.

Menendez had no problem with the fact that Dietrich was a rabid, unrepentant Nazi. Truth be told, the DAS commander found much to admire in what he'd read of Adolf Hitler's Reich, where state security was paramount and no one harbored any immature illusions about civil liberties. As for the Jews, he cared only for those who could put money in his pocket or assist him in some other way. Most of them did not matter to Menendez, one way or the other.

Now, Hans Dietrich had become a problem.

More specifically, the old man's enemies were causing problems that Menendez was required to solve. Failure would disappoint his sponsors, who might then encourage rivals to conspire against him, seeking ways and means to steal away the power it had taken nearly half a century for Menendez to claim.

The overnight mayhem did not concern him greatly. Bogotá had seen much worse, with higher body counts, although he granted that the mortar was a new twist. Car bombs, drive-by shootings and abductions were the normal stock-in-trade of various militias, death squads and cartels. So he would give the latest bloody bastards credit for originality.

And he would grind them into pulp at his first opportunity.

So far, he had two names.

Jorge Guzman was said to be a small-time smuggler, petty criminal, perhaps a state informer, though he'd never peddled information to the DAS. His modest flat had been ransacked before Menendez learned the address, so the search team he'd dispatched had come back empty-handed.

Still, his spies were everywhere, and they were watching. Wherever and whenever Guzman surfaced, he would be identified.

As for the second man, he seemed to be American, identified by his passport and Avianca reservation as one "Matthew Cooper." Checking out his background would require discretion and, perhaps, more time than Menendez could spare. He had people in Washington who could assist him, but it should be easier to trace the gringo in Colombia and kill him there.

Should be.

Menendez didn't know what Dietrich was involved in this time, and he cared only as much as the old Nazi's schemes might threaten his control of the empire Menendez had built for himself. As chief of the DAS, he was the nation's most powerful law-enforcement officer, answering only to the Colombian attorney general or the president. And they, of course, knew only what he chose to tell them about crime, conspiracies and insurrections nationwide.

It secretly amused Menendez that the logo for the attorney general's office was, in fact, a piece from a jigsaw puzzle. Menendez didn't know which idiot had chosen the peculiar symbol, or precisely what that moron had in mind when he selected it, but to Menendez it would always represent the fractured and chaotic nature of his homeland's politics.

In Colombia, the oldest rule was "Each man for himself." It helped if you possessed a private army to defend you and harass your enemies, as all the drug cartel commanders had.

As he, Menendez, had within the mighty DAS.

As long as he maintained control, guarded the secret information in his vaults that made some of the mighty tremble when his name was mentioned, then Menendez would endure. His personal idol, J. Edgar Hoover of the FBI, had dominated Washington, D.C., and pulled strings all around the world for almost fifty years. He still would be in charge today, if aging flesh and gray matter had not betrayed him.

Menendez had only ruled the DAS for seven years, and he was not prepared to watch it slip away from him. He would eliminate Hans Dietrich's enemies this time, because they threatened law and order—or, at least, the illusion of order Menendez created to bolster his own reputation. This he would do, but if Dietrich himself posed a problem, there were ways to deal with him, as well.

Despite his monthly bribes.

Despite his many influential friends in government and high society.

No person was invincible.

And if he caused Joaquin Menendez too much trouble, then that lesson might well be the last thing Dietrich ever learned.

Caquetá Department

TEN MILES WASN'T a killing march. On level, unobstructed ground a six-foot man could cover it with something like twenty-one thousand strides. Most healthy humans walked at speeds around three to four miles per hour, while race-walkers bumped that to five or six per. All things being equal, Bolan reckoned he could travel the ten miles to Hans Dietrich's compound in four hours, possibly four and a half.

Unfortunately, not all things were equal.

For starters, he wasn't alone. Cohen was fit and a decade younger than Bolan, but her legs were shorter, meaning that she used more energy to match his pace. As for Guzman, while he hadn't yet complained, the off-road adventure was taking its toll on a city boy's muscles and nerves, eating away at his stamina.

Another thing was the terrain, which bore no resemblance whatsoever to level, unobstructed ground. They were hiking through montane forest, which meant coping with altitude, radical slopes, unmapped rivers and streams, the crush of trees and undergrowth in places, widening thereafter into clearings. It was typical, in other words, but Bolan didn't know if either Cohen or Guzman had hiked enough to stay the course and still arrive in any shape to fight.

If nothing else, Bolan supposed they could assist him as decoys or bait. The sight of Cohen would distract most sentries long enough for Bolan to approach from a blind spot and make his kill.

Guzman would fight, he'd proved that much already, but he only carried two handguns, which meant that he was only dangerous within a radius of thirty feet or so. Cut that by half, perhaps two-thirds, for fighting in a forest, over ground familiar to their enemies, unknown to Bolan and his team.

Worst-case scenario, Bolan supposed that he could use Guzman as a diversion, send him off in one direction with instructions to be quiet, then trust him to make sufficient noise that any sentries in the neighborhood would flock to him, while Bolan slipped around behind them.

That would be the easy way.

And it was tantamount to murder.

If he chose that route, Bolan supposed it would be better, certainly more merciful, if he shot Guzman somewhere, anywhere, along their route of march. Thus he could spare his guide the pain of any awkward and debilitating wounds, much less the agony he'd suffer if Hans Dietrich's men took him alive.

He hoped that Guzman wasn't *that* dumb or naive. If faced with capture, Bolan hoped Guzman would save a bullet for himself and put away any religious scruples he'd been taught concerning suicide.

Bolan, a longtime connoisseur of death, new that a point-blank head shot was infinitely preferable to prolonged interrogation, when survival wasn't listed as an option. Dietrich's men would never let them go if Bolan and his team were caught alive. They would demand answers concerning motives and accomplices, but no response would save the captives' lives.

Dietrich had secrets to protect, and a ferocious reputation to uphold. He would no more release an enemy who fell into his hands than he would suddenly convert to Judaism and devote his final years to study of the Torah.

So, their options came down to success or death—at least, once they had penetrated Dietrich's private little world. Before that, if they turned back now, Bolan and Cohen probably could slip out of Colombia by one means or another, aided by their covert handlers. They could quit the game, escape and save themselves. It seemed unlikely that Dietrich possessed the manpower or influence outside Colombia to track them down.

In that event, of course, Guzman was screwed.

He was a native of Colombia, with no support system outside his homeland. Dietrich's men already knew his name, apparently, which meant their contacts in the DAS would know him, too. Unless their mission was completed, Guzman would be marked for death by Nazis and government agents alike.

And if they succeeded, what then?

Bolan was not assigned to kill Joaquin Menendez, and he wouldn't have accepted that assignment, even knowing what he did of the corrupt lawman's behavior and connections. Even if he managed to destroy Hans Dietrich and Colonia Victoria, wipe both the man and his creation off the map, Guzman was still at risk.

And at the moment, Bolan had no thoughts on how he might resolve that problem.

None at all.

"That's one mile," Bolan told his two companions. "Anybody need a break?"

"I'm fine," Cohen said. And she looked it.

"Do not stop for me," Guzman replied, sounding a bit fatigued, but able to continue.

"If we can hold this pace," Bolan observed, "we'll still have daylight when we reach the compound. That means time to kill, so we can spare a little on the trail if anybody needs it."

"Not yet," Cohen said.

Guzman just frowned and shook his head, swiping some perspiration from his forehead with one cammo sleeve.

"Okay," Bolan said. "Here we go."

Colonia Victoria

NASSER KHALIL PACED OFF the perimeter of Hans Dietrich's hundred-acre compound, followed and surrounded by the five men who'd accompanied him on this, his latest visit to the colony.

He was aware of Dietrich's sentries watching them, felt other members of the colony tracking his small party with vigilant, suspicious eyes. It was the same way everywhere he went inside Colonia Victoria, his dark skin and religion setting him apart from these self-styled defenders of the Master Race.

Khalil applauded Dietrich's hatred of Israel, his willingness to drown the Jewish state in blood, but his—Khalil's—disgust with Tel Aviv came from a different place inside him. He'd been born and raised in exile from his parents' native Palestine, uprooted and made homeless by the Zionists to whose destruction he devoted every waking moment of his life. Hans Dietrich, on the other hand...

What was the root of his extreme hatred for all things Jewish, to the point that he had gleefully participated in one of the greatest crimes ever committed by humankind? Was he insane? Were all these die-hard Nazis living in a dreamworld where their fair skin and the color of their eyes alone made them superior?

It makes no difference, Khalil thought. His danger lay in the real world, not in some realm of fantasy.

"You spoke to him?" Saghir El Haddad asked. He spoke in Arabic, as they all did when talking privately, to frustrate any listening devices Dietrich might employ.

"I did," Khalil replied, including all of them in his response. "Our host reports some difficulty, with the loss of several men in Bogotá."

They all knew it was worse than that. Khalil remained in contact with the outside world by means of his satellite phone and a compact shortwave radio. The news received from both told him of major violence in the Colombian capital, including the death or grave injury of some three dozen persons. Private inquiries told him all of them were Dietrich's men, and roughly half of them his pure-blood Germans.

"So, he lies to you," Najjar Baraka interjected sourly. Of all Khalil's soldiers, he most despised Colonia Victoria, its brash Teutonic atmosphere, the thinly veiled contempt that Dietrich's fascists felt for any dark-skinned guests.

"It's called diplomacy," Khalil replied. "All diplomats are liars, sugar-coating any news that threatens their authority. Our host—" he shied away from using Dietrich's name, since there was no way to disguise it "—believes that we may sever our alliance with him, if he is revealed as vulnerable."

"So we should," Baraka snapped. "I never understood why we collaborated with these madmen in the first place."

"They have money, influence, a sanctuary." As he spoke, Khalil surveyed the compound, built in the style of a quaint Bavarian village, festooned with flags and posters celebrating the Third Reich. Or would it be the Fourth, in Dietrich's mind, casting himself as Adolf Hitler's rightful heir?

Khalil snapped back from his distraction, pressing home his point. "They have assisted us on various projects, as you well know. Most recently, the new phase of our global war against the Zionists—"

"With all respect," Hamal Noura interrupted. "It may be that collaboration that has placed us all in danger now. I'm sure you have considered that, Nasser?"

"Of course," Khalil replied. "And if it's true, what of it? *They* are suffering the losses. No one from the Sword of Allah has been compromised or injured. We are free to leave at any time."

"You think so?" Baraka asked.

"Certainly. Why not?"

"Let's test it, then," Baraka said. "We should leave now. Get far away from here, before the men who bombed these lunatics in Bogotá show up and do the same thing to this white man's paradise."

"Where would you have us go, Najjar?" Khalil inquired. "Like me, you were convicted in absentia for crimes against Israel, and for the bombs we left in France. The British want us for a show trial, still insisting that I planned to kill their old, pathetic queen. And the Americans, let's not forget them, have decided they can kidnap anyone they want from any point on Earth, and pack him off before trial to some other country where they have no rules concerning torture. Where, exactly, would you have us go?"

"You make the world sound small," Wasim Riyad remarked. "We still have friends in Europe, in the Middle East, in Africa and Asia. There are many places we could go."

"And not be forced to smile at Nazis," Baraka added.

"White men despise us," Khalil told his men. "It is a fact of life. You should be used to it by now. *These* white men share our hatred for the common enemy. Right now, they help us strike against that enemy."

"I don't mind dying for the cause," Baraka said. "But it should be *our* cause, Nasser. Not some old German's pipe dream."

"No one's asking you to die," Khalil replied. "At least, not yet."

That brought a nervous laugh from most of them, but Khalil merely smiled.

Not yet, he silently repeated to himself. I am not asking you to die yet. Not today.

But soon, perhaps.

It could be true for all of them, and when the order came, no warrior could afford to hesitate. Whether the call came in Colombia or Palestine, the Sword of Allah had a sacred mission, and Khalil's soldiers were oath-bound to pursue it.

Even if it meant they had to smile and make nice with the crazy Nazis for a while.

Caquetá Department

"THAT'S MILE FIVE," Bolan announced. "We're almost halfway to the compound. In another hundred yards or so, we'll cross into the colony."

"There won't be any walls or fences this far out," Cohen said, "but we need to talk about security."

"You've checked it out, I gather?" Bolan asked.

"As far as possible," she said. "Which wasn't very far. Sales records show that Dietrich's purchased closed-circuit

TV, alarms, all kinds of toys, but we have no idea where he's installed them. Is he only covering the compound where his people live, or wiring the whole colony? The forest is too thick for decent satellite, and you already know about the men we tried to put inside."

"So, it's a crapshoot," Bolan said. "Once we're on Dietrich's turf, we take it slow and easy, watch our step, just like you would in any other combat zone. I doubt that he'd have cameras or listening devices five miles out from his CP, but with the new microtechnology, we can't be sure. Motion detectors are a possibility, and Nazis always seem to like their antipersonnel devices."

"Booby traps?" Guzman asked.

"Could be," Bolan replied. "Land mines, trip-wired grenades, on down to snares and pungi pits. Whatever they can think of to make drop-ins feel unwelcome."

"You mean, kill us," Guzman said.

"That comes as a surprise?" Cohen asked.

Guzman frowned and shook his head. "I simply don't like euphemisms. Call a thing by its right name."

"All right," said Bolan. "Once they know we're here, they'll definitely try to kill us any way they can. I thought that was a given, but I wouldn't want to minimize the risk. On Dietrich's game preserve, watch *every* step. Remember that he may be crazy, but he isn't stupid. Neither are his soldiers or technicians. If you give them any opening at all, they'll gut you like a fish. How's that?"

"Strangely," Guzman replied, "I am not reassured."

"I'm glad to hear it," Bolan said. "Short of a bullet in the head, the worst thing that could happen to you here and now is being overconfident."

"No worries, then," Guzman said as he forced a rueful smile.

"Ready to push on, then?"

"Ready," said Cohen.

"*Sí*," Guzman replied.

"The GPS will tell me when we enter Dietrich's dreamland," Bolan said, "but we should probably go red alert right now. Conversation only for necessities, and then in whispers. Be alert for wires or cables, triggers, pits or deadfalls, cameras—in other words, for *anything*."

"I hear you," Guzman said.

"Let's do it," Cohen urged.

Bolan nodded, turned without another word and led them on toward the border of Hans Dietrich's personal Reich.

There were no signs announcing the transition from Colombian soil, free in theory, to Nazi turf administered by men—and women? Bolan wondered—who believed that they were blessed by Mother Nature with the right to rule all other human races, creeds and colors on the planet. No alarms went off, or none that he could hear, at any rate. No flares or rockets arced into the sky, announcing the arrival of Hans Dietrich's enemies.

Bolan could understand the impulse toward extreme racism, spawned by human insecurity, fear of the strange and different, conviction that life's failures were the product of some vast conspiracy. A demagogue stepped in and offered simple, obvious solutions.

Blame the Jews, blacks, Arabs, Asians, gays, Muslims, or all of the above. Blame *them*. It's never your fault if you fail. Somebody sabotaged your best efforts, made you look foolish, stole your job, your home, your woman and your self-respect.

What do you do about it?

Make them pay. Get even, and then some.

Since you're never able to identify the individuals responsible for various imaginary crimes, you take it out on everyone with common traits.

It was the root of "ethnic cleansing," and as old as time.

Bolan had no illusion that eliminating Hans Dietrich would make the world a kinder, gentler place.

It might not even help perceptibly.

But, on the other hand, it couldn't hurt.

Colonia Victoria

"SIR, I SHOULD BE IN BOGOTÁ, conducting the search for our enemies."

"Nonsense," Hans Dietrich said. "It seems a miracle to me you're still alive. I need you here. The enemy is coming here. I feel it."

"As you say, sir."

Studying the man who stood before him, Dietrich thought it was a miracle that Otto Jaeger lived. Dark sutures closed a long wound in his scalp that had to have bled tremendously. A shaved strip, with the stitches and the burn ointment that glistened on Jaeger's left cheek, made him resemble something from a horror film. The cast on his left wrist seemed minor by comparison.

"While you were being resurrected," Dietrich said, "I've posted more sentries around the compound and increased the frequency of our patrols outside. I don't want to be taken by surprise a second time."

"No, sir."

As Jaeger spoke, he winced, whether from pain or the embarrassment of Dietrich's criticism, his commander couldn't guess. Jaeger had always been a proud man, rightly so, and failing twice within a single night had to hurt almost as much as his fresh wounds.

"On top of all the rest, our Arab visitors are discontent, I think," Dietrich observed. "Perhaps it's simply restlessness, but I believe they're worried."

"They should leave, sir," Jaeger answered. "We already have too many mongrels in the colony."

"You've never trusted them, eh, Otto?"

"No, sir."

"But they hate the Jews as much as we do," Dietrich said.

"With all respect, sir, they hate Israel. If it were destroyed tomorrow, no one in the Middle East would give a damn about the Jews in Europe or the West. It's not the same, sir."

"No? Perhaps not, Otto. But if Israel was destroyed tomorrow, *I* would celebrate as much as any Arab. In the meantime, you'll admit the Sword of Allah has been ruthless in its persecution of the Zionists?"

"Yes, sir. For their own ends, sir."

"But of course! Who but a suicidal altruist does anything not motivated by self-interest? Is there anyone? Outside—" his sweeping gesture indicated all the world beyond Colonia Victoria "—men purchase gifts for women when they want a little sex. Great industries contribute to lost causes for publicity and tax deductions. Armies 'liberate' their neighbors from oppression, in return for oil and other natural resources. It's the way of all life, Otto."

"Yes, sir."

"You have seen your wives since you returned?"

"No, sir. I came directly here."

"Good man. Go see them now, and let them see your battle scars. Take comfort from them for, let's say, an hour, then return to me. We have more preparations to discuss."

"Yes, sir."

"Perhaps you doubt me, Otto, when I tell you that I *know* the enemy is coming. But you'll see that I am right."

"I hope so, sir," Jaeger replied. "I want a chance to pay them back."

"You'll have it. This I promise you. Now, go. And don't forget, one hour!"

Jaeger clicked his heels and stabbed his rigid right arm toward the ceiling as he barked, "Heil Hitler!"

Dietrich smiled, returning the salute and watched his second in command march from the room, closing the door firmly behind him. He had been tremendously relieved to hear that Jaeger was alive and fit for battle, after the attack in Bogotá. For Dietrich, it confirmed that Odin and the other Nordic gods of yore were in his corner, pulling strings to help Dietrich destroy his enemies.

Granted, the first phase of the unexpected war had gone against him rather badly, but it often took a shock to motivate brave men who'd grown complacent during peacetime. Once they had been bloodied, seen their comrades slaughtered on the field, they fought with grim, fanatical determination to survive and to eradicate their enemies.

During the last world war, Dietrich had seen that principle in action, for himself. Hitler's Wehrmacht had plundered Europe, captured Scandinavia, invaded northern Africa and seized the western half of Russia by the autumn months of 1941. Their so-called allies in Japan had ruined everything with their attack on the United States, rousing a giant that had managed to ignore the war in Europe for two years, ensuring at a single stroke disaster for the Axis and its lofty dreams.

And tragically, the shock that came with changing tides of war had overwhelmed Dietrich's beloved Fatherland. His people might have rallied from the losses suffered on the Russian front, but round-the-clock bombardment from the skies destroyed their spirit. By the time that Allied troops rolled into Germany itself, the war was lost.

Hans Dietrich, meanwhile, had escaped to South America

and started life anew, using the spoils of war to build Colonia Victoria. His life had been a good one, lacking only final victory and installation of a Fourth Reich to resume the work that had been interrupted back in 1945.

Now Dietrich worried that he would not live to see that day, but he was not prepared to yield, lay down his guns and beg for mercy from his enemies. He would continue fighting in the only way he knew: scorched earth, no quarter asked or given.

With the strength of Odin and the Master Race, Dietrich believed that he could win. And if he died in the attempt, call it a sacrifice that guaranteed his entry to Valhalla.

Caquetá

"WE HAVE TWO MILES LEFT," Bolan announced, "according to the GPS. I recommend we split the difference, try to make another mile before the sun goes down, then stop while I go on to scout ahead."

"*We* stop, you mean," Cohen said.

"Right."

"You plan on leaving us behind?" she asked.

"If I thought I should ditch you, I'd have done it back in Bogotá," Bolan replied. "I need to see the target in advance and have a look around."

"Without us," Cohen stressed.

"Without somebody stepping on my heels or bumping into me. Reconnaissance is not the same as marching through the woods. You know that."

"I've been trained for both," she said. "Most of my job is some kind of reconnaissance."

"Okay, let's say you're qualified. You come along. Now, what about Jorge?"

"I'm happy to remain behind," Guzman said. "Don't think you will hurt my feelings."

"Stay behind alone," Bolan said, "while the other side is on patrol and hunting us."

"I'm not his baby-sitter," Cohen snapped. "Jorge's our guide, if you recall. *He* should be showing us the way, not you and your machine. Why is he even here?"

"Now you *have* hurt my feelings," Guzman said.

"Sorry," Cohen replied, not sounding it.

"We've lost time since we crossed the line to Dietrich's turf," Bolan explained. "That's understandable, and I expected some of it. But not this much. The river cost us. I'd expected to have the compound well in view by now."

The river had been wicked. It was seasonal, apparently, and so omitted from his map. A recent heavy rain at higher altitudes had turned it into foaming rapids five or six feet deep, and Bolan didn't have a day or two to wait for the wild water to subside. Instead, they'd crossed the torrent individually, Bolan leading with a rope that was supposed to make the crossing easier for his companions.

But it didn't work.

Despite the line, anchored by Bolan on one shore and Guzman on the other, Cohen had been battered, soaked and nearly swept away, clinging by one hand for an endless moment, Bolan knowing that he'd never find her if she dropped the line. She'd made it, finally, chilled to the bone and with chattering teeth, to help him haul Guzman across.

Near-miss disaster number two. Guzman had tied the rope around his waist, as ordered, then plunged in. He'd managed two or three steps, then went under, hurtling downstream with the current until Bolan's and Cohen's combined weight stopped him. Slowly, painfully, they'd reeled him in like some monster game fish, Guzman thrashing and gurgling cries for help instead of swimming. He'd been half dead when they beached him, and had only come around when Cohen gave him mouth-to-mouth.

Bolan still wondered if the last bit was a trick, but couldn't bring himself to ask.

Now, as the sun prepared to set, the two of them were still soaked to the skin. Soon they'd be shivering, as temperatures plummeted. There'd be no fire this night, no matter where they camped, and they'd brought no change of cammo clothing for the short excursion. Bolan wondered whether they were tough enough to battle hypothermia.

"We can't retrieve lost time," said Cohen, breaking into Bolan's thoughts. "We shouldn't split up, anyway, if there's concern about patrols."

They hadn't seen one yet. They'd seen nothing, in fact— no mines, trip-wired grenades, motion detectors, nothing. Maybe that was luck, or maybe Dietrich had been getting careless in his old age. Either way, Bolan was counting on some kind of opposition, getting ready for it in his mind.

"It might be better if you keep moving, at that," he granted. "I don't want the home team finding ice sculptures. They may be packing chisels."

"And if we meet a patrol, then what?" Cohen asked.

"Judge the situation. Take evasive action if possible, fight if we have to."

"You came to kill them, didn't you?" Guzman asked.

Bolan wondered if he'd warmed to the idea, or simply learned to live with it.

"We're after Dietrich, first," Bolan replied. "I'd rather not wade through the whole damned population of the colony, if we can help it. Take it one step at a time."

"But we all stay together," Cohen said, confirming it.

Bolan nodded. "Right. At least, for now."

With that point finally decided, he turned back in the direction of their target and began to walk once more.

CHAPTER EIGHT

Colonia Victoria

"Who are we looking for, again?" Henrich Brüner asked.

"The enemy," Ubel Waldron said as he wiped perspiration from his forehead with a sleeve.

It was approaching nightfall, and the temperature was dropping, but the night patrol still had him sweating. The exertion, coupled with the seeming urgency of his assignment, had put Waldron's nerves on edge.

"I *know* that," Brüner answered. "I mean, who exactly are we looking for?"

"If I knew that, you think I'd have to look for them?" Waldron replied. "I'd know where they were going, what they wanted, and we'd just sit down to wait for them."

"Sounds good to me."

"Go back and tell our leader that. See what he says."

"Hey, now! You know I'm only joking," Brüner offered in a nervous tone. "There's nothing to be gained by telling tales. I'd just like to have some idea who we're out hunting for."

"You heard the same orders that I did," Waldron said, craning his neck to catch sight of the scout he'd sent ahead to blaze their trail. "But if you're asking my opinion…"

"Go ahead, then," Brüner urged him. "Spill it."

Waldron glanced back at the straggling line of their patrol. He had ten native soldiers, with the scout, all armed and dressed in camouflage fatigues. They were no more than peasants, but he'd handpicked ten who followed orders and were not afraid to fight.

"You heard about what's happened up in Bogotá?" asked Waldron.

"Who hasn't? I saw Jaeger, looking like somebody kicked his ass and grilled it on the stove."

"Well, I think they're expecting the same people to attack the colony," Waldron said. "What else could it be?"

Brüner stood blinking at him in surprise. "You mean that? Who would even dare to try it? We're protected… aren't we?"

"Oh, the leader has his friends in government, no doubt. And pays them well, I shouldn't wonder. But if they could level Jaeger's place in Bogotá, why not come to Colonia Victoria?"

"We've always been secure here," Brüner argued. "This is our place!"

"And you think that's such a deep, dark secret? You don't think that must infuriate the Jews?"

"You're saying Jews killed all those men in Bogotá?"

Waldron slapped a mosquito that had settled on his neck. "Oh, not just any Jews," he said. "One of the death squads trained in Israel, maybe. That's most likely. But they're not all rag-pickers and clerks, you know."

"Why now?" Brüner asked.

"Are you sleeping when the leader speaks to us? You must have heard him talk about the new Reich and the end of Israel."

"Yes, I heard. But…"

"What?" Waldron stopped in the middle of the trail and turned, as if to challenge Brüner.

"Ubel, we've been hearing that each year since we were born here. I mean, it's like Jesus and the Second Coming. Whoever really thinks that it will happen?"

"That sounds like treason," Waldron said, then broke into a grin. "But I may not report you if, let's say, you clean my boots for two—no, three—weeks."

"Screw you and your boots," Brüner replied. "I asked a question, that's all. How are we supposed to find the enemy, if no one tells us who we're looking for?"

"This is Colonia Victoria," Waldron said. "Any stranger on our land is automatically the enemy. We'll be rewarded if we find someone. You wait and see."

"And if we don't? What then?"

"Then I suppose there'll be patrols around the clock, until the danger's passed."

"It isn't very well thought-out, if you ask me," Brüner remarked.

"Nobody asked you."

"All I'm saying is, we don't know who we're looking for, and won't know when we've found them. If we find no one, we have to keep on looking till the danger's passed. But if there's no one here, then there's no danger."

"Christ, you're like a damned old woman," Waldron said. "We've only been two hours on the hunt and you're already giving up."

"I'm doing no such thing! But if we're meant to meet the leader's expectations, we should be informed of all the relevant details. What's wrong with that?"

"They're classified," Waldron replied. "A matter of security."

"Oh, that again."

"You don't believe it?"

"We're assigned to guard the colony, Ubel. But they won't tell us who we're guarding it against. Does that sound rational to you?"

"Be very careful, Heinrich."

"Yes. I know. You'll go report me."

"No, I won't. But others might. They might report us both."

That silenced Brüner for a time. At length he asked, "So, what about the workers?"

"Give it one more hour," Waldron answered, "then we'll circle over to the village and collect them. By the time we get back to the compound, we'll have done our shift."

The slave run was a bit of drudgery, but someone had to do it. Once a week, a group of workers was collected from one of the two small native villages contained within Colonia Victoria. They were transported to the leader's compound, where they served the colonists as housekeepers, performing the domestic tasks that fell to servants. After their week was up, they went back home and others were collected to replace them.

Waldron never wondered why the natives took it, why they didn't fight. As peasants, he believed it was their rightful place in life, serving the Master Race. They had been born and raised for service, just as he was born and raised to serve the leader and his people.

Odin had decreed it. Who was Ubel Waldron to question the natural order of things?

"Another hour, then," Brüner said.

"More or less."

"Do me a favor, will you, Ubel? Try to make it less."

BOLAN SMELLED THE VILLAGE first. Something was cooking, up ahead, and when he checked the GPS, he found that they were more than seven miles from Dietrich's compound. Since no maps existed of Colonia Victoria, he couldn't open one and learn what lay ahead of them.

The only way to know was to approach and have a look.

"You smell that?" Bolan asked the others.

"Smoke," Guzman said.

"Someone cooking meat," Cohen added. "Don't ask me what kind."

"The main point is the cooking," Bolan said. "Somebody's in our way. I need to find out who and how many."

The Mossad agent shrugged. "All right," she said. "Let's go and see."

"I said *I* need to see," Bolan replied. "You two stay put, and I'll be back as soon as I finish the recon."

"You're not serious," Cohen said.

"Best believe it," Bolan told her. "I've done this a thousand times. It's delicate but doable, as long as I've got no one stepping on my heels."

"No problem," Guzman said. "I don't mind waiting here."

"And you'll be with him, just in case," Bolan told Cohen. "If anything goes wrong, I'll come right back."

"How would you know?" Guzman asked.

Cohen rolled her eyes. "He'd hear the gunfire," she explained as if to a slow child.

"Oh. Yes, I see."

The answer clearly didn't please Guzman. He looked around, as if expecting enemies to rush him from the forest's shadows any moment.

"Right, then," Bolan said. "Find some cover, but don't wander off."

Ignoring Cohen's sigh and pained expression, Bolan left them, following his nose in the direction of the fire that lay somewhere due east of where he'd stopped his team. A blind man could've followed it, and it was just as well, since nighttime in the forest offered precious little moonlight for illumination.

Warily, Bolan advanced, watching his step and taking full advantage of the night for cover. He had no suppressor for his Steyr AUG, but it would make no difference if he stumbled on an enemy encampment. Once the Nazis glimpsed him and got over their surprise, there'd be enough shooting to wake the dead.

Or, anyway, to give them some more company.

The scent of cooking meat, Bolan discovered, had to have traveled close to half a mile. When he had covered some three-quarters of that distance, he heard voices in the distance. Bolan guessed that they were speaking Spanish, but he wasn't close enough to verify it.

With audio contact, he slowed his pace. If he could hear the strangers up ahead, it meant that *they* might also hear whatever sounds he made, advancing on their company. It didn't sound as if they were expecting trouble, but there could be sentries posted. Bolan took his time, ensuring that surprise was on his side, not theirs.

When he was still a hundred yards away, he saw the fire. It wasn't huge, not bonfire-size, but large and bright enough for him to see when human forms passed by in front of it. Bolan continued his advance, doubly alert for any lookouts posted in his way.

At thirty yards, he knew it was a village, not a camp. The homes were little more than huts, and he could smell the not-so-distance effluence of an open latrine, but there was a crude permanence about the place. Its people stayed here and had put down roots into the unforgiving soil.

It puzzled Bolan, made him wonder why a colony of Nazis would permit a nest of dark-skinned natives in their own backyard, but that was someone else's problem. As he slowly circled the small village, staying just beyond the firelight, counting heads, he saw no weapons other than machetes, hoes and axes.

Definitely not a military outpost, then. And from the look of it, the villagers had no concern for gathering intelligence, guarding the western march toward Dietrich's forest lair.

Something was definitely roasting on a spit. It resembled a pig, but he couldn't be sure. Its aroma might have lured him in, if he was a hungry hiker, but Bolan had more pressing work to do, and forest picnics weren't on the agenda.

He was turning back toward his companions when a voice called out to the assembled villagers. It issued from the southeast, opposite Bolan, and it spoke in German.

Bolan froze, watched, waited, as armed men emerged into the firelight.

"THEY DON'T SPEAK GERMAN," Ubel Waldron said, after Henrich Brüner shouted greetings to the villagers.

"They understand me well enough," Brüner replied. "I want something, I point and then I take it. Simple."

"Just remember why we're here," Waldron said. "We're after workers, not a fight."

"That isn't all I do," Brüner said, grinning. "I'm a fighter and a lover."

Waldron scowled at that, but didn't answer as they moved into the camp. Brüner was crude, but like him, Waldron had been raised believing that the lesser peoples were created as a servant class. They were essentially useless, except where they were trained to serve the needs of Aryans.

And Aryans had many different needs.

The village had no name, as far as Waldron knew. A number marked it on the hand-drawn wall map in the leader's office. It was one of three small settlements that thrived under

Dietrich's generally benevolent dictatorship. Workers were drafted from a different village each week, in rotation, so those already used had ample time to rest, recuperate if necessary, and pursue the simple pleasures of their slow, idyllic lives.

It never crossed his mind to ask if they were happy.

Waldron simply didn't care.

When he was close enough to speak without shouting, Waldron addressed the villagers in Spanish. He was fluent in three languages, but Spanish always left an oily feeling in his mouth, for some reason. It lacked the gruff, decisive sound of German or the clipped, straightforward quality of English.

"As you know," he said, "it is the time when workers are selected for the compound. First, however, there are questions to be answered."

Nearly everyone regarded him with some mixture of curiosity and dread. The sole exception was an old man who'd been left to turn the spit, so supper wouldn't burn.

"Strangers are coming to Colonia Victoria," he said, stating the leader's supposition as a fact. "They may pass by your village, even stop to ask for help."

The natives glanced at one another, several of them muttering. Waldron gave them a moment, then continued.

"What we need," he informed them, "what your great leader requires, is a warning if strangers approach you. In that case, you must send the fastest runner from your village to alert the compound. Service to the leader is rewarded, as you know. Failure—which he will surely recognize—is punished. Any questions?"

In the front row, facing Waldron, a young man raised his hand, afraid to speak without permission.

"Yes?"

"How will we know them, sir?"

"They will be strangers, as I said," Waldron replied.

"But, sir, most of your people never visit us. They all are strangers to us, here."

He had a point, which irritated Waldron for some reason he could not define.

"First," Waldron said, "you will know strangers if they are not Aryan. None of our people have black skin, nor brown, like yours. Second, our soldiers and the natives we employ as fighters all wear uniforms like mine, with shoulder patches like this one."

He half turned toward the fire, leaned slightly forward, showing them the eagle with its wings spread, perched atop a world emblazoned with a swastika.

"You know us by this sign," Waldron explained. "Our enemies will not display it. Any other questions?"

To his left, another hand went up. An older man, this time.

"Speak," Waldron ordered.

"Will they come with guns?" the native asked.

"You're forgetting something!"

"Will they come with guns, *sir?*"

"Almost certainly."

"Then, how can we resist them, sir?"

"No one has asked you to play soldier. Send a runner to the compound. Take no other action," Waldron said.

"But, sir...who will protect us?"

"That is my job, after you alert us."

"Yes, but—"

"It is time to choose the workers," Waldron said, cutting off the villager's spiel. "Henrich, pick the twenty best of them."

"You lot form two lines," Brüner ordered. "Females to the left, males to the right."

His Spanish wasn't perfect, but they understood him well enough and hastened to obey. Some of the mén looked sour, fearing they would miss the pork smoking and steaming on the spit behind them.

They were right. Waldron had already decided he and Brüner should have first claim on the fragrant meat—assuming that his second in command for the patrol found nothing else to satisfy his appetite.

Brüner moved along the lines, inspecting each person in turn. He started with the females, which was no surprise. He always tried to mix pleasure with business, and would take the pleasure first, if possible.

"I don't remember this one," Brüner said, drawing a girl of sixteen years or so out of the line. "Wouldn't she stick in your mind, Ubel?"

Waldron made no reply. He did not share Brüner's attraction to inferior females, but he was loathe to criticize a fellow Aryan in front of peasants.

"She looks strong," Brüner observed. "I should find out before we take her, don't you think?"

"Be quick about it," Waldron said at last. "I'm not spending the night here, just so you can have your fun."

"There's no need to be jealous," Brüner answered in a mocking tone. "I don't mind sharing."

"Hurry up," Waldron said, "or I'll leave you here."

"All right, all right," said Brüner as he led the still-uncomprehending girl in the direction of the nearest hut. "We only need a bit of privacy, eh, sweetie?"

COHEN AND GUZMAN had found some nearby cover, but they both emerged at the sight of Bolan coming back to join them. They waited silently for his report and listened without speaking until Bolan had described the village and the group of Dietrich's men who had arrived moments before he left.

"A dozen men," Cohen said.

"Two Germanic types, with ten natives," Bolan explained. "I couldn't tell what they were saying, but they had the villagers turned out to listen."

"Should we take them?"

"Not unless you want the compound up in arms before we get there," Bolan said. "I couldn't tell if they had radios."

"What, then?" she asked.

"Bypass them," Bolan answered. "If they're looking for us in the village, we can slip around them while they're wasting time. We'll have to watch for them if they turn back, but maybe we'll get lucky and they'll be the only search party assigned to this sector."

"What of the villagers?" Guzman asked.

"What about them?" Bolan said. "They live on Dietrich's land. It's safe to say they've reached some kind of an accommodation with him. Anyway, we can't assume they're friendlies."

Guzman frowned, but kept whatever he was thinking to himself. Using his GPS device, Bolan picked out a course that would take them around the village, a hundred yards or so the north, then bring them back on track toward Dietrich's compound.

They still had the better part of seven miles to walk, and Bolan reckoned that Guzman, at least, would be exhausted by the time they reached their destination. He was wondering if they should find a place to camp, around the five-mile mark as they drew closer to the native village in the darkness. There was no escaping the aroma of the pork roast or the muffled sound of voices from their right.

Bolan was hoping the patrol might stop to have a bite to eat, maybe relax awhile and kill some time before they got back on the trail and started searching for intruders. Every minute he could buy put them a little closer to their target, and he doubted that Hans Dietrich would have two patrols working the same vicinity, with the inherent risk that they might meet and fire on one another in the dark.

He judged that they were nearly past the village when a woman started screaming. First, it sounded like an angry voice, but then it shifted into panic, rising through the octaves into unadulterated terror.

Guzman was the first to veer off course, in the direction of the screams. Bolan caught up with him inside of fifty feet and stopped him with a tight grip on his arm. When Guzman tried to wrench away, the Executioner hung on.

"Someone needs help!" the guide snapped at him, showing something almost feral in his eyes.

"And there's a way to go about it," Bolan answered. "Charging down a dozen guns is *not* the way."

"What, then?"

"Get back in line and follow me," Bolan commanded. "Watch our step, just like before. They haven't all gone deaf."

He led the way, guiding on screams at first, then on a rumbling sound of angry voices. They fell silent when a gunshot echoed through the night, but Bolan couldn't tell if it had been a warning or an execution.

Still the screams, though, as frantic as before, if somewhat muffled. Not the sounds of grief, in his experience, but fear. And, maybe, pain.

He reached the outskirts of the village, felt the others stop behind him, checking out the tableau ranged in front of them. The troops were more or less where he had left them earlier, facing a line of villagers that had been separated into men's and women's groups. The soldiers had their weapons leveled at the crowd, one of the fair-haired officers pacing between the hostile lines.

Where was the other German?

More screams from a nearby hut gave Bolan an idea of

what was happening. He might already be too late, in fact, but something in his gut told Bolan that he couldn't turn away.

"Stay here," he told his two companions. "Keep the others covered."

"Where are you—?"

He didn't wait around to answer Cohen's whispered question, circling to his right, along the tree line, toward the hut that seemed to be the source of the commotion.

Coming up behind it, Bolan had a heartbeat to survey the architecture. Thatched walls didn't offer much security, but he would make noise slashing through them. Once he started, it would all depend on strength and speed.

He withdrew his knife, felt for a soft spot in the wall and drove his blade into the heart of it. A moment later, Bolan's arm and shoulder lunged into empty space. He pushed off with his legs, a mighty shove, and started worming through.

The would-be rapist had his back turned, so distracted by his naked, screaming victim that he barely noticed Bolan hacking through the wall behind him. Barely, but enough to make him half turn as the Executioner lunged, old thatching dangling from his body like a sniper's ghillie suit, dragging one leg behind him as it snagged on twine or something used to build the wall.

The German squawked and sprang up from the sleeping pallet where he'd pinned the girl, lunging to reach his nearby weapon. He was fumbling with the safety, cleared it, had his index finger through the trigger guard when Bolan hit him, slammed him back against the nearest wall and plunged the knife into his throat.

ANOTHER GUNSHOT ECHOED through the village, silencing the woman's screams. It had a muffled quality, assuring Cohen that it came from the same hut where Cooper plainly thought he'd find the damsel in distress.

"Be ready!" she commanded Guzman, who stood tense beside her with a pistol in each hand.

It suddenly struck Cohen that they both should have brought rifles. Somehow, she had not considered jungle fighting with a group of well-armed paramilitaries when she had the chance to plan ahead and pick the weapon of her choice. The Uzi was familiar, and a proved close-range killer, but they were outgunned now.

It could be her last mistake.

In front of them, the German started barking orders at his men. Two of them peeled off from the skirmish line and double-timed toward what she thought of as the screaming hut, holding their automatic rifles at the ready.

Cohen didn't know if Cooper was inside the hut, if he had shot the other German or been shot. Perhaps the Nazi had grown tired of listening to screams and killed the woman before Cooper'd had a chance to intervene.

In any case, she thought, the answer would be known to them within the next few seconds.

"Don't fire unless I do," she told Guzman. And when he failed to answer, Cohen dug an elbow deep into his ribs. "Listen to me!" she whispered.

"I hear you!"

"Not a move, unless I—"

Cohen's thought was interrupted as a burst of automatic fire exploded from the screaming hut. The forward runner took it in his chest and stumbled backward, dropping with a dazed expression on his face.

His companion tried to change course, but the move came too late. A second short burst from the hut reached out to spin him like a twirling figure-skater. By the time he fell, three other swarthy paramilitaries had their rifles aimed at what had now become the killing hut.

"Hit it!" Cohen snapped as she stroked a short burst from her mini-Uzi.

It had the same range as the larger original model, at least on paper, but its barrel was 2.5 inches shorter, which *did* make a difference at ranges beyond twenty feet. In fact, the shorter barrel sliced one hundred feet per second off the smaller weapon's muzzle velocity, while the foot-long sound suppressor shaved off a little more. It hardly mattered at ten yards, but if her targets made it to the tree line and concealed themselves, it would be doubly dangerous.

Her first rounds struck a young man, slightly taller than the others, just as Guzman opened fire beside her. One of his shots struck the same soldier as he was falling, drilling through his left cheek and blowing out a fist-size chunk of skull behind his right ear.

"Get your own!" she ordered Guzman, shifting farther to her left to get away from him.

In fact, she worried less about the wasted rounds and duplicated effort than their muzzle-flashes. Cohen's suppressor reduced the mini-Uzi's muzzle-flare, but it might still be visible. Guzman's twin IMBEL pistols, meanwhile, were already flashing like a pair of signal lights, already drawing brisk fire from the eight remaining soldiers in the village.

I wish I had a rifle, Cohen thought again, but there was nothing she could do about it at the moment. Maybe later, if they won this fight—

A swarm of bullets rattled overhead, and the Mossad agent ducked behind a tree, hearing the slugs shred bark and underbrush around her. Guzman hit the deck, still firing, so she guessed he wasn't hit.

But how long would their luck hold out?

The German started shouting at his men in Spanish, losing Cohen, but she didn't need a translator. Under the circumstances, there were only two commands that he could issue: to attack or to retreat.

She waited for a heartbeat, heard the automatic weapons escalate, and knew the choice was made.

Cursing, she braced herself to meet the charge.

BOLAN RECOILED as automatic rifle fire ripped through the hut's thatched walls with angry crackling noises, like a giant piece of paper crisping in a fire. The girl he'd rescued still lay huddled in the farthest corner from the door, and she had sense enough to stay low as their enemies outside began to blast the hut apart.

The first barrage was interrupted, as he'd been expecting, by gunshots from somewhere off to Bolan's left, or east. He heard two different pistols, knowing it was Guzman, but with all the other racket Bolan couldn't hear reports from Cohen's mini-Uzi with its suppressor attached.

Outside, his enemies and many of the villagers were shouting, all in Spanish. Some of them were angry; most seemed frightened. Either way, they had begun to run in all directions, trying to avoid the deadly cross fire.

Bolan made it harder for the outside shooters when he rolled back toward the hut's doorway, leaned out and fired a short burst from his Steyr AUG into their straggling ranks. One gunman took most of it in his legs and crumpled, screaming, to the ground.

That brought the squad's attention back to Bolan, and another spray of bullets crackled through the hut. Bolan crawled past his first kill, toward the girl, and shook her out of her hysterics long enough to make her understand that she should exit through the gap he'd torn in the rear wall. When she understood, she nodded, muttered something heartfelt that he couldn't understand, then slithered through the opening as if she'd done it countless times before.

Bolan was right behind her, staying low, leaving the hut to its dead occupant. Outside, the once-alluring smell of roasting pork now vied with gunsmoke in a strange assault upon his nostrils. Villagers fled past him as he circled wide around the death hut and its nearest neighbor. Those who noticed Bolan veered away from him with cries or gestures of alarm, uncertain who he was and probably mistaking him for yet another enemy.

So much the better, if it made them clear his line of fire.

He crouched beside a slightly larger, still undamaged hut and peered into the village square. Of the original dozen invaders, half were either dead or hurt badly enough to keep them off their feet. The rest, five natives and another German type, were split between firing at shadows in the forest or continuing a strange one-sided duel with the silent hut Bolan had left behind.

A pair of them broke ranks and rushed the hut, both firing as they ran, hurdling the corpses of their comrades who had tried it first. Bolan lined up his shot and hit the nearer of them with a 3-round burst that dropped him, thrashing, to the ground.

The other runner heard or felt his comrade fall, half turning to see what had happened, even as he kept charging, kept firing, toward the empty hut. He never missed a step, until the next short burst from Bolan's autorifle ripped into his chest, mangling his heart and lungs for a near-instant kill.

Momentum and reflexes kept the runner going two more wobbling strides, then he collapsed across the threshold of the death hut, lying with his legs and boots outside. Bolan dismissed him instantly and swung back toward the four remaining members of the Nazi rat pack.

One of them had fallen in the short time Bolan was distracted, leaving three still on their feet. Of those, three bronze-skinned native gunmen kept their eyes and weapons focused on the tree line, while their taller, blond commander drew a bead on Bolan.

The Executioner rolled back under cover of the hut as bullets from the German's rifle chewed the thatch to tatters. Up and running in a heartbeat, Bolan circled back the way he'd come and ducked in through the rough back door he'd carved into the first hut, now containing two dead men.

He rushed the doorway, barely reached it with the Steyr at his shoulder when he found his mark and took the shot. Dietrich's man, mouthing curses, was replacing a spent magazine, still facing the Executioner's last vantage point, when Bolan stitched him with a rising burst and put him down.

He turned to rake the other two, in time to see them twitching, taking hits and crumpling to the ground. A muffled ripping sound from somewhere to his left pegged Cohen and her mini-Uzi as their nemesis.

Bolan emerged, checking the bodies of his adversaries to confirm that all of them were dead. One of the native troops, still moaning softly, took a mercy round between the eyes and shuddered into silence.

Stepping from the forest shadows into firelight, Cohen called to him, "What do we do with these now?"

"Leave them," Bolan said. "We don't have time to dig a dozen graves. But first, check them for radios."

Guzman found one on Bolan's second German, clipped to his web belt. It was turned off, but only seconds were required to send a message, sounding the alarm.

"Did either of you seem him use it?" Bolan asked.

"Not me," Cohen said, "but he could have."

Guzman simply shook his head.

It seemed unlikely, in the circumstances, that the German could have called home base, made his connection, passed his message and replaced the two-way handy-talkie on his belt while trading shots with Cohen and Guzman.

Unlikely, right. But not impossible.

The village was deserted but for Bolan, his companions and the dead. He had no way of knowing when, or if, the villagers would drift back to their homes, and while he hated leaving corpses on their doorsteps, Bolan had no choice.

"Grab anything you want to take along," he said. "I'd recommend a couple of these rifles, with spare magazines, but suit yourselves. We need to split."

Guzman and Cohen both took rifles from the dead, then wrestled bandoliers of ammunition from their former owners. Bolan noted Cohen switching out the nearly empty mag on her new rifle and advising Guzman to do likewise. While she was at it, Bolan helped himself to several hand grenades.

"Ready," confirmed the lady from Mossad.

"Okay, then," Bolan said, "assume a call was made, and that we're being hunted. If we aren't right now, we will be when the news of this gets back to Dietrich."

"Maybe he'll be dead by then," Cohen said.

"Maybe we'll strike oil along the way and stumble on a gold mine," Bolan said. "But I'm inclined to doubt it."

CHAPTER NINE

Colonia Victoria

A native runner stumbled into Dietrich's compound shortly
after ten o'clock. The sentries nearly shot him, then relented
as he babbled at them in rapid-fire Spanish, explaining his
mission between gasps for breath. Another ten minutes was
wasted before a sergeant of the guard brought the winded native to Hans Dietrich's quarters and rapped on the door.

Now, having listened to the story and dismissed the weary
villager with orders for the kitchen staff to feed him, Dietrich
summoned Otto Jaeger to his office. While he waited, the
commander of Colonia Victoria drank schnapps and paced the
hardwood floor.

Jaeger arrived within two minutes, thus confirming
Dietrich's guess that he'd been waiting in the wings. The
bruising underneath his eyes had darkened in the interval
since Dietrich saw him last, as had the reddened patches of
his facial burns.

"My leader!" Jaeger snapped to full attention with the
usual stiff-armed salute.

"At ease, Otto. You've heard the news, I take it?"

"Yes, sir. I'll miss Waldron. He was a good man. Brüner was…how shall I say it…?"

"He was lax, in terms of discipline. I grant you that. Still, two more of our soldiers lost, Otto."

He didn't count the native losses, though their numbers might be missed if adversaries moved against the compound.

Make that when, he thought. Not if.

Jaeger appeared to read his mind. "The enemy is coming, then."

"Closing upon us as we speak," Dietrich replied. "It's what—six miles from here, this village?"

"Roughly, yes, sir."

"And this native's come to us already. Running, from the look and sound of him. No small achievement, in the dark. I doubt our enemies will move as swiftly, but must be nearly here."

"Unless the skirmish broke their nerve, sir," Jaeger offered. "There's a chance they've turned around."

"After their victories in Bogotá? Then coming south, finding their way inside the colony, and killing more of our people? I doubt it very much, Otto."

"No, sir. You're right, of course."

"This native said a strange thing, Otto."

"Sir?"

"If we can trust him, Waldron's team was wiped out by two men—one white, the other native—and a woman."

"Sir?"

Dietrich could only shrug. "It's what he says. I think he understands the risk involved in lying to me. Still…"

"It's difficult to judge, sir, without seeing them. I'd recommend patrols throughout the area between the compound and the village, certainly. If we can intercept them—"

"Yes, by all means. See to it at once."

"Yes, my leader!"

Jaeger turned to leave, but stopped as Dietrich said, "And find Khalil. I wish to speak with him as soon as possible."

"Yes, sir. He's in the mess hall, I believe. Something about pork sausage."

"Good God. See to the patrols, first. Then, see if our guest can stop his whining for a moment, to discuss matters of life and death."

"Yes, sir!"

The Arabs had been difficult from the beginning, with their strictures against alcohol and food their scriptures branded as "unclean." Dietrich often wondered why they hated Jews so much when their religions were so similar.

Another fifteen minutes passed and Dietrich was about to give up on Khalil, proceeding with the phone calls that he felt compelled to make, when muffled rapping on his door distracted him from morbid thoughts.

"Come in!"

Nasser Khalil entered the office, solemn-faced, and closed the door behind him. "We have more trouble, I understand," he said.

"You've heard the news, then."

"Everyone has heard by now, I'm sure."

"I think," Dietrich said, "that we may regard this as a positive development."

"How, so?"

"The enemy will come to us, and we shall be prepared for him. Rather than searching all of Bogotá—or all Colombia—we simply have to watch and wait."

"It seems you have few men remaining, for a search in Bogotá," Khalil replied.

Dietrich swallowed the shriek of rage that welled inside him, and instead said, "I appreciate your generous concern, Nasser. But I assure you, I have everything under control."

"And yet," the Arab said, "you've lost a dozen tonight, within a few short miles of where we stand."

"Two men," Dietrich corrected him.

"I understood—"

"The rest were merely peasants," Dietrich interrupted with a smile.

Khalil was frowning deeply as he asked, "You have a different arithmetic for natives, then?"

Dietrich's patience was stretched tightly. He longed to draw the compact Walther pistol from the pocket of his quilted dressing gown and give Khalil a third eye that would never close.

Instead he answered, "You appear distraught, my friend. If it's your wish to leave before our common enemy has been eliminated, naturally I won't detain you. As it happens, sadly, there is a malfunction with the helicopter, but I'll happily provide a native guide. If you leave now, I'm confident that you can reach Solano by…what? Noon tomorrow, at the very latest."

"You suggest my men and I walk out of here tonight?"

"It wouldn't be my choice, of course," Dietrich replied. "But if I've lost your confidence and you are set on leaving, I'm afraid it is the only way."

"I never mentioned leaving."

"Oh? It must be my mistake, then. I assumed you were dissatisfied with my security precautions and preferred to trust your luck outside. Alone."

"I think not," said Khalil. "You may need all the hands—and guns—that you can get to solve your latest problem."

"Once again, the altruist," Dietrich replied. "What can I say, except to thank you for your offer of assistance. And your sacrifice."

"Excuse me?"

"Of your time and energy," Dietrich said, smiling hugely. "What else?"

"If you'll excuse me," Khalil stated stiffly, "I must consult with my associates."

"In which case, I shall not detain you."

When he was alone once more, Dietrich unleashed a stream of curses toward the Arabs. If it weren't for their efficiency at killing Jews, and their propensity for swift revenge, he would have executed Khalil and his stooges, then told their superiors that they were victims of a tragic hunting accident.

But, wait!

His enemies, no doubt advancing on the compound even now, might give Dietrich an even better alibi. Khalil insisted on participating in the camp's defense. Of course, there would be casualties. A hero's funeral. Profound regrets dispatched to those who ran the Sword of Allah from afar.

Cooperation would continue, and he'd never have to see Khalil's thin, sneering face again. Not after he was planted in a forest grave.

So be it.

Now all Dietrich had to do was to wait for one of his patrols to meet the enemy, defeat them and convey their corpses to the compound. If they took one of the team members alive, so much the better. Questions would be answered, vengeance plotted.

Waiting was a game Dietrich knew well.

He had been playing it since 1945.

THEY HAD DECIDED NOT to camp, agreeing that they needed distance from the village more than rest. Bolan assumed that even in a village where the people were enslaved, abused, treated like livestock, there would be at least one spy for Dietrich's side. When they were safely out of sight, if not before, that traitor would be racing to inform his master of the latest carnage.

That meant more patrols, more sentries at the compound by the time they reached it. Bolan was already thinking past the compound and around it, but he hadn't briefed his two companions on Plan B.

When they had put a mile and change between the village and themselves, Bolan signaled a rest stop. Even Cohen seemed relieved, as if the killing, more than hiking through the woods at night, had sapped some of her energy.

"I've been rethinking our approach," Bolan said while the others caught their breath.

"Don't tell me that you're giving up," Cohen suggested with a cautionary tone.

"It never crossed my mind," he said. "But Dietrich could find out about our skirmish while we're still out here, trudging along. That gives him all the time he needs to reinforce the compound, make it that much harder getting in."

"So what do you suggest?" Cohen asked.

"He'll be looking for us to the west," Bolan replied. "We need to circle wide around the compound—north or south, it shouldn't matter—and come back at Dietrich from another angle."

"You mean, east?" Guzman asked.

"I don't have any specific point in mind," Bolan explained. "The point is not to be where he expects us."

"Won't he simply add more guards on every side?" their guide inquired.

"No doubt," Bolan said. "But I'm betting that he still thinks like an army officer. Which means he'll likely send out more patrols to intercept us, hoping he can either kill us in the bush or bring some of us in alive for questioning."

Bolan imagined he saw Cohen shiver as she said, "He won't take me alive."

"I wouldn't recommend that route for anybody," Bolan

said. "But every search party he sends into the field weakens the home team. And his guards—most of them, anyway—will still expect us to attack from westward, even if they're posted on the far side of the camp. If one or two relax, even a little bit, it could be all the edge we need."

"I wish we had your mortar, still," Cohen said.

"That's because you've never carried one for ten miles, through the woods."

"All right," she said. "So how much mileage are we adding to our journey, then, before we catch a glimpse of Dietrich?"

Bolan double-checked his GPS reader. "We're five-point-four miles from the compound now," he said, "due eastward, as the bullet flies. Figure another two miles, three at most, to give the place a wide berth and come in from Dietrich's blind side."

"But he won't be blind on any side," the lady from Mossad reminded him.

"Figure of speech. I'm thinking of the blind spot in his mind."

"You think somebody from the village ran ahead to warn him," Guzman said.

Bolan nodded. "I'd be surprised if no one did."

"A traitor, then."

"To his own people, not to us. He doesn't owe us anything."

"You helped the girl," Guzman replied.

"That won't make any difference to him—or her."

"I wonder," Cohen interjected, "if he will describe us, tell Herr Dietrich that we're only three?"

"There's no way to predict that," Bolan said. "The villagers were scattered by the time you two broke cover, but that doesn't mean they weren't around and watching from the shadows."

"If he knows we're only three," she said, "he'll feel contempt for us."

"I hope so," Bolan told her. "It could be his last mistake."

DAS Headquarters, Bogotá

JOAQUIN MENENDEZ CURSED the jangling telephone. It was his private line, the one that he could least afford to walk off and ignore. No more than twenty people in the country knew that number, and to insult any one of them might pose a risk to his career, if not his life.

He answered on the third ring, ready for more bad news in a week that seemed to be composed of nothing else. Someone needed a favor, or was calling up to complain about something, expecting Menendez to fix it. And he would do everything within his power to oblige, no matter how bizarre or dangerous the task might be.

That was the downside of selling your soul.

Once it was done, you had to deal with devils every day.

"Hello?"

"Señor Menendez, do you recognize my voice?"

"Of course."

It was Hans Dietrich on the line. He always played this cloak-and-dagger game, refusing to identify himself by name, although Menendez repeatedly assured him that his private line was swept for taps three times each day.

"Shall I engage the scrambler?" Menendez asked.

"Yes, please."

When Menendez pushed a button on the bulky cradle of his private telephone, a small light at the bottom switched from red to green. Even if someone found a way to tap his line now, or should somehow snatch his conversation from thin air, they would hear only clicks and squealing static, like the last gasps of a dying robot.

"So, Señor Dietrich, how may I assist you?"

It came out in a frantic rush, now that the line was perfectly secure.

"The enemies who killed my men in Bogotá are here, inside Colonia Victoria," Dietrich said. "They've already killed more people!"

Menendez scowled and mouthed a silent curse. "You have soldiers and weapons to defend the compound," he reminded Dietrich.

"Yes, but maybe not enough! Another dozen dead already, I now have. I can't live under siege on my own property. I won't!"

Menendez knew where this was going, and he saw no way to head it off. Instead he beat the aging Nazi to the punch.

"I have a small team I can send," he said. "They're trained to deal with insurrectionists. Most of my people, as you know, are mere policemen."

That was an exaggeration, as they both knew, but his offer seemed to pacify Dietrich a bit.

"When can you send them?"

"They can fly within the hour," Menendez replied. "Then, with their flight time, I would estimate arrival somewhere in the area of…shall we say midnight? Maybe one o'clock?"

"They'll come here to the compound, yes?"

"If you still have the helipad," Menendez said, "I can arrange that."

"Excellent! Thank you, Commander. I shall not forget your generosity."

Meaning the very opposite, of course. Dietrich had funneled a small fortune to Menendez, through the years, and now he meant to get his money's worth.

"It's nothing, Señor Dietrich," Menendez said, though he was well aware he'd have to justify fielding his crack antiguerrilla team.

"Be sure they radio ahead before they try to land," Dietrich instructed. "We don't want any unfortunate mistakes."

Saying that he might shoot the helicopters down if they approached without permission. And he likely would, too, in his present mental state.

"They'll call ahead as usual," Menendez answered.

"Commander, thank you, thank you."

"Certainly, Señor Dietrich. If there's something more that you require?"

Relief swept over him as Dietrich said, "No, no. That should be quite enough." And once again, "I won't forget this."

I won't let you, Menendez thought, as he said good-night and broke the link.

Goddamn the man!

Before he had time to consider all the risks and consequences it entailed, Menendez made the necessary phone call to alert, rally and send Escuadrilla Especial de la Acción— EEA—off to hunt and kill unknown targets, on behalf of a foreigner he should have thrown in prison.

Life was strange, and getting stranger all the time.

Menendez only hoped that it would be a long strange life for him, a painful short one for his enemies.

Colonia Victoria

HANS DIETRICH PLACED his next call to Naldo Aznar. He didn't worry about waking the drug lord; such people stayed up "partying" throughout all hours of the night, and sometimes didn't go to bed for days on end.

In any case, he needed help. And Aznar would provide it, whether he was half asleep or not.

Dietrich had learned a great deal in his youth from Adolf Eichmann, the bookkeeper who had risen to command the chain of Polish camps designed to carry out Der Führer's final solution to the Jewish question. While he climbed the Nazi

Party's ladder, gaining ever-higher rank, Eichmann had documented every foible of his fellow fascists, filing details of their secret hobbies, weaknesses and sins—enough, in most cases, to topple them from power and ensure an agonizing death.

Eichmann had rarely used those precious files, which was the point, of course. Knowledge was power. Blackmail was a tool like any other, oftentimes more deadly than a knife or gun.

Dietrich had watched, listened and learned. When he had fled the crumbling Reich and wound up in Colombia, he started files on every politician, judge, policeman, soldier, socialite and criminal he'd bribed or otherwise done business with along the way. Those files were safe, scanned onto CD-ROMs with the advent of computer age, and any leaks would ruin those who'd served Hans Dietrich's cause while fattening their bank accounts.

In Aznar's case, the method was a little different. Most people in the Western Hemisphere knew that he was a drug dealer and murderer. He could not be attacked by sending files to the police, since most of them, at one time or another, were accomplices to Aznar's crimes.

Still, there were certain things that Aznar wished to keep out of the public eye, facts that would weaken and perhaps destroy him, should they be revealed. His taste for children was a prime example—gender didn't seem to matter—and the fact that he sometimes fed information on his competition to the Yankee DEA. If the former secret was exposed, there'd be a public hue and cry that might result in prosecution or exile. If Dietrich leaked the latter, it would mean another war between the drug cartels, which, at the very least, was bad for business.

One of Aznar's flunkies answered on the second ring, heard Dietrich's code name—Valkyrie—and went to fetch the master of the house. A moment later Aznar's voice came on the line.

"Señor Dietrich," he said, "I have no answer for you yet, concerning the events in Bogotá."

"I have a new concern," Dietrich replied.

"Which is…?"

In simple terms, Dietrich explained his problem and the scope of Aznar's contribution to resolving it. "How many soldiers can you spare?" he asked in closing.

"Twenty, perhaps," Aznar replied. "I'll have to find the jungle fighters, if I have any. Otherwise, you'll just be stuck with city boys who wouldn't know a viper from a garden hose."

"How soon can they be here?" Dietrich asked.

"You're lucky, there," said Aznar. "I have people in Caquetá who can help you. Otherwise, they'd be delayed for several hours, possibly until tomorrow afternoon."

"Will they arrive by air, or travel overland?" asked Dietrich.

"As to that, I'll have to check and call you back. Within the hour I should know something."

"Thank you, Herr Aznar. I was sure that you would not abandon us in this grim time. I shall look forward to their swift arrival."

Telling Aznar, without saying it out loud, that he had a responsibility to keep Colonia Victoria intact and thriving, for his business and for personal security.

"I'm always glad to help, *señor*," the drug lord said.

"And we shall see you for the celebration, yes?"

"Of course," Aznar replied before he severed the long-distance link.

Dietrich had done his best. Help would be coming from Menendez and Aznar, both of whom he trusted to make good on what they'd promised to him. As to when the reinforcements might arrive, Dietrich could only estimate and hope. Whatever happened, he had to hold the colony until the help he'd summoned was delivered.

Hold it against whom?

The villager's report disturbed Dietrich, but he was not sure he could trust it. Certainly, three shooters could destroy a dozen men, if they had the advantage of concealment and surprise. That part did not surprise him. Rather, it was the supposed composition of the ambush team that gave him pause.

Two men—one white, one native and a woman?

Anything was possible, of course. The damned Israelis trained women for combat and expected them to do the bloody killing work of men. Dietrich himself had known some women in the Reich who outstripped any man for bloodlust and ferocity. So why not send a woman for the job, if she was capable?

The part that troubled Dietrich, giving him a headache in that place behind his eyes, was not the composition, but the number of the team. It made him sick to think that three shooters had reached such havoc with his men in Bogotá, and now had threatened him within Colonia Victoria itself.

What did that augur for the Master Race?

What was the damned world coming to?

Grumbling, Hans Dietrich went to pour himself another brimming glass of schnapps.

HAL BROGNOLA TOOK THE CALL from Stony Man at home. He hadn't changed for bed yet, wasn't sleepy in the normal sense, although the day had left him feeling tired, rundown. Lately, he felt that way most days.

He had been doing paperwork and sipping cocoa—Helen's thoughtful gesture, on her way to bed—when the phone rang. It was his private line, the one that automatically scrambled conversations as soon as he lifted the receiver. Anyone who had the number and was authorized to call him also had a scrambler on their end. Wrong-number dialers and random solicitors received a shrieking high-pitched tone that guaranteed earaches and no call-backs.

Brognola grabbed it at the end of the first ring, "Hello?"

"News from Colombia," Barbara Price said.

"I'm listening."

"Starting in Bogotá, the broadcasts claim at least a dozen dead and twice that many wounded. First, there were eight men shot in the factory district, around the time Striker was due to touch down. Our contact with the DAS—their FBI— thinks they were tracking someone from the airport when the hit went down, but there's no evidence to prove it."

"So," Brognola said, "he's made contact."

"And then some," Price replied. "A couple hours later, someone leveled Dietrich's home-away-from-home in Bogotá with high-explosive rounds from—get this—an army-surplus 60 mm mortar. Basically, they blew his house down, killed at least four more. Others are hanging on in critical condition."

"That's our boy."

"The trouble is, it's all gone quiet now," Price said.

"Too quiet?"

"Well, I figure that he took some time to sleep last night, then hit the road with Guzman navigating. If they drove, call it three or four hours from Bogotá to the nearest jumping-off point for a march into Dietrich's backyard. I'm guessing that he wouldn't just drive up to the front gate and ring the bell."

"Not likely," Brognola agreed.

"So, then, I lose them on the trail, with no idea exactly where they'd start from or how long the march should take."

"That kind of thing, I never had much luck," Brognola said. "You don't know who he's met, or what goes on along the way. Is there some kind of opposition, or an easy run?

Mountains? Clearing a trail where no man's gone before? You'll get an ulcer from the guessing games."

"Did you?" she asked.

"Not me. I gave up guessing and went with the flow."

Price actually laughed at that, surprising him. "Sorry," she said. "You caught me by surprise, there. I was worried that you might've lost your sense of humor."

"Hey, I'm serious," the big Fed said. "You mean, I don't go with the flow?"

"Not even close, boss," she replied. "Hell, you'd reroute the Mississippi if it didn't flow to suit you."

Brognola couldn't decide if he should take that as an insult or a compliment, so he decided to ignore it.

"Anyway," he said, "my point is that on deals like this, clock-watchers seldom go the distance, and they're nearly always disappointed. Try relaxing, if you can. Whatever's going on will happen when he's ready."

"Right."

Price didn't voice her secret fear, but Brognola already knew it. He had lived with it for years on end.

What if, the grim scenario began, Bolan went off to do a job and never called again, never reported back? What if he simply disappeared without a trace? What then?

Brognola thought about it every time he sent Bolan halfway around the world to do his dirty work, to clean up someone else's mess. And always, he suppressed the fear, answered those questions in the only way he could.

Not this time. Please, God, not this time.

And so far, it had worked.

"I'll be in touch, as soon as I hear anything," Price told him, signing off.

"Sounds good. Thanks for the update."

"'Bye for now."

"Good night."

He cradled the receiver, slumped back in his chair and felt world-weariness envelop him like steam inside a sauna. They could use some help, some luck, as soon as possible.

"God bless us, every one," Brognola said, and turned back to his paperwork—then, he was struck with an idea.

It might not work, might not even be feasible, but it was worth a try.

Why not?

Smiling, he reached for the telephone.

Colonia Victoria

BEFORE SOME GENIUS invented GPS technology, Bolan had navigated jungles with a compass and the stars to guide him, trusting his gut and his sense of direction. He'd been lost a time or two, but only for a little while, and never when it mattered.

Now, Bolan was right on course, making good time, and shared the feeling of his two companions who were wishing that he'd lead them straight to Dietrich's compound. That would be the easy way, with no diversions, no delays. Go for the jugular, and see what happened next.

Most likely, they would all be killed.

Hans Dietrich had to be on full alert by now. He couldn't possibly be unaware of the events in Bogotá, and Bolan guessed that he'd been briefed about the village skirmish by this time, as well.

Would he react as Bolan had predicted, beefing up his guard on the perimeter and sending more patrols out to the west? If so, they had a decent chance of slipping into Dietrich's compound. If he went some other way—deciding, for example, to forego further patrols and put all of his soldiers on the compound's firing line—their task would be more difficult.

But would it be impossible?

Bolan hated to use that word, but he was also realistic. And there were, in fact, some things he couldn't do.

He couldn't stop a charging rhino with a water pistol. Couldn't fly without mechanical contraptions to support him. Couldn't guarantee a happy ending, full of peace and love, for everybody in the world.

Bolan was only human, after all.

But he could do his best, and in the past, that had been good enough.

This time? He'd have to wait and see.

Jorge Guzman was near exhaustion, from the look of him, and even Gabriella Cohen had begun to show fatigue around the edges. She was strong, determined, and would tough it out until she dropped—but *she* was only human, too.

That was the problem he kept running into. Everyone around him, all of them, were human beings, with the frailties and the wicked streaks that had retarded humankind's progress through the ages. Every time it seemed humanity was on the verge of some great breakthrough, lowly humans screwed it up.

Bolan remembered as a child, how he'd been so excited by the Race for Space. He'd dreamed of colonies on Mars and Jupiter, of explorations in the farthest galaxies. Instead, the space shuttle went up a couple times per year and circled Earth, then came back down again with no great fanfare. Lonely footprints on the moon had gathered dust.

Humanity, for all its progress in the fields of medicine and science, hadn't really changed much in the past millennium or so. People lived longer, and in many cases better, but the civilized still walked in fear of predators who might appear and strike them down at any time. The courts, police and prisons all were swamped and losing ground.

The Executioner would never be without a job.

"How far?" Guzman asked, sounding winded.

Bolan checked the GPS and answered, "Six point one."

They'd covered nearly two miles from their last stop, and his legs were feeling it. Guzman was dragging, but he followed Cohen doggedly, refusing to be left behind. Would he be fit to fight when they arrived if nothing happened to him in the meantime?

Bolan didn't know, but they had passed the point of no return. For Guzman, giving up now meant a six-mile walk back to the car—if he could find it on his own, lurching through darkness.

Would he make it?

Bolan would have bet against it, but it didn't matter. Guzman wasn't giving up. He saw that in the man's expression, read it in his body language. Guzman wouldn't quit, because he had something to prove, if only to himself.

And after finishing the hike, would he survive what happened next? Would any of them make it out the other side alive?

Bolan had never been a fortune-teller, but he thought their odds were fair.

And if it seemed that they might fail, he'd take as many of the Nazis with him as he could.

CHAPTER TEN

DAS Headquarters, Bogotá

Joaquin Menendez hated working nights. He'd done enough of that when he was younger, in the army, later with the DAS, when he was rising through the ranks. Nightfall brought trouble, crime and violence, the same way it brought predators from hiding in the jungle, searching for an easy kill.

During his long career he'd raided rebel camps and suspect native villages, kicked in apartment doors and ransacked houses, lain in wait to ambush men he'd never seen before—most of it in the middle of the night.

These days, now that he was in charge, Menendez liked to spend his evenings more creatively. Late suppers, firelight, bottles of expensive wine and women who would yield to him because of who he was, including some who never would have given him a second glance in ordinary circumstances.

Menendez did not deceive himself that they allowed him to possess them out of love, because they found him irresistibly attractive. He could not have cared less how or why they found their way into his bed, as long as they fulfilled his private needs.

It had surprised him when he first became an officer, the way some women took for granted that he had the power to help their loved ones who had been arrested, even those imprisoned after trial. Some would do anything to make him feel more kindly toward their brothers, husbands, sons or lovers.

Anything at all.

Now that he actually had the power to release detainees, transfer inmates from one lockup to another, or arrange early parole, the friends and relatives were even more insistent that he take their money, jewelry, family heirlooms. That he plunder them in every way imaginable, for the sake of inmates in his custody.

A shuffling sound of footsteps from his outer office jarred Menendez from his reverie. His secretary had gone home three hours earlier. Perhaps it was the janitor making his nightly rounds.

Menendez took a step in the direction of his office door, then reconsidered it and doubled back to take the pistol from his desk. He had already locked the desk, of course, and as he fumbled with his keys, knuckles beat a tattoo upon the door.

Menendez dropped his keys, was stooping to retrieve them when the door opened. Two men of roughly equal size and build entered his office and advanced to stand in front of his desk.

He left his keys and rose, so that they would not tower over him. When he was on his feet, he judged the stranger on his left—gray suit, gray briefcase, matching hair—to be approximately six feet tall. His companion, standing five-eleven, wore a navy blue suit and had close-cropped sandy hair.

In unison, they both produced credentials, holding up their laminated IDs for Menendez to inspect. It struck him that they could as easily have drawn pistols and killed him where he stood.

The IDs looked authentic, but he really couldn't tell without performing certain tests. What startled him almost as the appearance of two total strangers in his office after hours, was the information printed on those ID cards. He was processing it when one of the intruders—Gray Suit—spoke.

"Colonel Menendez—"

"It's Director, now, *señor.* I left the army years ago. The DAS does not use military ranks."

"Of course, Director. I am Arthur Grant, third secretary from the U.S. consulate in Bogotá, and this is Ezra Benjamin, from the Israeli consulate."

Menendez didn't know if the American was DEA or CIA, but he assumed that the Israeli was Mossad. "I don't recall that either of you telephoned for an appointment," he said.

"This is urgent," Grant replied.

"We assumed you would not wish your staff to know that we are here," Benjamin added.

"Why *are* you here?" Menendez asked.

"To show you something," Grant replied.

Without a by-your-leave, Grant placed his briefcase on the desk and opened it, withdrew a fat manila file folder and passed it to Menendez. Printed neatly on the cover was Gunter, Hans Dietrich.

Menendez raised his eyes and asked, "Am I supposed to read this now?"

"Most of it, you already know," Ezra Benjamin said, speaking for the first time.

"What are you saying?"

"Simple English," Grant replied, "you're in this file, along with the old Nazi and his friends. In fact, you are one of his friends."

"I know Señor Dietrich, of course," Menendez said. "He also knows Supreme Court justices and the attorney general, members of parliament, perhaps even the president. To say that we are friends, however, is inaccurate."

"Okay," Grant said, "we'll call you partners, then. How's that?"

"Again, you are mistaken. If you think—"

"I think you shouldn't say another word until you've read that file and seen the photographs. They've got some nice ones of you killing time with Dietrich, having lunch, boating, riding around in his Mercedes limousine. Cozy."

"Why are you here?" Menendez asked again.

Benjamin answered with a question of his own. "Were you aware that Dietrich raises coca on Colonia Victoria and runs cocaine processing labs?"

"That is a serious—"

"He sells directly to Naldo Aznar," Grant interrupted Menendez. "You haven't had much luck arresting Aznar since you took over the DAS. Why is that?"

"Investigations are ongoing, and—"

Benjamin cut him off, asking, "Were you aware of Dietrich's intimate connection to the Sword of Allah?"

"I don't—"

"At this moment, he is harboring a fugitive from justice named Nasser Khalil, wanted on murder charges in Israel, the U.S.A. and Germany. Two of Khalil's present companions, Najjar Baraka and Wasim Riyad, have been convicted by a French court, in absentia, on three counts of murder."

"Assuming all of this is true, how do you know?" Menendez challenged.

"Simple research and investigation," Grant replied. "The kind most people would expect the DAS to do, before you climbed into bed with a Nazi war criminal."

"I'm not required to stand and listen to your insults," Menendez said. "You believe that I can be intimidated with a file and photographs? You threaten…what? To speak with my superiors? Perhaps the very men who introduced me to Señor Dietrich? I think you will be disappointed, gentlemen."

"You're right," Grant said. "That would be disappointing. So we thought we'd take our information to the media. Start with the papers and the TV stations here in Bogotá, then copies to the *New York Times* and *USA Today*, try CNN and all the major networks in the States. You'd like to be a star, right? A celebrity?"

Menendez felt his stomach twisting into knots.

"And while we're at it," Benjamin remarked, "we may as well release our files on several of the others whom you mentioned earlier. The judges, the attorney general, who knows? As far as the reporters are concerned, those files all come from you. I doubt they'll name you personally. Something like, 'A well-placed source within the DAS,' I should imagine."

"Stop! What is it that you want?"

"I thought you'd never ask," Arthur Grant replied.

Colonia Victoria

"ABOUT FOUR MILES remaining," Bolan told his two companions when they took their next short break for rest and water.

"When you say 'about,' how far is that?" Cohen asked.

Bolan didn't have to check the GPS a second time. "It's four point three," he said.

"So, four and one-third miles," she verified.

"That's right. We could stop sooner, or go on a little farther, if we find a spot that looks good, where we have a chance to breach security."

"It will be light by then?" Guzman asked.

"Getting close, if not already daylight," Bolan told him. "Yes."

"It seems impossible for us to get inside the compound in broad daylight," Guzman said.

"We'll have to wait and see," Bolan replied. "If it's too hairy getting in, we'll sit it out and wait for nightfall."

"Could we sleep, then?" Guzman asked him, almost plaintively.

"As long as someone's standing watch."

"I wonder if they'll celebrate this year," Cohen mused, as if talking to herself.

"Celebrate what?" Bolan asked.

"It's a Nazi holiday today," she said. "Didn't you know?"

"I must've missed the memo from the Führer," Bolan said.

"You're nearly right, although he couldn't send the invitations out himself. And he won't be attending, naturally, even though the party's in his honor."

"Hitler? What about him?"

"It's his birthday," Cohen replied. "All over the world, neo-Nazis will celebrate. Most just get drunk. Some will vandalize synagogues, graveyards, whatever they can find that seems to them most Jewish."

"I'd have thought they would be getting over it, by now," Bolan said.

"Poison never dies. It never rests. Do you remember Frank Spisak?"

"It doesn't ring a bell," said Bolan.

"He's a neo-Nazi from your Cleveland, in Ohio."

"Not my Cleveland," Bolan said.

"In any case, he is in prison for the murder of three strangers, shot at random. One was black, the other two he thought were Jews, although he'd never met them. He was wrong, of course. The murders happened the year I was born. He was sentenced to die, but he's still living, still filing one appeal after another."

"Does it make a difference how he dies, as long as its in prison?"

"Not to me," Cohen said. "But to others, I believe so, yes."

"And yet, if memory serves, Israel has no death penalty," Bolan said.

"Except for genocide and treason during wartime, that's correct. The only man we've ever hanged was Adolf Eichmann."

"So, you're out of step with your bosses on that point," Bolan said.

"On others, too, I think," she answered, smiling. "Why, if they knew—"

Bolan frowned as Cohen left the comment dangling.

"Go on and finish it. If they knew what?"

"All right, why not," she said. "If they knew I was here, they would be furious."

"They didn't clear it?"

Cohen shrugged. "I didn't ask."

"You're off the grid," Bolan said.

"The grid was too restrictive, in this case," she said. "They sent me here to *watch* Dietrich, report back what he does and who he sees. What good is that? The only way to stop him is to stop him."

Bolan thought about that for a moment, Cohen watching him, while Guzman stared at her.

Their guide said, "So, you *want* to be here?"

"Jorge, there is nowhere on this planet that I'd rather be right now." She turned to Bolan then, frowning, and said, "So, what now? Would you send me back?"

"Too late," he said. "We're past the point of no return."

THE TWIN BELL 412 HELICOPTERS cruised in tandem at an altitude of seven thousand feet. Below them, the montane forests of Caquetá might have been mistaken for a deep shag carpet dyed in varied shades of green. One step onto that carpet from their present height, however, meant a screaming plummet to the ground far below, flayed alive by countless limbs along the way.

Inspector Arturo Obregon hated flying. Above all else, he hated helicopters, with their mostly open cockpits and the vulnerability to drafts—up, down, sideways, it was all the same to him. And if God had wanted people hovering in mid-air like dragonflies or hummingbirds, He would have given them wings.

Still, flying was part of his job, and he did it without one complaint, without letting his superiors or subordinates know how much it frightened him. It was expected of him, and he dared not disappoint those who depended on him for results, or for his leadership.

This mission, in particular, set Obregon's teeth on edge. He understood the urgency of flying off at odd hours to chase guerrillas, or to seize a drug shipment—though he was seldom called on to do that—but *this* assignment struck him as preposterous.

Why should he and twenty-three armed agents be detailed to guard a group of German immigrants, living on their own in the middle of nowhere? They weren't even citizens, as far as Obregon could tell, and rumor had it that their leader was an old, decrepit Nazi who had fled the Fatherland before he could be hanged at Nuremberg. Why was he even in Colombia? Why had a long series of presidents permitted him to stay for fifty years or more?

Arturo Obregon knew better than to ask such questions. His job was not to reason why. His mission was to do as he was told, regardless of the damage suffered by his conscience or morale.

Señor Dietrich had friends in power, that was obvious.

And Obregon believed that one of them was the director of the DAS, Joaquin Menendez. In which case, Obregon had only two choices: he could obey orders or he could quit and try to find another job.

Of course, if he displeased Joaquin Menendez, there would be no other job in government for Obregon. Nothing of any importance in private security, either, unless he chose to leave Colombia. And even then—

"Five kilometres to go," one of the pilots announced, his words crackling through Obregon's earphones.

Since his men had none, and they were deafened by the roaring of the Bell's twin engines, Obregon raised his right hand, fingers splayed, and shouted, "Five kilometres!" as loud as he could.

Obregon's left hand clutched his M-16 rifle, holding it upright, its butt on the metal floorboard. Vibrations from the helicopter traveled through the rifle, along Obregon's arm, and made him feel as if his heart was palpitating. Sweat beaded his forehead, even though there was a chill inside the chopper that raised goose bumps on his arms.

He thanked the uniform designers who had put long sleeves on the DAS field uniforms. When they were safely on the ground, he might sweat through his shirt in fifteen minutes, but at least his men would not know he was terrified while they were airborne.

Moments later, traveling at speeds in excess of 150 miles per hour, the pilot announced, "There it is." Obregon remained firmly strapped in his seat, made no attempt to glimpse their destination prior to touchdown. He had seen the compound once already, and had hoped never to make a second trip, but here he was.

He wondered whether they were meant to guard the place or to go out on patrol in search of whoever or whatever had

Dietrich in a panic. Obregon found it distasteful either way, but he would do as he was told—presumably by Dietrich, since his orders from Menendez were extremely vague.

They landed on the compound's helipad, one whirlybird behind the other, leaving ample room between them for the twenty-three-foot rotor blades of each. That placed the helicopters nearly fifty feet apart as Obregon removed his headphones, rose and scrambled from the airship that felt like a flying coffin.

Dietrich came to meet him, hand outstretched, his white hair whipped chaotically by rotor wash. Behind the old German came a younger man with bandages and fresh burns on his face. If Obregon had met the second man before, he did not recognize the singed and battered face.

As he was shaking Dietrich's hand, one of the pilots shouted at him through an open cockpit window, waving Obregon back to the helicopter.

"Pardon me," he told Dietrich, and jogged back to the chopper, climbed inside, asking the pilot, "What is it?"

"Message for you, sir."

"Message? Where? From whom?"

"Use these," the pilot said, passing another headphone set to Obregon.

He wedged them on and spoke into the small stalk microphone. "Hello? Who's speaking?"

"Listen carefully, Arturo," the unmistakable voice of Joaquin Menendez commanded. "You must get your men back on the helicopters and return to Bogotá at once."

"Return, sir? But—"

"Don't question me! Just do as you are told!"

"Yes, sir. What shall I tell Señor Dietrich?"

"Refer to some emergency. Tell him whatever comes to mind. I don't care what you say, just get back here as soon as possible."

"Yes, sir! I understand."

Which was a lie, of course. He understood nothing.

Obregon dismounted, walked back to where Dietrich and the younger man stood waiting for him, putting on a rueful smile that honestly conveyed his confusion.

"Señor Dietrich, I regret that we must now return to Bogotá. Director Menendez requires our presence in the capital without delay."

"But…but…you just got here!" Dietrich sputtered.

"Yes, sir. I apologize. It seems that there is some emergency."

"I'm in the midst of an emergency right here!" the German snapped.

"Señor, I fear I have no choice. Feel free to contact the director for an explanation. Once again, I do apologize."

Before the German could say more, Obregon rounded on his men and ordered them back aboard the helicopters. They went, with some typical grumbling among themselves. Obregon quickly boarded his chopper and found his seat, fastened the safety straps and donned his headset.

"Let's get out of here," he told the pilot, "before someone has another change of heart."

He risked a glance below as they were lifting off, and saw Dietrich retreating toward his headquarters. The old German was running, or attempting to. The bandaged man limped rapidly along behind him, looking like a mummy that had just escaped from a museum.

Arlington, Virginia

BROGNOLA TOOK THE LATE CALL on his scrambled line, at home. A deep, familiar voice told him, "It's done."

"How did he take it?" Brognola inquired.

"About like you'd expect," the caller told him. "If he wasn't paranoid before, he will be now."

"And the support for Dietrich?"

"Pulling back," the caller said. "At least, he promised. Too much riding on the line for him to bluff, in my opinion."

"Good," Brognola said. And then again, for emphasis, "That's good."

"We're all square, then," the caller said, not making it a question.

"Square on what, exactly?" Brognola asked.

"That's the answer I was looking for."

The line went dead.

It was impossible to work in law enforcement—or in any branch of government, for that matter—without incurring debts and doing favors. No reformer from the farm belt or the inner city ever mastered flying solo through the bureaucratic maze; none ever would.

Brognola, in his many years of service to the letter and the spirit of the law, had logged entries on both sides of the ledger. More than he could count, in fact. One heavy item on the credit side had just been canceled out, with the result—he hoped—that Bolan might be faced with fewer enemies when it was time for him to penetrate Colonia Victoria.

In fact, Brognola thought, the Executioner was likely there already, looking for his angle of attack, weighing the odds, choosing his moment. Dietrich had a small army of Nazis whom he'd brainwashed from the cradle up, both to believe his Master Race insanity and act upon it, without mercy or remorse, when called upon to kill or maim.

Add to that tight goose-stepping army any men Dietrich could beg, borrow, or steal from Naldo Aznar's drug cartel, and the old Nazi had a formidable combat force. Likely too much for any average soldier to evade, much less defeat.

Mack Bolan was no average soldier, granted, but he *was* a human being. Hal's mind had rebelled at having agents of the DAS arrayed against him, in addition to the brownshirts and the narcokillers. Most especially, he needed to remove the DAS from the equation, since his oldest living friend would rather die than drop the hammer on a cop.

They'd argued that point time and time again, with Brognola surprised to find himself opposing Bolan's conscientious stand. He'd pointed out the obvious—that some supposed lawmen had sold their badges to the Mob or other rotten syndicates and thus lost any right to be regarded as police. Others—not many, but enough to make the big Fed sick at heart—were simply thugs with badges, who would kill, rape, rob and brutalize the innocent without compunction.

Why not kill them, in those circumstances? he had asked.

And Bolan always said the same damned thing: "They're soldiers of the same side, Hal, even if they've forgotten it."

So, if he couldn't run away from lawmen bent on killing him, Bolan would stand and take a bullet rather than defend himself with deadly force. Some might've called it crazy, even suicidal, but Brognola didn't waste his time on labels.

He was simply doing what he could to make sure that scenario was yanked out of the script, this time around.

And if his caller was correct, Brognola had succeeded. Blackmail was a potent weapon, and Joaquin Menendez was one vulnerable bastard. If he lived up to his bargain in this instance, the big Fed would let him slide.

But if he pulled a double-cross…

Brognola had some people on his team who'd never sworn off killing dirty cops. And if Menendez tried to screw him, he'd be meeting some of them before the week was out.

Colonia Victoria

GERALDO SANCHEZ SIPPED tequila from a silver flask and nestled in the Hummer's shotgun seat, thankful for air-conditioning that kept the morning's heat at bay. The armored vehicle might not provide the smoothest ride available on four wheels, but it sure as hell beat walking.

Sanchez was a city boy who shunned the wilderness whenever possible, leaving the forests and the swamps to creatures that belonged there—caimans, vipers, scorpions, tarantulas and leeches. To them, he was the enemy, for some an item on the menu, and he did not trespass into their domain if it could be avoided. Sometimes, though, a side trip through green hell was mandatory.

Like this day.

Naldo Aznar had chosen—ordered—him to lead this team. Three Hummers, fifteen men and all the weapons they could reasonably carry. Sanchez was commanded to assist Hans Dietrich in eliminating certain trespassers on his rural estate, thus keeping Dietrich happy and his cocaine flowing freely at the normal contract price.

Sanchez regarded the assignment as an inconvenience, not a problem. Half the men he'd chosen for the job were natives of Caquetá, and they knew its woods as well as Sanchez knew the barrios of Medellín. Besides which, Dietrich's crazy gringos had been living on the land for fifty years or something, meaning they should be familiar with its every nook and cranny.

It should be no special challenge, then, to find a group of strangers blundering around the property and either kill them on the spot or take them into custody. Knowing Hans Dietrich as he did, chiefly from third- and fourth-hand rumors, Sanchez thought the prowlers would be lucky if they died fighting. The stories that were told about Colonia Victoria, its secret laboratories and religious rituals, made Sanchez wonder why Aznar was even doing business with such a maniac.

The answer, as he well knew, was cocaine.

In any given year, Dietrich produced roughly fifteen percent of the cocaine Aznar sold through to the United States, to Canada and Western Europe. How much was it worth? Perhaps one and a half billion dollars.

Any way you counted, it was money well worth fighting for.

The narrow access road leading to Dietrich's compound was unpaved, coating the three black Hummers with a khaki-colored layer of dust. None of it reached Sanchez or his companions, riding with the windows tightly shut and air-conditioning cranked to the max. Sanchez believed that even if your destination was the seventh ring of hell itself, you ought to ride in style.

"Three kilometers," his driver said to no one in particular.

"Last chance to check your weapons," Sanchez told his backseat passengers.

None of them stirred. Being professionals, they would have checked the hardware when they received it, not waiting until they were out in the middle of nowhere, with no exchange options. They were stoic, staring silently ahead or out the nearest tinted window, watching trees and more trees seem to march away as they rolled toward their target.

Dietrich had gunmen posted where the road entered the compound, at the point where Sanchez always thought some kind of gate belonged. Sanchez counted five instead of the usual two. Elsewhere, as far as he could see, sentries with automatic weapons covered the compound's perimeter.

Dietrich had not walled-off his compound from the forest acreage surrounding it. The net result was spacious, with a sense of freedom to it, but it had to have been a nightmare to defend. Wild animals could come and go at will, scavenge for garbage, even stalk and kill prey on the compound's grounds. Three guard towers, positioned in a rough triangular formation, let machine gunners command the streets, the helipad and playing fields, but it would only take a moment of fatigue or apathy to let an enemy slip past one of the towers, worm his way into the heart of Dietrich's Aryan community.

That's why he needs us, Sanchez thought. He's either running short of lookouts or he wants more guns out on patrol.

Sanchez hoped it was lookout duty, so he wouldn't have to lead his men around in circles through the goddamned forest, but he wasn't counting on it. He supposed the odds were fifty-fifty, at the very best. But he would do as he was told, please Naldo Aznar by cooperating with the crazy German.

To a point.

Sanchez would not partake of any scientific or religious mumbo-jumbo that the aged Nazi might suggest. Killing the trespassers, or catching them alive and handing them to Dietrich, was the limit of his job description.

Keeping that firmly in mind, Geraldo Sanchez forced a smile as he stepped from the Hummer into muggy heat and saw Hans Dietrich rushing toward him, hand outstretched. From the expression on the German's face, he either had bad news to share, or breakfast had been off.

Sanchez stood fast and braced himself to hear the worst.

"WE CAN TRY HERE," Bolan announced after another consultation with his GPS device, "or we can hike another half mile to the next-best place."

"Try here," Guzman said, sounding winded.

"This seems fine," Cohen stated.

"I should point out that we haven't seen the compound yet," Bolan reminded them.

"A minor detail," Cohen said, before she sat on a mossy rock.

Sunrise had tinged the forest treetops with their first pale blush of pink and orange. Soon it would be full daylight. Bolan had marched his team straight through the night.

"We can rest here awhile," he said, "and wait to see the compound when we have more light."

"Can we afford to sleep?" Cohen asked.

"Taking it in turns should be all right," Bolan replied.

Guzman put on a brave face, saying, "I can push on, now."

"Jorge," Cohen said, "if it's all the same to you, I need to rest."

"Well, if we must."

Bolan suppressed a smile. Machismo might keep Guzman on his feet and moving, but exhaustion made for careless soldiers, who were dangerous to both sides. Cohen was adept enough at reading others to decide that Guzman needed sleep.

"I'll take the first watch," Bolan told them. "Say two hours."

"Then you'll sleep?" Cohen asked.

"Right," he lied.

Two hours should refresh them, but he wouldn't sleep while they stood guard. Two hours was enough time wasted, when they had a job to do.

Bolan wished they'd been able to obtain aerial photos of Hans Dietrich's compound. Even some rude sketch of the layout might help, but none had been available when Bolan left the States. Colonia Victoria was blank on standard maps, although they bore the standard symbols indicating montane forest.

Nothing had prepared him for the streams they'd crossed, much less the village where they'd clashed with Dietrich's men. Bolan had no clue as to whether penetration of the Nazi compound might require wire cutters, rubber gloves for an electric fence or climbing spikes to scale a stockade wall.

Maybe it's just as well, he thought, since he had brought none of those things.

His training for the U.S. Army Special Forces had taught Bolan how to improvise, adapt and turn most situations to his own advantage with a little thought and elbow grease. He knew there had to be some way inside the compound, since it took deliveries of food and other staple items trucked in from outside. If nothing else, there'd be a gate, and he would find some way to open it. Take out the guards Dietrich had posted. Make his way inside.

And then?

Bolan could only plan so far ahead, and he had reached his limit until he'd laid eyes upon the target. Before moving in, he had to mark his targets: generators and communications links, Dietrich's command post and his quarters, motor pools and arms repositories—anything at all, in fact, that made the compound viable and self-sufficient.

Bolan hadn't flown into Colombia to simply kill one man, or any certain group of men. As he read Brognola's instructions, he'd been sent to wipe a plague spot off the map. Scorched earth.

He couldn't kill the Aryan mystique or the impulse to subjugate "inferiors," but with some planning and a dash of luck he could eliminate a focal point of orchestrated hate and violence. Some Nazis might survive his strike, but if he played his cards right, they'd be scattered to the winds and likely driven from Colombia by bad publicity, forced to seek other havens where their cancer of the soul could put down roots and grow.

And there would always be such places, Bolan realized. No evil every truly died or was eradicated from the Earth. Wounds could be cleaned and cauterized, but poison ran throughout the bloodstream of the human race, infecting new victims as soon as other carriers were isolated or eliminated.

Such was life.

Such was the Executioner's unending war.

CHAPTER ELEVEN

Colonia Victoria

So here he was, goddamn it, in the middle of the woods, exactly as he'd feared. Geraldo Sanchez spit into the ferns that edged the narrow game trail and dug in his pocket for a handkerchief to wipe the perspiration from his face.

Hans Dietrich had insisted that his men join in the cycle of patrols around the aging Nazi's forest hideaway, despite the fact that they were neither dressed for hiking in the wilderness nor trained in tactics of guerrilla warfare. Naldo Aznar, curse him, had told Dietrich they would follow his instructions, which meant craziness Sanchez was only now beginning to appreciate.

Still, he could draw a line. If Dietrich and his people started in on any of their weird religious mumbo-jumbo, Sanchez would have none of it. He might be a drug runner and a murderer, but he was not about to help these Nazi heathens worship any god except the Jesus dangling from a tiny silver cross around his neck.

Sanchez had managed to convince himself that Jesus

would forgive him for the drugs, the killings, all the other sins related to his chosen line of work, but never for adopting other gods. That would be pushing things too far, and he was not about to take that risk with his immortal soul.

If they could only find these bastards lurking in the woods and kill them, everything would be all right.

Like Dietrich and his scar-faced second in command, Sanchez had no idea who he was looking for. *Perhaps* three people, but there could be more. *Maybe* one of them was a woman.

Useless shit.

He understood this much: the interlopers, male or female, three or thirty-three, had already killed twelve of Dietrich's men before Sanchez arrived. That told him they were well armed, probably well trained, or else had taken Dietrich's slackers by surprise. In either case, they had evaded search parties and might be running for their lives away from Dietrich's little Nazi factory by now. But Dietrich didn't think so, and since Aznar was permitting him to call the shots, Sanchez was stuck.

Some kind of flying insects buzzed around his head, tormenting him. Sanchez slapped at them, missed, and then felt foolish, like one of the crazy homeless people who were everywhere in Bogotá and Medellín. At least he wasn't talking to himself, unless you counted muttered curses when he stepped in clinging mud or a stray branch slapped him across the face.

Hell must be like this, Sanchez thought. Marching through mud and heat and swarming bugs, searching for something that you never find. Searching forever, without end.

It was almost enough to make Sanchez give up his life of crime.

Almost.

But then he thought about the bonus Aznar offered for performance of this unaccustomed and unpleasant duty, and the insects didn't seem so bad. He could afford another pair of shoes, new clothes. And next time he would *ask* about the dress code and equipment first, before he jumped into some business unprepared.

At least they had the weapons for the job. Each member of his team carried an automatic rifle and a pistol, with spare ammunition magazines for both. Some of them also had grenades clipped to their belts, and while Sanchez thought that was going overboard, he'd let them go ahead. Better to bring grenades, then take them home again, he thought, than wish they had grenades when there were none.

The more he thought about it, Sanchez almost felt a stir of pity for the prowlers he was hunting. If he found them, it would be no contest. He had picked the deadliest, most vicious gunmen he could find upon short notice, choosing some who knew the woods and all for their ability to kill without remorse or second thoughts.

They were perfect.

Now, if only he could find the goddamned people they were seeking.

Dietrich's flaw, Sanchez decided, was the scattershot approach. His men had missed their adversaries in some nearby native village—had been killed to the last man, in fact—and now Dietrich was panicking, sending patrols in all directions without any clue to where they should be searching. Sanchez saw the problem, but he had no answer for it, since he didn't know the territory or the enemy.

His first instinct had been to reinforce the compound, watch and wait for an opponent to reveal himself. Dietrich had overruled him on that point, insisting that the new arrivals join in foot patrols—and so they had.

What if the enemy was already behind them?

What if someone raided Dietrich's compound in his absence, killing the old Nazi and his followers?

Sanchez wouldn't bat an eye. He had been told to follow Dietrich's orders, and it wasn't his fault if the orders were defective.

He would double back, of course, if they heard firing from the compound, but they were an hour out and counting. By the time they reached Dietrich's retreat, the battle could be over.

Better yet.

If Sanchez came out of this job with nothing worse than insect bites, he would be happy.

"How much farther, boss?" one of his gunmen inquired.

"A little more," Sanchez replied, with no idea of how far they should march or when they should return to camp. "I'll let you know."

But who would let *him* know?

Cursing under his breath, Sanchez slogged on through the forest, chasing phantoms.

THE OTHERS STILL HAD twenty minutes left to sleep when Bolan woke them, shushing both of them with fingers pressed against their lips. Stooping, he whispered to the pair of them at once, "Somebody's coming."

Both sprang to their feet, ready to fight, as if one hundred minutes spent unconscious had restored their energy completely. Bolan wasn't sure if that was true, but staying where they were was not an option.

From the south, perhaps southwest, he heard the sounds of a patrol advancing through the woods. The trees and undergrowth weren't thick enough for them to use machetes, but they still made noise—jostling the shrubbery, stubbing their toes, dislodging stones, stepping on twigs, the usual. A voice raised, sounding like a question asked in Spanish, though he couldn't make it out.

"Which way?" Cohen asked, whispering.

The GPS device confirmed their adversaries were approaching from a south-southwesterly direction. To avoid them, without straying too far from the Nazi compound, Bolan chose a course that would take them due east and presumably out of harm's way. Once they'd shaken the hunters, they could turn south again and approach Dietrich's lair from the east, for—he hoped—a dramatic surprise.

First things, first.

When they had shouldered all their gear, policed the area for any traces of themselves, Bolan led Cohen and Guzman eastward, setting a pace he knew would tax them, but which also should permit them to avoid their enemies. Bolan took care to make as little noise as possible, trusting the others to do likewise, even though they lacked his skill at fighting in the wilderness.

As Bolan marched, he thought about the day—framed it as Adolf Hitler's birthday in his mind—and couldn't calculate the misery that had been spawned by one event. Were Hitler's parents glad to see him on his first birthday? Bolan knew that the father hadn't lived to see his son grow up. What of the mother? Had she watched her child display the first signs of a raving psychopath?

What difference did it make, so long after the fact?

Hitler was dead, and while he'd had no children, he left heirs aplenty who had carried on his hateful cult of personality, preserving it to modern times. One such disciple was Hans Dietrich, and while he was too old now to count for much alone, his offspring—physical and psychological—still posed a clear and present threat to humankind at large.

And that was unacceptable.

The answer: take them out.

Bolan slogged on, hating the interruption that prevented him from turning south immediately, checking out the compound. They were wasting precious time, but if they didn't dodge the hunters, they were finished.

Stand and fight, a voice inside his head suggested.

He ignored it, pushing onward.

There was nothing to be gained by an engagement this close to the compound. Even if the gunfire didn't warn Dietrich and his defenders in their camp, it could attract other hunters to the battle site, result in Bolan and his two companions being trapped.

Better to duck and dodge, he thought, than to die before he even had a chance to glimpse his target in the flesh.

He needed to be extra-cautious now. Fleeing one enemy too hastily could put him in another's path, and Bolan knew an ambush on the trail could be disastrous. Even if he somehow survived, what of Guzman and Cohen?

Take your time, he thought, but not too much.

The hunters he had heard weren't chasing him, just roaming through the woods in search of targets, tracks, some other kind of leads. Unless he drew them to him, made some critical mistake, they ought to be all right.

For now.

But still, the compound beckoned him. He'd never seen it, but it drew Bolan the way a magnet drew iron filings. He was looking forward to the time when he could study its perimeter, find weak points, take advantage of them and destroy as many of his enemies as possible.

It was not killing that he craved, although he knew it to be mandatory. Long ago, he'd learned how to detach himself from any death and suffering he meted out to human predators. They lived by terror and would die the same way, if the Executioner had anything to say about it.

But he never loved the killing, like some twisted soldiers he had known. He killed because he could, and because sometimes it was necessary. Guarding the herd meant stopping predators in such a way that they could not return to wreak more havoc.

Take them out and see what happens next.

But first, he had to dodge the hunters who were tracking him and make it to the Nazi camp alive. From that point onward, Bolan knew, all bets were off.

HANS DIETRICH WATCHED a group of young people hoisting a giant banner, seven feet by twelve feet, careful not to let it brush the ground. He paid as much attention to their eager faces as the flag itself, feeling no anger when he noted that the swastika was crooked.

"Slightly higher on the left," he told them. "Possibly six inches."

As his children made the last adjustment to the flag behind his podium, flanked by two different portraits of Der Führer, Dietrich felt a presence hovering behind him, to his right.

A quick glance from the corner of his eye showed him Nasser Khalil. The Arab was alone, his men for once not trailing him around like ducklings following their mother. Dietrich made him wait until the flag was perfect and he had applauded the young Nazis for their sterling effort. Only then did he acknowledge Khalil's presence.

"*Ach,* my friend," he said. "You come to join us with the decorations for the festival, perhaps?"

"I had supposed, under the circumstances," Khalil answered, "that the party might have been postponed."

"And let the Jews dictate our holy days?" Dietrich's personal indignation was not feigned. "Never, while I'm alive!"

"Will not the mass assembly of your followers present a tempting target for your enemies?" Khalil inquired.

"Perhaps, but they have homes, towers and vehicles to fire on, if they find no people. It is all the same. This is our home. We will defend it to the death."

"By singing songs and eating birthday cake?" Khalil replied, sounding incredulous. "Why not just put a pistol to your own head, and avoid embarrassment?"

Dietrich's blue eyes turned gunmetal as anger surged inside him. "I will tolerate no further disrespect!" he snapped. "You are a guest here and are free to leave at any time. You are *not* free to mock our customs or beliefs. I hope we understand each other, Herr Khalil."

"I meant no insult," Khalil said. "Our own young men are glad to sacrifice themselves for God, whether carrying explosives to the enemy or facing troops in battle. We do not, however, court death by continually underestimating our opponents."

"I will not pretend, sir, that mistakes have not been made," Dietrich said stiffly. "I was not present in Bogotá, when the attacks occurred there. Ubel Waldron, although like a son to me himself, clearly was negligent in letting adversaries ambush his patrol. I will not make the same mistake."

"And yet you decorate the compound for a celebration, when you could be manning barricades," Khalil replied. "If there *were* barricades. When the Israeli murderers attack our villages in Palestine, they find the dwellings fortified, our people armed."

"And so our common enemy will find this compound, Herr Khalil. I have the tower guards in place, sentries on the perimeter, patrols out scouring the forest. Furthermore, our celebration of Der Führer's birth allows each individual above the age of twelve years to present arms, offering him- or herself as a willing sacrifice to nurture and preserve our race."

"A sniper in the forest," Khalil said, "could decimate your ranks."

"Only if he survives to make a second shot," Dietrich replied. "You see only the obvious precautions, not the *other* preparations I have made. You cannot look inside the hearts of men and women bred for war. Their dedication to the cause of pure blood eludes you."

"I admit," Khalil said, "that I do not share your fascination with genetics. Far too often, I have seen mistakes made by commanders who habitually underestimate their enemies."

"That's where we differ," Dietrich said. "I know that Aryans are the best warriors in the world."

Khalil frowned and replied, "Logic dictates, then, that it is impossible for them to lose a battle. Yet…"

He left the statement hanging in the muggy air between them. Dietrich wasn't sure whether the Arab had insulted him, his soldiers or the Third Reich, which had clearly lost the last Great War. Dietrich wanted to slap Khalil, punch him and throttle him for such damned insolence, but he controlled himself.

"No soldier is invincible, of course," he said after a long moment of stony silence. "Even proud Achilles had one vulnerable place upon his body."

"And an enemy used it against him, when he least expected it," Khalil reminded Dietrich.

"That won't be a problem," Dietrich said, "since I expect our enemies to find us and have made arrangements to receive them…shall we say, warmly?"

"No walls, no fence—"

"No need," Dietrich replied. "Trust me, comrade. When it is time, you will be safe."

"You won't mind if my men unpack their weapons, all the same?"

"It is as if you've read my mind," Dietrich said. "I was just preparing to suggest that very thing."

THE PROBLEM, BOLAN REALIZED after the fact, was that he had no way of knowing how many patrols Dietrich had sent into the woods. In fact, no one from Brognola through Stony Man to Gabriella Cohen had been able to inform him how many loyal Aryans resided in Colonia Victoria. That was a problem he had recognized from the beginning, coupled with the likelihood of children living in the Nazi compound, but he'd hoped to work it out in time, when he was on the scene.

At 8:13 a.m. on Adolf Hitler's birthday, Bolan's time ran out.

The true, decisive moments often weren't predictable. They came out of left field, caught human beings absolutely by surprise, and sometimes were not even recognized for their importance, at the time.

Mack Bolan glanced at his GPS device, plotted a corrected course and turned to signal his companions. When he turned back to face the trail, he saw a gunman standing there.

The shooter saw him; there could be no doubt about it. Wide-eyed, gaping, the young man stopped dead in his tracks, his gaze locked with Bolan's. Whether he had seen Guzman or Cohen, Bolan never knew.

In combat, such split-second choices were routine. The shooter on the trail had three options: to fire, to turn and flee or to alert any companions yet unseen with shouted warnings.

Any of those choices could mean death to Bolan and the other members of his team.

Which meant that Bolan had no choices left.

Before his startled adversary could react, Bolan shouldered his Steyr AUG and squeezed the trigger once. A single 5.56 mm bullet left the rifle's muzzle, closing the thirty-yard gap between shooter and target in less than a second.

Bolan saw it strike his target in the throat and almost felt the bullet clip his spine. The man collapsed without a gasp or wheeze, but Bolan's gunshot echoed through the forest loud and clear. It would be audible to anyone within a mile or two, at least.

"Cover!" Bolan snapped at his companions, setting an example for them as he dodged off to his left, leaving the meager trail and ducking behind a large tree that had fallen months or years ago, nearly concealed by rampant ferns.

Behind him, Bolan caught a glimpse of Cohen and Guzman lunging for cover. He hoped they'd both make it, but couldn't assist them. He had to focus on the trail ahead now, and the enemies who might be waiting for him there.

There was a slim chance that the man he'd dropped had been a solitary scout, but Bolan wasn't counting on it. Dietrich didn't strike him as the kind of field commander who, under the present circumstances, would send troops into the forest one by one.

Two other options: one, another long shot, cast the dead man as a straggler separated from his team, and maybe lost. Viewing the body now, his shoes and street clothes *did* seem poorly suited for a long tramp through the woods and mountains.

The final option: there would be a team somewhere behind him, likely crouching in the forest and weighing *their* options, whether to send another scout forward, advance en masse, stay where they were and wait it out or cautiously retreat.

No leader worth a damn would leave his scout behind, not even knowing if the point man was alive or dead. Whoever chose that option was a coward and a fool. Bolan likely would have no problem killing him, or any other member of his team.

From somewhere in the shadowed forest up ahead, a voice called out in Spanish. *"¿Paco? ¿Donde éstas?"*

No answer from the corpse.

Bolan sat still and waited.

In another moment, came the disembodied voice once more. *"¡Paco, contestarme! ¿Qué se está encendiendo?"*

Whatever they were saying, Paco's friends had to know by now that he wasn't about to answer.

Bolan waited through a full long minute, worried that Paco's companions might be flanking him, using the time to better their position, but he heard no telltale movement in the woods to either side.

Then came muttering, a brief exchange too muted for his ears to capture. Finally the man in charge settled the argument with a decisive command of some sort.

Whatever he'd said, it got the troops moving. Bolan heard them now, at least two men advancing slowly, cautiously, toward the point where their scout had fallen.

Bolan raised his rifle, bracing it across the mossy log.

Waiting.

GERALDO SANCHEZ FELT AS IF his head might burst at any second. Crouched behind a tree, his shoes and trouser cuffs beslimed with mud, he waited while two of his men advanced to see what had become of Paco Salazar.

He was their best woodsman, and so Sanchez had ordered him to take the point, find them a trail that they could follow through the forest without trashing every stitch of clothing that they wore.

So far, the route had been no simple stroll, but Sanchez knew it could get worse.

In fact, it had.

After the gunshot froze him in his tracks, he'd hope Paco had fired it. Maybe taking out a snake. God knew there had to be thousands of them crawling through the woods, waiting to bite some city boy who lost his way.

But Paco hadn't answered when Sanchez called out to

him, not even in the face of threats and curses. That told Sanchez that his scout was either dead or gravely injured, probably unconscious.

Sanchez thought about the gunshot that had startled him. In retrospect, he knew it hadn't come from Paco's AK-47. It was higher-pitched, a smaller caliber, though powerful. He thought he recognized it.

Perhaps an M-16, or something similar?

Sanchez dismissed that question for the moment, and refocused on survival. Someone had shot Paco Salazar. That someone was still lurking in the woods nearby, perhaps drawing a bead on Sanchez at that very moment.

Cringing in the shadows, Sanchez almost wished that it was night once more, so that the darkness could conceal him. He felt suddenly exposed, wondered if the eleven men ranged out behind him on the narrow game trail would be any use at all against an unseen enemy.

Now he was waiting for a signal from the two men he'd sent out to find Paco. If only they could—

Two more rifle shots rang out.

Sanchez waited for a moment, then could hold himself in check no longer.

"Hey, Ernesto! Julio! Where are you?" he called in Spanish.

If they could hear him, they weren't saying anything.

He tried again. "Ernesto! Julio! Respond!"

But they didn't answer. Only silence greeted his command.

Sanchez edged backward, creeping toward the nearest of his eight surviving men. He was intensely conscious of the danger now, expecting any second that the unseen sniper might squeeze off another round and drop him in his tracks.

He reached the next shooter in line and beckoned for the others to advance. They joined him slowly, cautiously, some crawling, some duck-walking through the undergrowth. Their eyes were everywhere, seeking a target for the weapons clutched in their white-knuckled hands.

When all of them were close enough to hear him whispering, Sanchez told them, "We have three soldiers dead or wounded. I won't leave them here, like this. We can't go forward or retreat safely until we find the sniper and eliminate him."

There it was. He would appeal to both their sense of honor and their fear.

"What can we do, boss?" one of them asked.

"We must fan out, locate the sniper and encircle him. When he's surrounded, he will show himself. We kill him, then."

"Or he kills us before we get that far," another said.

"If you're afraid to fight," Sanchez gritted, "then go! Leave now! And if you live to see the city, pray that Naldo Aznar never finds the cowards who abandoned us."

"Where do we find him, boss?" someone asked him.

"If I knew that," Sanchez answered, "he'd be dead already. See where Paco and the rest were shot, then go from there. Slowly and quietly."

"Are you coming with us?" one of them inquired.

"Of course, I am," Sanchez said. "I'm not some stinking coward who stays behind!"

The others shifted nervously, exchanging anxious glances. None of them was happy with the order, but they all feared what would happen if they left Sanchez and he survived to tell Naldo Aznar.

A swift death in the forest, possibly. Long nights of screaming on a meat hook, in the city, if Aznar should punish them for cowardice.

At last, with visible reluctance, they began to separate and move off through the forest, in the same direction they'd been marching when the shooting started. Sanchez clenched his teeth and followed them, clutching his gun so tightly that his fingers ached.

BOLAN FOUND COHEN WITH HIS EYES and tried to warn her that the trackers were advancing. First, he cupped a hand behind one ear, then pointed in the general direction of their creeping, rustling sounds, sweeping his index finger left and right to indicate a spread-out skirmish line.

He couldn't see the hunters yet, but Bolan knew what they were doing. He'd been part of similar engagements, on the other side, and recognized the tension they'd be feeling, knew some of them would be wound up to a fever pitch, ready to fire at the first sight or sound of opposition.

Bolan couldn't kill them, if he couldn't see them. Cohen and Guzman were at an even greater disadvantage, limited as their experience of woodland fighting was.

He only knew one way to spook the opposition, in the present circumstances. Bolan hoped it wouldn't spark some foolish action on the part of his companions, but he had to play the only card he held.

Trying to pick one source of sound, he zeroed in as best he could and fired a single shot into the forest on his left front, then ducked back to take advantage of the log he'd chosen for his cover.

Automatic weapons opened up at once, raking a firing line some thirty yards across. Bolan had no time to count muzzle-flashes from the shadows, concentrating on the nearest as he thumbed the AUG's selector switch to 3-round bursts.

He squeezed the trigger once, then pivoted and fired again. Off to his right, at the same time, he heard the larger rifles captured by Guzman and Cohen hammering away at targets barely seen.

Before Bolan could judge the impact of his shots or fire another burst, bullets began to shred the ferns around him, forcing him to burrow down behind the fallen log that sheltered him. Low-flying slugs drummed on the log itself, sounding like strokes delivered with a golf club or a hatchet.

Bolan started crawling to his left, digging with knees and elbows, careful to stay below the dead tree's mossy upper rim. He didn't know what kind of tree it was, but judged its length at forty feet or so before the trunk began to taper, branching into spindly, broken limbs that offered Bolan no concealment or protection from incoming rounds.

When he had covered twenty feet, approximately, he stopped and risked a glance over the log. He thought that there were fewer hostile muzzle flashes in the forest, but if true, that didn't mean his other adversaries had been killed or wounded. Some of them could be reloading, swapping out their empty magazines, or simply hiding from the storm of fire his two allies were laying down.

The good news: Cohen and Guzman were drawing all the hostile fire right now.

Bad news: ditto.

Bolan sat up and found a target, clearly human as he blundered through the brush and shadows, firing short bursts at his two companions. Bolan stitched his mark with three rounds on a rising angle, 5.56 mm tumblers slapping home between the stranger's hip and armpit.

Bolan saw the dying shooter drop, and framed another target in his sights before the stalkers could adjust and bring him under fire. The second man had seen his partner fall and was half turned toward Bolan when a 3-round burst ripped through his chest, delivering a death as close to instant as human technology allows.

Someone in front of him shouted.

It didn't sound like the commander's voice from moments earlier, but the attackers who were capable of running turned and fled, firing wildly as they ran.

Bolan was on his feet a heartbeat later, pounding after them and shouting to the others, "We can't let them get away!"

He caught a glimpse of Cohen leaping up to follow him, then Bolan's focus narrowed to the three men fleeing northward, confused by the woods and their fear, running away from Dietrich's compound. When they turned to fire, he'd duck behind a tree and catch his breath, while bullets whistled through the muggy air.

One of the runners stumbled on a root or something similar, threw out an arm for balance, but he never found it. Bolan used the split second of weakness as a weapon, slammed a 3-round burst between his shoulder blades and dropped him facedown on a bed of ancient rotting leaves.

Which still left two.

One of them wheezed and sputtered like an old jalopy's engine, running out of steam, while his companion pulled ahead. Bolan sighted on the straggler, marked him just as he was turning for a final stand, and stole it from him with a burst that turned his sweaty face into raspberry jam.

Bolan spun, still moving, and found the last runner sighting on him, down the barrel of an automatic rifle. In the fraction of a heartbeat left to him, he chose to duck and roll beneath a shot that seemed to echo mainly in his right ear, from the wrong angle.

He waited for another beat, then faced toward where the shooter had been standing. And saw no one. A flicker movement on his right brought Bolan's AUG around, to cover Gabriella Cohen standing there.

"I think that's all of them," she said without emotion.

Bolan rose and scanned the secondary killing ground. "Jorge?" he asked her.

"Stayed behind," she said.

As Cohen spoke, another gunshot echoed from behind them. Bolan and the Mossad agent jogged back in that direction, watching both for hostile stragglers and for Jorge Guzman, both hoping he wouldn't fire upon them by mistake.

And Bolan saw him first, Guzman standing above a prostrate human form. Guzman glanced up at their approach but didn't raise his weapon.

"This one wasn't dead," he said to no one in particular. "But now he is."

Bolan glimpsed gray matter extruding from a shattered skull and didn't question Guzman's diagnosis.

He surveyed the corpses visible from where he stood, then walked around to check the others. There was not a German face among them.

"No Nazis," he said. "No standard uniforms."

"Who are they, then?" Cohen asked.

"No idea, but we should get away from here," he said, "before another team shows up."

"I'm ready," Guzman told him.

A simple nod from Cohen, as she fed her rifle a fresh magazine.

Bolan consulted his GPS tracker and pointed due south. "This way," he said. "It's time we had a look at Dietrich and his playground for the Master Race."

CHAPTER TWELVE

DAS Headquarters, Bogotá

Joaquin Menendez heard the telephone ringing as soon as he entered his office. At home, the night before he had unplugged his landline and switched off his cell, to keep Dietrich from reaching him. Of course, he'd known that the relief was only temporary. Now, he would be forced to pay for it.

"It's him again," his secretary said as Menendez walked past her desk.

"I'll take it," he replied. "Give me a moment."

Menendez had slept little overnight, busy drafting and rehearsing a speech for Dietrich. He could almost hear the old bastard's voice now, whining and threatening by turns, demanding favors and protection. Normally, Menendez folded and complied with the demands.

But this was not a normal day.

He kept Dietrich waiting a few minutes longer, removing his jacket and hanging it up on a wall hook behind his office door. Then, having poured himself a cup of strong black coffee, Menendez sat at his desk and lifted the telephone receiver.

"Señor Dietrich? How are you?"

"Under siege, is how I am!" the German snapped. "You were supposed to send me reinforcements. They arrived, then left again at once, without an explanation."

"*Sí.* I ordered that," Menendez said.

"For God's sake, why? The enemy is all around us here! I need your help!"

"Sadly, *señor,* I must decline this time."

"Decline?" The German sounded like a man who thought he had been cursed in some language he did not understand. "What do you mean, *decline?*"

"*Señor,* at this time it's impossible for me to send you any men."

"But this time is the moment when I need your help, Herr Menendez! Tomorrow or the next day, it will be too late!"

"With all respect—" the words nearly choked him "—I am unable to assist you."

"Why? Why, dammit?"

"Frankly, because I have too much to lose."

"You have… Explain yourself!"

Menendez knew it would feel wonderful to simply hang up on the ranting old man, but he did owe Dietrich some sort of explanation, if only to protect himself.

"It seems, Señor Dietrich, that our…relationship…has been exposed."

"Exposed? What do you mean?"

"I had two visitors late yesterday," Menendez said. "My men were airborne when they came into my office. One from the United States, and one from Israel. Diplomats or spies, I can't be certain. They had a dossier detailing every phase of our collaboration since I was appointed as director of the DAS. And there were other things, as well, which I can not afford to have exposed."

"You fear embarrassment? Are you forgetting that I also have a dossier?"

"Indeed, it seems that I am damned in any case. Since you can only harm me, Señor Dietrich, it is only wise for me to minimize the damage, eh?"

"You think I am an idiot? Someone you can easily ignore? I will release the information I possess, Herr Menendez!"

"And the Americans or the Israelis will release it if I help you," Menendez said. "Why should I add more crimes to the list?"

"You are worthless!" Dietrich snapped at him. "I should have known you had no honor. I will destroy you, if it is the last thing that I do!"

"Perhaps," Menendez said. "If you have time. If someone doesn't kill you, first."

"Is that a threat, Menendez?"

"Not at all. You've said that you are under siege. Your men in Bogotá are dead or wounded. How much longer can you last, I wonder?"

"You may be surprised," Dietrich rasped.

"What would you do in my position, then?"

"I would be loyal! Keep my promises! Stand for the right!"

"Today, I'm standing for myself," Menendez said.

"I may be forced to speak with your superiors," Dietrich said.

"As you wish," the DAS commander said. "But you may find them less than willing to cooperate, after the bad publicity you've brought to Bogotá these past few days."

"I have done nothing!" Dietrich said.

"Dead Nazis in the streets," Menendez replied, and now a smile lifted the corners of his mouth, beneath his thick mustache. "The president and the attorney general aren't amused, I can assure you. Both are facing reelection in the new year. Neither of them wants a German millstone tied around his neck."

"They take my money, then abandon me? Is that what you're implying?"

"They are politicians," Menendez said, feeling stronger now. "What else would you expect? You think they'd sacrifice themselves? For you? What would they gain from that?"

"I'll send them all to prison!" Dietrich snapped. "Yourself included."

"Perhaps," Menendez said. "If you survive. Then again, when we consider it, who would you tell your story to? Will the attorney general prosecute himself? Will judges implicated in your dossiers admit them into trial as evidence? Who will admit that he's accepted bribes from Nazis, to promote their ideology within Colombia? Why not simply go home and drink a quart of poison? It would have the same effect."

"The media!" Dietrich said. "They will print the story!"

"If you send it to the Communists, perhaps. Or maybe to that rag in Medellín that prints the stories about flying saucers. But I have one question, Señor Dietrich."

"Question?"

"Simply this—if you survive this week and burn your bridges in Colombia, where will you go to make a fresh start with your little Aryans?"

Dead silence on the line.

"Goodbye, *señor*. Feel free to call again, if you are able, when your problems are resolved."

Menendez cradled the receiver, feeling better than he had in days.

BOLAN WAS DOUBLY CAUTIOUS as he led his two companions southward through the forest, drawing ever closer to Hans Dietrich's compound. He saw nothing to suggest an enemy pursuit, but almost wished the woods around them had been lowland jungle, where a distant sniper would have less chance of detecting them and squeezing off a well-aimed shot.

At least, he thought, there were no straggling survivors from the strange patrol they'd met and vanquished on the trail. Bolan still wasn't sure why they were dressed in urban street clothes rather than fatigues like those worn by the squad his team had blitzed the previous night. Another question nagging at his mind was the complete absence of any German-types commanding the patrol.

What did it mean?

At first, he thought of mountain bandits, then decided that could not have been the case. For one thing, he supposed a group of rural outlaws would dress more appropriately for their natural environment. For another, Bolan doubted whether Dietrich's Nazis would permit encroachment on their land by such "inferiors."

What, then?

Not soldiers or police, since they had worn civilian clothes and carried mismatched weapons. Dietrich might have ties to some right-wing militia groups, but once again, guerrillas would have known the proper clothes and boots to wear.

That only left drug smugglers, and the notion put a frown on Bolan's face. He knew from Brognola's briefing that Dietrich was allied with the Aznar cocaine cartel. Would Naldo Aznar loan some shooters to a business partner in his time of need?

Why not?

More to the point, what were the odds that Aznar would attend Dietrich's strange birthday celebration for a long-dead Nazi psychopath? If it was such a big deal in the murky world of neo-fascist crime and politics, who else might turn up for the weird festivities?

Bolan remembered film clips he had seen, some years ago, of a similar celebration at some "Aryan" survivalist compound in Idaho. Most days, the place was just a rural eyesore, home to a hundred or so redneck families, but on their special weekend they were inundated by a mob of lunatics from all over the States, plus more from Canada and several European countries.

Would Dietrich's bash draw a similar crowd?

And if so, what did it mean to Bolan's mission?

More targets, he thought, but the easy answer wasn't always best. No one was sure how many people normally resided at Colonia Victoria, but he had come to expect two or three hundred, including the women and children. If visiting nutcases bumped that figure, even if they only doubled it, the odds against Bolan's survival increased accordingly.

The women and kids were another problem. He knew that some women were criminals, including terrorists and contract killers. If they crossed his path and tried to take him out, Bolan would drop them without thinking twice. Conversely, he had never gunned a man or woman down strictly for their beliefs, however vile or strange, and he had never harmed a child for any reason whatsoever.

Never would.

Unless...?

There was the flip-side argument, of course. In foreign wars, from Southeast Asia to Iraq, U.S. soldiers had learned that children could be lethal enemies. Teach them to shoot, or turn them into walking bombs, and there was no age limit on lethality. A bullet didn't know who pulled the trigger, and a brick of C-4 didn't care who pressed the detonator's plunger.

Dead was dead.

So he would have to judge the situation once they reached the camp and found some way to get inside. He had no wish to fire on women, much less children, but he also hadn't come this far to let himself be slaughtered by a modern version of the Hitler Youth.

To clear his head, he checked the GPS tracker again.

Another mile and change before they reached the compound proper. Anytime now, he should start to watch in earnest for alarms and booby traps, sentries, surveillance gear—in short, whatever he could think of that Hans Dietrich might've used to help ward off invaders.

None of it would save the aging Nazi now.

Bolan had made that promise to himself.

A RUNNER CAME TO FETCH Hans Dietrich on the very stroke of nine o'clock. A helicopter was approaching, and the pilot's message had identified its passengers as friends. Encouraged for the first time in the past two days, Dietrich chewed breath mints to disguise the smell of schnapps as he walked from his quarters to the helipad.

This day was most auspicious, in his mind. It marked 120 years precisely since the birth of the most vital and commanding figure known in modern times. Such epic anniversaries were rare indeed, and Dietrich had no reason to believe that he would live to see Adolf Hitler's 130th birthday.

In fact, he might be lucky to survive this one.

Guests had been straggling in over the past week, pitching tents where necessary, helping where they could with daily chores. So far, the foreign celebrants included three Canadians, all members of the Western Vanguard; half a dozen Ku Klux Klansmen from South Carolina; two French members of the Blueshirt Legion; and a paunchy resident of Kansas, U.S.A., lately released from jail in Hamburg, where he'd been confined for smuggling Nazi literature into Germany.

All friends and allies in the struggle.

The brave smile on his face, as he approached the helipad,

was all for show. Behind that bold facade, he was beset by fear that made him feel ashamed. It should not matter that his enemies were coming for him. Dietrich knew that he should welcome any chance to crush them and to prove himself a worthy object of their hatred. He should relish the campaign.

He heard the helicopter now, and turning toward the west saw it approaching, looking like a dragonfly above the tree-tops, growing into something from a prehistoric nightmare as it closed the gap between them. Finally it reached the helipad, hovered, descended, whipping Dietrich's hair to snowy tatters with its rotor wash.

"They're here at last, then," Otto Jaeger shouted from beside him. With the helicopter's thunder in his ears, Dietrich had not heard him approach.

"I hope our other guests won't get their noses out of joint," Dietrich replied.

"They all hate Jews more than the ragheads," Jaeger shouted back at him. "But I'll have people watch them, just in case."

"Do that."

Dietrich pressed forward with a broad smile and his hand extended, as the helicopter's passengers deplaned. The first man off, Muhunnad Qadir, was ranked in CIA and Interpol files as the Sword of Allah's second in command. He was a fugitive from terrorism charges filed in Israel, Britain, France and the United States, subject to state-authorized abduction if he could be found and it could be accomplished without sparking international hostilities.

Qadir shook Dietrich's hand and introduced him to three other Arabs. Dietrich filed their names away in short-term memory, knowing it was unlikely that he'd ever see them again once they left the compound. Muhunnad Qadir, on the other hand, was a force to reckon with, an ally with whom

Dietrich had plotted his late-life campaign against the Jewish state of Israel.

"Welcome to Colonia Victoria," Dietrich told all of them, turning his head to favor each in turn with his prodigious smile. "Your quarters are prepared. No doubt you'll wish to freshen up before the midday meal."

"First," Qadir said, "I wish to see Nasser Khalil."

"Of course," Dietrich replied. "I can't imagine why he is not here to greet you personally, but I'll have him fetched at once. Otto?"

"Yes!"

In fact, Khalil was missing from the helipad because Jaeger, acting on Dietrich's orders, had informed him that Qadir and company were scheduled to arrive at half-past one o'clock. A simple miscommunication, on its face, and yet sufficient to take Khalil down a peg or two in front of his superiors.

In short, a job well done.

As Dietrich led Qadir and his companions to their bungalow—no tents for these guests, even if they were accustomed to them in the desert—he observed the Arabs checking out the compound's decorations. Swastikas were everywhere, their number nearly equaled by portraits and photos of Der Führer in his glory days, unbeaten by the Allied war machine or traitors in his own glorious party.

And he saw them checking out the guard towers, the sentries on patrol, the automatic weapons everywhere around them. There could be no question in Qadir's mind as to who retained the power in Colonia Victoria.

Dietrich felt better now, despite his screaming match with the pathetic oaf Menendez. He would stage an epic demonstration for his allies, kill the enemies who had been sent against him, then deal with Menendez in his own sweet time.

The DAS commander might believe himself secure. Hans Dietrich was prepared to prove him wrong.

NALDO AZNAR PREFERRED Learjets to helicopters, but he had no choice for this excursion to Colonia Victoria. Despite the fact that he had occupied his forest stronghold for a full half-century, Hans Dietrich had not bothered to construct a landing field that would accommodate planes larger than a Piper Cub.

This day, with all that had occurred, Aznar wanted enough loyal soldiers at his side to deal with anything that might arise, however unexpected. So it was that he approached Colonia Victoria in an Aérospatiale 322 Super Puma helicopter, with a two-man crew and seating for twenty-one passengers. Counting the pilot and copilot, that gave Aznar twenty-two guns, once they were safely back on solid ground.

The flight from San José del Guaviare was supposed to take forty minutes, cruising at the helicopter's top speed of 165 miles per hour. Aznar glanced at his diamond-encrusted watch and found ten minutes still remaining. And how many hours at the compound, for the silly celebration?

Never mind, he thought. It was a cost of doing business with the lunatics who ran Colonia Victoria. It cost him next to nothing, and a few toasts to the memory of Adolf Hitler helped ensure that Aznar would retain his monopoly on Dietrich's top-grade cocaine.

Besides which, last year's birthday cake, baked in the shape of a huge swastika, had been one of the best Aznar had ever tasted.

His only cause for hesitation, this year, was the trouble Dietrich had attracted to himself—and, by extension, to his business partners. Murder was a daily fact of life throughout Colombia, but something else was plainly going on with Hans

Dietrich. Two wholesale massacres in Bogotá, within a single day, was excessive even by Aznar's own standard.

He hoped Geraldo Sanchez and the other men he'd sent ahead to Dietrich were cooperating with the German, and not aggravating him unnecessarily. Aznar had made it crystal clear to Sanchez that the job, while clearly undesirable, was critical to the cartel's prosperity. Anyone who jeopardized Aznar's relationship with Dietrich, except on Naldo's direct and unequivocal order, could expect unpleasant repercussions.

Meaning death.

Naldo Aznar did not believe in half measures. In his personal experience, any embarrassing or painful punishment that left people alive also created enemies for life. He had enough of those already, by the very nature of his business, and did not need any more.

Therefore, while he might offer mild verbal correction to a colleague or employee if they were alone, he never lectured, threatened or harangued in front of witnesses. A bullet to the brain was simpler, quicker and more economical than a protracted argument that might result in mutiny or all-out war.

If Aznar ever chose to terminate his contract with Hans Dietrich, he would have to terminate the ancient German, too. That would mean trouble, since he couldn't count on any of Dietrich's subordinates to roll over and side with Aznar against their master and strange father figure.

For the moment then, Aznar was still on Dietrich's side. He would assist in the destruction of the Nazi's enemies, if possible. More to the point, he would discover who they were, who'd sent them to Colombia, and whether they posed any threat to Aznar's drug cartel. If they arrived while he was having cake and lager at Colonia Victoria, his men could have some target practice.

"Five more minutes, boss," Aznar's pilot said.

Instead of shouting, which would only strain his voice, Aznar held up one hand, the fingers splayed, to warn his men. A couple in the front rows nodded, while the others double-checked their guns.

Aznar had warned Dietrich that he was bringing soldiers with him, though he hadn't said how many. Dietrich had not asked. If the contingent rattled Dietrich, Aznar was prepared to make some personal excuse—troubles in Medellín or San José del Guaviare—and fly home again directly if Dietrich protested.

That, of course, would be an insult, and since Dietrich was as well versed in the art of criminal diplomacy as Aznar, Aznar doubted that the subject would be raised.

Besides, Aznar thought, Dietrich's Nazis and their native mercenaries had his team outnumbered roughly twenty-five to one. Even with Sanchez and his fifteen guns, it would be no contest in the event of any violence.

But Aznar was determined that it wouldn't come to that. If he had any killing grudge against Dietrich, he would not walk into the spider's parlor and attempt to kill him personally. Aznar had progressed beyond all that, when he'd become a billionaire.

The Super Puma hovered, gently settling on the camp's large helipad beside two smaller whirlybirds. Hans Dietrich stood there, waiting for him, when Aznar deplaned. They shook hands, but the solemn look on Dietrich's face did not reflect Aznar's feigned pleasure.

"Herr Aznar," the white-haired German said, "I am afraid I have bad news."

THE LAST QUARTER MILE WAS the slowest. Bolan placed each step deliberately, all the while scanning the landscape around him for lookouts, traps or surveillance devices. So far, he had come up with nothing.

Cohen and Guzman moved with equal caution behind him, matching Bolan's pace on a winding course through the forest. Bolan trusted his sense of direction, but still checked his GPS every ten minutes to reassure himself that they were still on course.

Arriving in daylight, presumably with Dietrich's camp on full alert, made the approach more delicate. Surveillance of the target was imperative, but any serious approach would have to wait for nightfall—meaning that they'd have to find someplace nearby to pass the daylight hours. Somewhere close enough for the convenience of their mission, yet secure enough that Dietrich's hunters didn't stumble over them by accident.

Bolan could not be sure that such a place existed, but he had to find it, anyway.

The mission, and his team's survival, would depend on it.

When they were still five hundred yards from the compound, Bolan called a halt and huddled with his two companions. Whispering as if an enemy was crouched behind the nearest tree, eavesdropping, he explained his plan.

"We'll have a quick look at the compound now," he said, "then find someplace to dig in for the day. I don't know when this birthday party is supposed to start—or if they'll even go ahead with it, considering what's happened—but I'm hoping it's supposed to be a nighttime bash. The more noise Dietrich's people make, the better it will be for us when we go in."

"And what then?" Guzman asked him, sounding nervous.

"Taking Dietrich out is top priority. If we can tag his contacts from the Sword of Allah while we're at it, so much the better. Beyond that, raise hell with the party and get out alive."

"I'm not sure I can do this," Guzman said.

"Don't sweat it," Bolan told him. "You've fulfilled your

contract, coming this far. No one told you you'd be taking on an army. You can sit it out."

Bolan could not have said if Guzman blushed, but his embarrassment was obvious. Machismo cut both ways, inflating pride and wounding egos. Guzman shot a sidelong glance at Cohen, then appeared to stiffen, drawing back his shoulders.

"I did not mean to suggest that I would leave you," he replied, though Bolan had the feeling he was speaking more for Cohen's benefit. "It's simply that I'm not a soldier. I was never trained for anything like this."

"You've done all right, so far," Bolan reminded him.

"It all seems accidental, somehow, if you understand me," Guzman said. "Men try to kill us, and I fight. It's only natural. But planning strategy, invading military camps… I worry that through some mistake of mine, you'll both be injured."

"Okay, how's this," Bolan said. "When the time comes, you decide if you're prepared to go in with us, or if you'd prefer to stay outside the compound, maybe help us out with a diversion. Any way you slice it, when the shooting starts, it won't be hard to find a target."

Guzman nodded, his shoulders slumping. By accepting Bolan's plan in principle, he obviously felt diminished, but at least he had a shot at saving face. He didn't have to drop out now, with Cohen staring at him in the light of day.

In fact, Bolan observed, the Mossad agent had turned away from them while they were talking, seemingly engaged in some adjustment of her rifle's shoulder sling. She didn't make it obvious, as if shunning Guzman, but rather gave him a degree of privacy, so that he wasn't forced to meet her gaze as he confessed his fear.

Having forestalled one problem, Bolan faced the next and larger one. "We've almost reached the compound," he informed them. Pointing, Bolan added, "It's about five hundred yards in that direction. Every step we take from this point on is critical. Along the way, be looking for that hideout. If we have to climb a tree, we'll need one or more with optimal cover."

Guzman nodded. Cohen, finished with her rifle sling, said, "We should hide as close to the compound as possible. Dietrich will have his sentries posted, and he won't like duplicating effort with patrols on the perimeter. The old German efficiency we hear so much about."

"That's good," Bolan said. "Let's go see what's waiting for us."

CHAPTER THIRTEEN

"All dead? Sanchez and all of his men?"

Naldo Aznar was rarely taken by surprise, which could prove fatal in his line of work, but Dietrich's news had literally stunned him.

"I'm afraid so," said the ancient Nazi. "We heard gunfire in the forest, to the north. Another of my patrols found the bodies. I sent natives to retrieve them. We have burial facilities on-site, although I must admit they're somewhat overtaxed at present."

"What of those who shot them?" Aznar asked.

"My men are searching for them as we speak, of course," Dietrich replied. "Unfortunately..."

"What?"

Dietrich was visibly embarrassed. With a little shrug he said, "Regrettably, the signs appear to be confused. My trackers had no difficulty following the trail left by your men, because their footwear was...unusual."

"And, possibly, because you found their bodies." Aznar fairly sneered.

"Of course. As to the others, those responsible for the

atrocity, their boots are very similar to our own standard issue. It's a common brand, you see. Sold by the thousands and—"

"And your best trackers can't tell one set from another," Aznar finished for him.

"We—that is, my men—patrol the colony routinely," Dietrich said. "Since the events in Bogotá, of course, patrols have been increased. They follow no set pattern and the tracks became—"

"Confused. Yes, so you've said. What's being done to sort out the confusion, then?"

"I have more men out searching," Dietrich answered. "If the enemy attempts to breach this compound, obviously they will be eliminated."

"As they were in Bogotá?"

Color flushed Dietrich's cheeks. "We had no reason to expect those incidents, although I grant you that my people should have paid closer attention to security. We are on full alert now. The mistake will not be replicated."

"Full alert," Aznar replied, "and yet I see the trappings of a celebration everywhere I look."

Dietrich stepped closer as he drew himself to full attention. "We observe Der Führer's birthday as a sacrament, Herr Aznar. Nothing will deter us. If our enemies attempt to interfere, they will provide us with the perfect sacrifice."

"When you say 'sacrifice'…"

"I mean precisely that," Dietrich replied. "An offering to Odin and the Führer on this holiest of holy days."

Aznar had questioned Dietrich's thinking in the past, although he'd kept it to himself. Now, he began to doubt the German's sanity.

"Do you suppose these people who have killed—how many is it, now? Two dozen, with my men included?"

"There was another incident, before the ambush of Herr

Sanchez and his comrades. At a native village on the property."

"How many?"

"Altogether," Dietrich answered, "twenty-seven in the colony."

"Plus those in Bogotá?"

"Correct. Of course, the first attack was staged before we knew the enemy had come so far. We're ready for them now, I can assure you."

"Why were my people in the forest?" Aznar asked his host.

A frown creased Dietrich's forehead as he said, "You may recall instructing me to use the men you sent to strengthen our defenses. Armed patrols are the first line of our defense against these interlopers. Clearly, it is preferable to locate and eradicate them in the woods, before they reach the compound."

"I agree," Aznar replied. "If it had worked."

"Your men seemed capable enough. Herr Sanchez seemed quite confident that he could deal with any problem he encountered on patrol."

"It's plainly his fault, then," Aznar remarked.

"I simply meant to say—"

"Señor Dietrich, I'm trying to determine why fifteen of my best men are dead. Beyond that, I must now decide whether to stay and see who's slaughtered next, or fly back home to San José del Guaviare now."

"Herr Aznar, I shall personally guarantee your safety."

"Can you guarantee your own?"

That brought another angry flush to Dietrich's cheeks, but his response was measured, well under control.

"You know a little of my history, perhaps," the German said. "I served Der Führer in the glory and the dark days of the Reich. I faced the Russians, the Americans, yet here I am. The Zionists assassins who have tried to kill or kidnap me are dust in unmarked graves. I have a talent for survival. It is in my blood, supported by my training and my faith."

Aznar understood that there was nothing to be gained from arguing with a fanatic. His decision, whether to remain or flee, had to be based on logic. Influenced, perhaps, by Aznar's craving for revenge.

Someone had slaughtered fifteen of his men. Their high-priced vehicles were parked outside, waiting for passengers and drivers who would not return. If word of that defeat leaked out—as it was sure to do, somehow—Aznar could not be seen as one who took it lying down.

He had to have blood for blood.

And he could not offend Hans Dietrich, unless he was ready to cut all their business ties, effectively declaring war.

"You have convinced me," Aznar lied. "I'm here, with my companions, and we may as well enjoy the celebration. If your enemies should interrupt the festival, however, then I must insist that you allow me to participate in their extermination."

"Herr Aznar," the smiling Nazi said, "nothing could please me more."

BOLAN'S FIRST VIEW of Dietrich's compound came as a surprise. He'd been expecting stockade walls or barbed-wire fences, something on the order of a fort or concentration camp, but Dietrich's layout had a small-town feel about it. That is, if you overlooked the guard towers and sentries on patrol.

The uniforms his soldiers wore were Third Reich chic, updated versions of the Wehrmacht gray from World War II. The higher-ranking officers wore classic SS black, complete with jackboots, swastika armbands and silver death's-heads on their caps and collars.

"It's a bad old movie," Cohen whispered from his left.

"Except that the director's crazy," Bolan answered, "and they won't be firing blanks."

The compound had been decorated for a celebration, hung with Nazi flags, posters of Hitler, and large banners painted with slogans in German. Bolan couldn't read them, but he guessed that none of them promoted brotherhood or peace on Earth.

In what appeared to be the center of the compound, children were collecting scrap wood for a massive bonfire. They already had a ten- or twelve-foot heap, and showed no sign of slackening their efforts.

Bolan was pleased to see the work in progress. In his personal experience, bonfires were typically reserved for ceremonies or festivities occurring after nightfall, when the flames were showed off to their best advantage. Torching such a pyre in daylight would produce more smoke than spectacle, making the effort a colossal waste.

He scanned the camp from right to left, eyes tracking north to south. The first feature he noted was the compound's motor pool, including several sedans, two midsize trucks, four motorcycles, one gray bus and three new Hummers parked together at the far end of the line. Those vehicles, each with its tank of gasoline or diesel fuel, had the potential for one hell of a diversion when the time was right.

Scanning, he recognized a spacious mess hall with kitchen attached, fragrant smoke wafting out of its stovepipes. Latrines had been constructed on what had to be a downhill slope, likely with gravel trucked in for the drainage system. An adjacent structure, standing in the shadow of a water tank, apparently housed showers. Dish antennae fingered the communications center. Hammer strokes and sounds of power tools echoed from a machine shop.

Bolan counted three separate generators, each with its own chugging gasoline engine. Floodlights were mounted on poles at various points around the compound, while others on swivel mounts served the three guard towers. Scattered tents concealed their secrets behind canvas and nylon.

Bolan knew he'd have to walk the compound's perimeter to see it from all angles, but he had a feel for Dietrich's small community already. Living quarters were divided between barracks, for the single men or women, and bungalows for families or higher-ranking officers. There was no sign of Dietrich yet, but Bolan pegged his CP as the bungalow that stood beside a twenty-foot flagpole, surmounted by a flapping Nazi battle flag.

Off to the south, trees had been cleared to build an obstacle course reminiscent of those found at military training camps the world over. Those who completed it would scramble over walls and crawl beneath barbed wire, climb ropes, leap from an elevated platform into low-slung cargo netting and perform assorted other tasks. Beyond the course, trees had been cleared and concrete laid to make a spacious helipad. Two choppers presently inhabited the pad, a Super Puma built by Aérospatiale, and a streamlined Agusta A109 Hirundo, with seating for one pilot and seven passengers.

Han Dietrich's private air force?

Bolan realized that he would have to take the choppers out, to keep Dietrich within the compound and available for killing. Any move against the motor pool was secondary—or, ideally, should be carried out at the same time. But Bolan needed to eliminate the helicopters early on, before there was a general alarm.

He could not let Hans Dietrich fly.

By contrast, if the camp's top Nazi tried to drive away, there was at least a fair chance—three fair chances, if he counted Cohen and Guzman—that they could stop his car and take him out before he reached the forest access road.

Because once Dietrich was airborne, he was gone.

"Has everybody seen enough from this viewpoint?" Bolan asked.

Silent nods in his peripheral vision, left and right, supplied affirmative responses.

"Right, then. We'll be circling to the south, one-quarter turn, to get another angle. Slow and easy, follow me."

NASSER KHALIL WAITED until he and Muhunnad Qadir had something that approximated privacy. They stood together, thirty yards beyond the shower building Dietrich's workers had constructed out of cinder blocks. No listening devices were in evidence, and their men surrounded them, paired off for seeming idle conversation that prevented any German from approaching close enough to eavesdrop.

And to guarantee security, they spoke in Arabic.

Despite his agitation, Khalil kept his wits about him and remembered protocol, showing respect to his superior.

"I am surprised to see you, sir," he said.

"You knew that I was coming for the German's celebration," Qadir said.

"Yes, sir. That is, I knew someone was scheduled to attend. But in the light of all that's happened, I supposed it would be canceled."

Qadir frowned at him, seemed confused. "Canceled? What is it that has happened? Please explain yourself!"

Now it was Khalil's turn to look confused.

"Commander, I reported all of this by radio, to headquarters."

"Then, no doubt you remember it and can repeat it for me now."

"Yes, sir."

Where to begin? At the beginning, with a deep breath that, Khalil hoped, would remove any suggestion of a tremor from his voice.

"The camp is under siege, apparently," he said. "It all began in Bogotá, the day before yesterday. Someone killed a dozen of Dietrich's men and wounded many more. His villa in the city was destroyed, from what I understand, by mortar fire."

"Within the capital itself?"

"Yes, sir. And then, after a long day waiting for the stragglers to return here, more of Dietrich's men were shot while patrolling the forest, a few miles from here. None survived. Dietrich requested help, and more Colombians arrived in those." He nodded toward the three black Hummers in the nearby motor pool. "They're all dead now, as well, shot down perhaps three hours ago."

Qadir maintained his usual composure, but his frown had turned into a scowl. "And you reported all of this to headquarters, you say?"

"Yes, sir. Using the satellite phone issued when we left Damascus."

"And your calls were completed? No question?"

"Reception was perfect. Of course, I engaged the scrambler."

"But you're certain that headquarters understood what you were saying?"

"Absolutely, sir. I made four calls in total, beginning yesterday at 6:00 a.m., Greenwich Mean Time."

"In that case, Nasser, it appears that there has been…how shall I say it? A communications breakdown within headquarters itself."

Khalil had no idea what that meant.

"Sir?"

Qadir paused to consider his response. When next he spoke, his voice was calm, almost amused.

"It seems that someone made a conscious choice not to inform me of your news," he said. "Does that seem odd?"

"Yes, sir! Extremely so."

"Would it surprise you to be told that bitter rivalries divide our leadership?"

Khalil knew he was stepping onto shaky ground. No matter how he answered that question, he could make trouble for himself.

"Of course, sir, there are always rumors. I try to ignore them."

"Keep your ears open in future. That's my best advice to you. Assuming we get out of here alive, and you still have your ears."

"Sir?"

"I won't burden you with names or details, if you've managed to avoid them this long, Nasser. Rest assured that there are men around our leader who resent my influence upon him and would love to see me dead—or, at the very least, embarrassed and discredited. I have no doubt that one of them diverted your communications, with the aim of sending me into a war zone unprepared."

"But, sir…I mean…"

"You don't believe it, eh? Your faith is still that pure?" Qadir produced a weary smile. "Nasser, what do we do with every waking moment of our lives, except conspire, scheme and destroy?"

"Sir, we are fighting for the liberation of—"

"Yes, yes. I know all that by heart. I wrote some of it, while you dreamed inside your mother's belly. I'm not speaking of our cause, Nasser. I'm asking you to tell me what it is we do."

"Make war against the Zionists and their pig allies," Khalil said, as if reading the answer from a textbook.

"And, sometimes, against each other. It's dispiriting, I grant you. But it's still a fact of life."

"Sir, if you name your enemies, I promise you—"

"They're far beyond your reach," Qadir said, interrupting him. "We may not live to see them, much less plot revenge.

Before there's any time or hope for that, we must survive the present."

"Yes, sir."

"So, Nasser, tell me everything you know about this place, about Hans Dietrich and these enemies who have him under siege."

THEIR SOUTHERN VANTAGE POINT provided an entirely different view of Dietrich's compound. Gabriella Cohen studied the approaches to the helipad and its three aircraft, judging that the nearest of them had to be fifty yards from the tree line where she, Cooper and Guzman stood.

"It shouldn't be too difficult," she whispered, "after nightfall. Since the trees are cleared, we'd have to crawl, of course."

"They won't remove the guards," Bolan replied.

Four men with automatic rifles stood at the four corners of the helipad. It was too large for them to speak without raising their voices, so each sentry stood in solitude, watching the forest or the compound for a hint of danger to the choppers.

"They'll never see me coming," Cohen promised. "When I'm close enough, I'll use the Uzi with its silencer."

"You won't have line of sight on all four sentries," Bolan said.

"I'll manage," she assured him. Never doubting it, despite a little thrill of dread that shivered down her spine.

"And what about the choppers?" Bolan asked.

"I can disable them by one means or another," she replied. "Borrow some of your hand grenades, or shoot up the engines. It doesn't take much to disable an aircraft."

"I'll think about it," Bolan said, then fell silent. Cohen saw him studying the compound's layout from this new angle, and joined him in the exercise.

She *could* take out the helicopters. There was no doubt whatsoever in her mind. Or, if Cooper preferred, she could attack the motor pool. Those vehicles would make a bonfire far more satisfying than the pile of scrap wood growing in the middle of the compound.

At her shoulder, Jorge Guzman said nothing, but she could almost hear his mind at work, counting the enemies arrayed before them. Certain of the men were not in uniform and did not seem to fit in well with the community, although they paused from time to time and snapped salutes in front of this or that portrait of Adolf Hitler. Those would be the neo-Nazis who had flown in for the party from Europe or North America to frolic with their fascist friends.

And she had seen the Arabs, too.

She'd drawn Cooper's attention to them, saw him recognize Nasser Khalil. The older man who huddled with Khalil could only be Muhunnad Qadir, ranked as second- or third in command of the Sword of Allah, depending on the source of latest information.

Cooper had not recognized Qadir, but nodded when she'd briefed him on the terrorist's identity.

"One more we shouldn't miss, if we can help it," he'd replied.

She thought about the hundreds of her countrymen whom Qadir and Khalil had killed during their long war against Israel. Going further back, she felt the weight of thousands, millions, slaughtered in the Holocaust, a burden on her conscience that would never leave her if she missed this golden opportunity to strike a blow against the murderers.

And if it cost her life to strike that blow, to make it count, what of it?

Gabriella Cohen didn't want to die—and least of all to die here, in Colombia—but she'd been raised and from birth to answer duty's call, to stand for Israel and be counted when it mattered, even if the whole world stood against her.

Jorge Guzman, on the other hand, just wanted to go home.

Cooper, she already trusted to the point of being sure that he would fight, and sacrifice his life if necessary for his mission. Guzman was an unknown quantity, although he'd fought and killed in self-defense. The man himself admitted that he wasn't sure of his own capabilities.

But Cohen would be watching him as much as possible. She didn't mind if Guzman ran away, as long as he was not assigned to a position of responsibility. Running was fine, if no one else depended on him for survival.

But if Guzman's fear or inexperience somehow should threaten to betray them, foil their mission, then he had to die. Before she let him ruin everything—help Dietrich or the Arabs slip away, however inadvertently—she was prepared to shoot him, even strangle him with her bare hands.

"Let's try the western view," Bolan said, barely whispering. "Remember that they've sent most of their armed patrols in that direction, so far."

Cohen followed him, placing her feet deliberately in the tracks that the big American made, hearing Guzman behind her as they made their way around the camp's perimeter. The woods concealed them from Hans Dietrich's sentries in the compound, but they'd have no cover if they blundered into a patrol returning from the latest sweep.

So many ways to die, she thought.

But when the time came, only one would be required.

OTTO JAEGER LISTENED to the sergeant who had led the last patrol, lately returned from a two-hour circuit through the forest lying northwest of the compound. Boil it down and throw out the excuses, they'd found nothing.

How could that be possible?

No tracks that could be linked to any strangers on the property.

No evidence that anyone had camped or hidden in the area examined.

Nothing in the nature of a cigarette butt, cast-off candy wrapper or a pile of feces that would help them locate their elusive enemies.

And yet the enemy was there.

Jaeger had all the evidence he needed, in the form of twenty-seven bullet-punctured corpses and the testimony of his runner from the village where the first slaughter occurred.

Two men, the spy had said, and one young woman.

Looking for a smaller party made the search more difficult, but it should not have been impossible. Jaeger's incessant headache had returned, and suffering from burns around his face and elsewhere. Mental aggravation added to his injuries, combining to depress him, threatening his very will.

Jaeger had not been privileged to serve Der Führer in the great war that had shattered the Third Reich. He had been born in 1963, one of Colonia Victoria's pure-blooded children, schooled throughout his life to uphold Aryan ideals. And now, he wondered if that privileged upbringing might have somehow weakened him.

What could he do, in this grim situation, that he had not tried already?

There was no one to interrogate or threaten. No one in the compound knew the enemies who threatened them. There were no traitors in the ranks.

He thought about some of the late arrivals for the birthday celebration. Was it possible that the drug dealer, Naldo Aznar, might have some motive for trying to destroy Colonia Victoria? It seemed insane, given his yearly profits from the colony's cocaine crop and the fact that fifteen of his men lay stacked up in the compound's modest morgue.

No, Jaeger thought. If this was Aznar's plot, it had to be the most irrational and convoluted scheme that any human mind had yet produced. Why jeopardize a multibillion-dollar business and kill his own men for no apparent benefit?

Impossible, Jaeger thought. But he'd keep an eye on Aznar and his people just the same.

The Arabs were another problem. Jaeger did not trust them. They were inferiors and adherents of a strange religion, even if they hated Jews with every fiber of their being. He regarded them as allies of convenience.

They were convenient, not trusted.

Scarcely even human, really.

Nasser Khalil, the parasite who had attached himself to Hans Dietrich, complained incessantly about life in the compound, daring even to presume that he could dictate policy and military strategy. Jaeger had offered more than once to get rid of Khalil and his companions, but his leader had demurred. Now, rather than eliminating them, more Arabs had been welcomed to participate in this most solemn, honored ceremony of the Nazi year.

And just as they arrived, Colonia Victoria was under fire.

Coincidence? Or part of a conspiracy?

Jaeger supposed that most psychiatrists would claim that he was paranoid. He cared nothing for judgments made by men whose families and lives had never been uprooted, cast adrift by Bolsheviks and Zionists, hounded halfway across the world for "crimes" that would have saved the human race, if only they'd been able to complete their work.

To Jaeger, "paranoia" simply meant that he was conscious of his enemies and ready to destroy them, given half a chance. He'd failed in Bogotá, and would be years living that down, but failure only made him more determined to succeed next time.

This time.

Jaeger would watch the Arabs closely, monitor their every move. And if it seemed to him that they were linked in any way to the attacks upon Colonia Victoria, he might not even ask his leader's blessing before taking action.

There were twice as many of them now, as when Khalil and his companions were the only Arabs in the compound, but Jaeger still had them heavily outnumbered and outgunned. He would confine them to their quarters if the compound was directly threatened, and it would be that much easier to kill them all together in one place.

The prospect made him smile as he dismissed the sweaty sergeant and prepared to launch two fresh patrols. Jaeger did not know where his enemies were hiding, but he meant to find them, one way or another. He would not rest until they were located and battle had been joined.

This time, he meant to do it right.

"AND NOW," BOLAN WHISPERED, "we've seen it all."

They were crouched on the northernmost edge of the compound, having carefully negotiated passage by the nearest guard tower. The sentries upstairs, with their gray uniforms and coal-scuttle helmets, reminded Bolan of actors in an old World War II film. All they needed was a goofy sergeant and they could play out a sketch from *Hogan's Heroes*.

It was funny, like a bullet in the gut.

"Any thoughts?" Bolan asked, before he turned his mind toward the location of a hiding place for the remainder of the daylight hours.

"Obviously," Cohen said, "we need to hit their transportation. Helicopters should be top priority, then rolling stock. I count four generators, so we'll have a problem blacking out the compound. Anyway, the bonfire will provide sufficient light for fighting, if we let them light it."

Bolan nodded in agreement with the points she'd made, an echo of his own grim thoughts. "Given a choice," he said, "I'd rather hit them with the party in full swing. They'll be distracted, that way, plenty of them drinking, and the noise level should work against their sentries. It's too bad we can't take one of the towers."

"Why is that impossible?" Guzman asked.

"We're short-handed," Bolan replied. "Between us, I and Cohen have to take out their transport, then make a strong run at Dietrich, his friends from the Sword of Allah and Naldo Aznar."

They had glimpsed the cocaine baron when he stepped out of a bungalow near Dietrich's quarters, spoke briefly to sentries posted on the door, then vanished back inside. Bolan had been surprised to see Aznar at Adolf's birthday bash, but he was not about to waste a golden opportunity, if there was any way at take Aznar out of the picture.

Any way at all.

They would be spread thin, as it was, without trying to seize a guard tower and—

"I can do it," Guzman said.

"Hold on a second," Bolan cautioned.

"No, I mean it. I am not afraid of heights, and I shoot well enough. Not in your league, perhaps, but still…"

"Those are machine guns in the towers," Bolan told him. "Have you ever fired one?"

"No. Before last night, I'd never fired a rifle, either."

"There's a difference," Bolan said. "I can't tell the model of their weapons, from down here. I couldn't coach you on the trigger or the safety mechanisms, anything about reloading, whether it's belt-fed or feeding from a magazine."

"So, I will try their gun, and if it doesn't work, I have my rifle and my pistols."

"What about the two men in the tower?" Bolan asked.

"They'll be distracted by the celebration, as you said," Guzman replied. "I'll climb the ladder, go in through the hatch—or knock, if it is locked—and say in Spanish that I've brought them something from the party. They have many Spanish-speakers in the camp. If they don't understand me, all the more reason for them to open the trapdoor."

"And then?" Bolan asked.

"I will shoot them, take their place and do what must be done."

Bolan was seeing Jorge Guzman in a whole new light. He hoped their guide and translator had guts enough to match his battle plan, but Bolan wouldn't know until the time came.

On the flip side, in his cold-as-ice strategic mind, he knew it wouldn't hurt appreciably if they lost Guzman in his attempt to take the tower. It would be one more diversion to distract his enemies, while he and Cohen hit the helipad, the motor pool, and started hunting their selected targets in the compound.

Still…

"We'd need to synchronize," Bolan said. "Make sure that you've got the tower covered when we blow the choppers and the motor pool."

Bolan noted Cohen's anxious look and asked, "How did you plan on getting down and out?"

"There will be much confusion," Guzman answered. "When I think it's safe, I will climb down and lose myself among the others, make my way back to the forest."

Bolan nodded, saying, "Well, it's something to consider. We can talk some more about it when we've found a place to spend the afternoon. Speaking of that, we'd better get it done."

CHAPTER FOURTEEN

Naldo Aznar was restless. He had flown in early for the stupid birthday celebration, knowing that the main bit would not happen until after nightfall. At the time, of course, he hadn't known that fifteen of his men were dead, a fact that would have made him cancel out completely had he known.

Too late.

He was already on the spot, and fleeing now would mark him as a coward, even if it was the wisest thing to do. Somehow, somewhere, the word would spread that Aznar had lost men and done nothing about it. That he'd run away.

It was unthinkable.

He would remain with Dietrich overnight, at least. Perhaps longer, if more time was needed to avenge Geraldo Sanchez and the others. Aznar did not care about them personally, would not miss them unless some job came up in the future that they could have done for him, without additional expense for bringing in another contractor. It was the insult to his pride and his authority that made Aznar determined to exact revenge.

"What if they don't come, boss?" one of his assembled soldiers asked.

Aznar frowned at the question, which he had already asked himself.

"They'll come," he answered. "Why kill forty men like that, and then give up? They haven't lost a man yet. They've been winning."

Aznar's soldier shrugged, suggesting, "Maybe it's enough."

The drug lord's frown deepened. "What do you mean?" he asked.

"Maybe they never meant to kill the German. It could all be done to weaken him. Let others know he can't control his territory, eh?"

"And our men?" Aznar queried. "What of them?"

"Maybe it was the wrong place and the wrong time. If these contractors come from somewhere else, they wouldn't know the German's men, eh? He uses locals, too. Geraldo and the others come along, maybe they even start the shooting. Who knows? These outsiders drop whoever threatens them."

Aznar considered it. If that turned out to be the case, and he—his men—had not been targeted, if there was no ongoing threat to his domain, Aznar could leave Hans Dietrich to his enemies and still sleep well at night.

Except.

Whether or not he'd been the target when the unknown shooters killed his men, the end result was still the same. In San José del Guaviare, in Cali and Medellín and Bogotá, his enemies would hear the story. They would know if Aznar had not punished those responsible. And they would surely act upon what they perceived as weakness.

Aznar could avenge Geraldo Sanchez and the others, here and now, or he could wait to prove himself with each competitor who challenged him in turn.

Maybe they'd come for him one at a time—meaning one

private army at a time. Or, maybe some of them would team up to increase their strength, attack him from all sides at once. In either case, he thought his odds were better here.

And he could make them better, still.

He could send the helicopter back to fetch another load of shooters, bring his numbers up to forty-three soldiers. And if the old Kraut didn't like it, that was too damned bad.

Aznar picked up his sat phone, speed-dialed one of the numbers programmed in its memory and waited for an answer on the other end. He recognized the voice that answered on the third ring, wasted no time on preliminaries. When his order was acknowledged, he cut off the link.

"Antonio! Filipe!" Aznar summoned his two pilots. When they stood in front of him, he delivered his instructions, heard their crisp affirmatives without debate.

"Boss," Filipe said, "we'll need more fuel for the return trip."

"Fine. Buy what you need, but make it fast. The sooner you get back with reinforcements, the better off we'll be."

"And leaving," Antonio said, "we'll need two round-trips for the men."

If all of them are still alive, Aznar thought. But he said, "No problem. It's just gasoline and money, right?"

"Yes, sir!"

"Take off, then. And no stalling on the ground in San José del Guaviare, understand?"

Their nods were quick and energetic. Neither of those trusted men was likely to displease him in a dire emergency, and risk a bullet to the brain.

Well pleased with his decision, Aznar watched the pilots leave, then turned back to the eighteen men who packed his bungalow. Two others were on guard outside the building's only door.

"We'll soon have more help than we need," he told them,

hoping it was true. "We'll mop these bastards up tonight, to-morrow at the latest, and be home tomorrow night."

If any of his soldiers doubted him, he couldn't see it in their faces or their attitude. He had not failed them in the past, and there was no reason for them to think that he would fail them now.

How could he?

In their strange and narrow world, he was a god.

THE TREES WEREN'T PERFECT, but they'd have to do. In the absence of tunnels or caves—which their enemies would have scouted thoroughly, in any case—Bolan's team could only seek cover above ground.

In this case, twenty feet or more above.

They chose two forest giants, situated ten or fifteen yards apart, whose sturdy limbs should easily support their weight, while leafy foliage would conceal them from at least a casual appraisal by searchers passing below.

Again, it wasn't perfect.

Bolan knew that die-hard trackers could determine whether anyone had climbed the tree, from scuff marks on the bark, disturbance of its mossy outer layer, whatever. Some might even tell how long ago the climbers went aloft, but that part wouldn't matter if one of Dietrich's patrols picked out their trees.

In that case, there'd be nothing left for them to do except fire down upon the hunters, maybe drop a couple of grenades, and hope like hell that none of them was blasted from their perches into freefall.

On the upside, Bolan didn't think that Dietrich's trackers would be spending much time studying the scuffs and scratches found on tree trunks. Not with close to thirty of them dead already and their enemies still roaming free around Colonia Victoria.

They would be beating bushes, definitely. Poking under logs and boulders, absolutely. But investigating treetops? Bolan hoped not.

Part of it was human nature. Walking through the woods, most people didn't stare up into trees unless something attracted their attention—birds, monkeys, a falling coconut, whatever it might be. Hunters were used to seeking spoor around ground level, tracking prey by means of hoof or paw prints, droppings, places where an animal had pawed the soil or cropped a batch of leaves.

Hunters of men were much the same, particularly in the wilderness. Now that the trackers had been seriously bloodied, they would be alert for traps and ambushes, expecting more of what their friends had already received.

It was a funny thing, the human mind. Despite best efforts to protect its fleshy host, it was conditioned by its rearing and environment, sometimes to overlook the obvious.

And that could get a soldier killed.

Bolan took one tree for himself, yielding the larger of the two to Cohen and Guzman. The lady from Mossad had cocked an eyebrow at him when he issued the assignments, but said nothing. If she thought there was some motive to his choice, she was right.

He wanted time to think, without the burden of explaining what he planned to do. Further, he thought that Cohen would have more influence on Guzman, concerning his idea to capture a guard tower at the compound. Bolan thought the odds for his success were less than fifty-fifty, but he didn't feel inclined to argue.

It might cost Guzman's life to follow through, but they were all at risk, had been from the beginning. Guzman was as likely to be killed while blundering around the compound if he had no plan; perhaps more so. If he succeeded in his plan, Bolan would benefit.

And if he failed?

Same thing, perhaps, as some of Dietrich's soldiers were distracted by a stranger firing at them from on high.

In either case, it couldn't hurt.

How could he reach inside Hans Dietrich's compound and cause problems for the aged Nazi? One thought immediately came to mind, evolving from the look he'd seen on Naldo Aznar's face during the smuggler's brief discussion with his bodyguards. Aznar seemed anything but peaceful and relaxed in his surroundings at Colonia Victoria. If Bolan had a chance to tip him over, from distrust to homicidal fury, it would be too good to miss.

He palmed his sat phone, glanced across toward Cohen and Guzman, but couldn't see them huddled in their tree. She had provided Bolan with her cell-phone number, and had set the phone to vibrate without ringing, but he had nothing to tell her at the moment.

Leaning back against the tree trunk, Bolan tapped a dozen digits with his fingertip and waited for a distant telephone to ring.

Washington, D.C.

SOMETIMES IT SEEMED to Hal Brognola that paperwork made up the bulk of his existence. All day long, five days a week, he wrote and answered memos, sent e-mails, read letters and dictated answers, studied files and dossiers. He often took work home on weekends, even though he'd pledged a hundred times to stop it or at to least cut back on the volume.

And when it wasn't paperwork, it was the telephone.

Like now. His private line again.

The big Fed grabbed it on the second ring. "Hello?"

"It's me."

He had no problem recognizing Bolan's voice despite the gruff whisper.

"What's up?"

"I want to shake things up a little here," Bolan replied. "Reach out and touch someone."

"Unlisted number?" Brognola inquired.

"I'd bet on it," Bolan replied. "It's Naldo Aznar's private sat phone."

"Ah." Brognola's mind was off and running as he said, "I'll have to go through Stony Man for that. Whether they'll try to piggy-back on NSA or go some other route, I couldn't guess. What kind of deadline are you on?"

"We roll at nightfall, or a little after," Bolan answered, "but I want the pot boiling before we join the party. ASAP on that number, if it's even possible."

"I'll get them cracking on it. Shall I call you back?"

"I'll call you," Bolan said. "Right now, I'm literally up a tree in no-man's land."

Which would explain the whisper, Brognola decided.

"Okay," he said. "Give me an hour, anyway, then call back when you can. I'll either have the number or an estimate of how much longer it should take to nail it down."

"Assuming that it's possible," Bolan said, voicing Brognola's unspoken question.

"Most things are, these days. But off the top, I don't re-member trying this before. We'll see."

"One hour, then."

"I'll be here."

Brognola didn't bother cradling the receiver, simply waited for the dial tone after Bolan cut their link, then speed-dialed Stony Man's command center. The voice that answered him was Aaron Kurtzman's.

"Hey, boss," he said, before Brognola had a chance to speak.

Caller ID, Brognola thought.

Cutting directly to the bottom line, the big Fed said, "I got a call from Striker, asking for a private sat phone number in Colombia. Can do?"

"Whose sat phone?"

"Naldo Aznar's."

"Ah. I don't suppose we know his service provider? Globalstar? Iridium? Inmarsat?"

"Beats me."

"It wouldn't be Tharaya, on this side of the Atlantic. Okay, let me work on it. What's Striker's deadline?"

"ASAP for the maximum effect," Brognola said. " He'll be calling in an hour for a progress check. Forget about it after sundown."

In his left ear, through the telephone, computer keys rattled like tiny tap dancers.

"Where he is," Kurtzman said at last, "sunset gives us eight hours and thirteen minutes. Make that twelve minutes."

"So, it's doable?" Brognola asked.

"Should be. We've done it two, three times before, that I recall."

"I'll leave you to it, then," the Justice man said. "Call me."

"Will do."

Another link broken, but Brognola knew he could dial that number anytime he needed to for an update on his request.

Brognola pictured Bolan up a tree in no-man's land. That meant he'd penetrated Dietrich's territory and was sitting out the daylight hours, waiting for a chance to move at nightfall. After that…

If Bolan planned to stir the pot by calling Aznar on his private sat phone, that told Brognola the drug lord had to be visiting Hans Dietrich. It was handy, letting Bolan bag two vultures for the price of one, but the big Fed knew that security would likely be increased, particularly after Bolan had already shaken up the locals.

Would the Mossad agent teamed with Bolan help or hinder him when it was time to blow down Dietrich's Nazi theme park? Could their native guide carry his weight or would he leave them in the lurch?

Was there time and opportunity enough for Bolan to dismantle fifty-odd years' work within eight hours and change? Would this be the assignment where his luck ran out?

Cursing the damned uncertainty, Brognola turned back to his paperwork and waited for the telephone to ring.

THE HOUR DRAGGED FOR BOLAN, waiting until he could call Brognola back to see if Stony Man had conjured Naldo Aznar's sat phone number from thin air.

He knew Dietrich's soldiers would be searching for them. There could be no doubt of that. After his team had wiped out two patrols, the manhunt should be unrelenting, leave no stone unturned.

And yet he doubted whether Dietrich had enough men left to scour every square yard of Colonia Victoria, without leaving the main compound unguarded, open to attack. He guessed that wasn't Dietrich's style, particularly on a special day when celebrations had been organized.

He wondered if the helicopters flying in and out meant reinforcements, party guests or some of both. In either case, he was relieved that Dietrich seemed intent on going ahead with his weird birthday bash. It was madness, of course, but this time around the insanity might work to Bolan's advantage.

He understood the psychological basis of racial and religious bigotry: a deeply seated sense of personal inferiority and failure that sent angry losers in search of scapegoats, someone whom they could objectify and blame for all their problems, label them subhuman and inflict upon them all the angry violence that couldn't be directed safely toward some figure in authority.

He understood it, but it still amazed him that so many otherwise-rational people swallowed the bait. Millions in Germany had followed a dumpy, dark-haired psychopath who told them tall, blond, blue-eyed folk were the human ideal. Stranger still, not one of Adolf's top lieutenants fit the mold they championed. His inner circle had included an obese drug addict, a club-footed dwarf and a myopic chinless chicken farmer.

What the hell?

What would Hitler think of Hans Dietrich's Colonia Victoria, with its supposed polygamy, occult religious rituals and trafficking in drugs? Would he approve and say ends justified the means, or would it be too much even for Adolf's twisted mind?

And in the end, what difference did it make?

Hitler was dead, and Bolan hoped Hans Dietrich would be joining him before the sun rose on another day. Eliminating Dietrich wouldn't end the Master Race charade, by any means, but it might finally eliminate one focal point of antiquated Nazism in the modern world. Without Colonia Victoria, the kooks would have to gather somewhere else. Perhaps some of them would be desolate from loneliness and eat their guns.

The butterfly effect?

Bolan could only hope that it spread far and wide.

He checked his watch, saw that he still owed Brognola two minutes, but decided it was close enough. Taking the sat phone from one of his cargo pockets, Bolan hit redial and waited through two rings.

"Hello?"

"I'm checking in," Bolan said.

"Right on time," the big Fed said. "You have a pencil handy for that number?"

"I'll remember it," Bolan replied with a smile.

CHAPTER FIFTEEN

Colonia Victoria

The droning buzz of his satellite phone caught Naldo Aznar with a glass of tequila at his lips. He drained the shot glass, grimaced and reached for the phone as it buzzed once again.

It had to be Antonio, reporting on his progress with the re-inforcements. No one else would call Aznar at Dietrich's camp unless it was the most severe emergency.

He thumbed the button marked HABLAR and said in Spanish, "Tell me you're on the way."

"I didn't catch that," a strange voice replied in English.

"Who is this?"

"Someone trying to save your life," the voice replied.

"Explain."

"You're in a world of trouble, Naldo. Maybe you know that already, though."

"What trouble?"

"Sitting in the middle of a Nazi camp on Hitler's birthday? Think about it. When the Aryans get all worked up, will you be white enough to pass inspection?"

"Who is this? I want your name!" he snarled.

"Why waste your time? You wouldn't recognize it, anyway. My message—"

"I am hanging up now," Aznar threatened, but he made no move to do so.

"Suit yourself," the caller said. "But if you're smart, you'll keep an eye on Dietrich and the Arabs. Most especially the Arabs."

"Why? What are you saying?"

"Think about it, Naldo. Do you suppose Dietrich regards you as an equal? Does he even need you to continue in the coke trade?"

Aznar felt the angry color rising in his face. "I don't know who this is, or what you're saying about drugs, but—"

"Now you're sitting in the middle of his compound, waiting for his Nazis to get liquored up for Adolf's birthday. All of them with guns, I'm betting. Are you part of the fireworks show they're planning, Naldo? Do you wind up on the bonfire when it's over?"

Aznar realized that whoever the caller was, he had to have seen the compound with its pile of lumber waiting to be set alight. Could he be calling from inside the camp? If so, who was it? What could be his motive?

And if he was not inside the camp, then where?

"I don't suppose you know about my men, eh?" he inquired.

The caller answered with a question of his own. "Why, are you missing some? It wouldn't be fifteen, by any chance?"

"You didn't guess that number!"

Aznar felt his people watching, moving closer, but he waved them back and turned so that they could not see his face.

"Maybe ask Dietrich or the Arabs. Don't forget the Sword of Allah, Naldo. They hate drug dealers almost as much as they hate Jews. And Catholics. You think they don't remember the Crusades?"

"You're here, aren't you? Inside the camp!"

"You think so? Maybe you feel someone watching you?"

"I want a name, goddamn you!"

"Talk to Dietrich. Ask about those fifteen men."

The line went dead. Aznar was on the verge of shouting at the caller when he heard the droning hum of dead air in his ear. He flicked the HABLAR switch again and turned to face his men.

"What is it, boss?" one of them inquired.

"A call," he said, then realized he sounded foolish. Obviously it had been a call. "I think it came from somewhere in the camp."

"What did he say?" another asked.

Aznar spun toward him. "He? How did you know it was a man?"

His soldier paled and took a quick step backward. "Boss, I don't know! I never heard you curse a woman on the telephone."

Aznar stopped in his tracks and took a deep breath, willing himself to be calm and to think rationally. Of course the men surrounding him were not involved in the disturbing call. How could they be?

"Someone close by is watching us. He claims to know who killed Sanchez and his men."

"Who, boss?" a number of them asked in unison.

"I'm not sure yet," Aznar replied. "It seems we should trust no one hereabouts."

"Boss—"

"No more questions! Two of you come with me. You, there! And, you! We go to see our host."

Trust no one.

That was simple. It was Naldo Aznar's private mantra, and had been since he was ten years old, an orphan running through the streets of Medellín and stealing anything that he could carry. All that differed now was his position and his wealth.

No, there was something else.

He was surrounded by potential enemies, cut off from all escape until Antonio and Filipe returned with the helicopter and his reinforcements. Then, and only then, he could decide whether to flee or to stay and fight.

In the meantime, he was trapped, and he had done it to himself.

The very least that he could do was speak to Hans Dietrich again, press him for further information on the murders of Geraldo Sanchez and his other men.

And he would also keep a close eye on the scheming Arabs. Yes, indeed. Aznar would keep a very close eye on them all.

DAS Headquarters, Bogotá

JOAQUIN MENENDEZ WAS a troubled man. He had begun to doubt himself, and that was dangerous. In fact, as he well knew, self-doubt was often the beginning of the end.

Some men are troubled by their consciences, but that was not the case with Menendez. If he had ever had a conscience, something which he frankly doubted, it had been suppressed and overridden by survival instincts sometime during adolescence.

No.

He felt no guilt, except as it pertained to self.

And at the moment, Menendez was worried that he'd made himself look weak.

The visit he'd received from the American and the Israeli had shaken Menendez. He'd broken his agreement with Hans Dietrich to protect himself, but he was having second thoughts.

It would be foolish, he admitted, to commit troops in defense of Dietrich's Nazis when so many foreign eyes were watching, and to thereby place his own career at risk. But now that he'd had time to think about it, without anyone haranguing him, Menendez worried that it might be just as dangerous to sit back and ignore the trouble brewing in Colonia Victoria.

How would it look if he did nothing, while the German settlement was raided, possibly annihilated, by guerrillas? Dietrich was a wealthy man, with widespread influence, and while some of the politicians he had bribed might be relieved to see the last of him, they would not countenance a public act of terrorism. Some of them would doubtless ask Menendez why his men were not on hand to stop the bloodshed or to at least pursue and kill the terrorists responsible.

What would he say?

Clearly he could not tell the president or the attorney general that he had dropped his guard because a Yanqui and a Jew had threatened him in his own office. How could he explain that he had crumbled in the face of blackmail, fearing the exposure of his personal corruption?

It would make more sense to take the pistol from his desk drawer, place the muzzle in his mouth and spray his brains across the room. At least, that way, he would not have to face the shame of being fired, then prosecuted and imprisoned.

How long would he live in jail? A month? A week? Even a day?

There was an answer to his problem, though. Menendez was convinced of it.

His visitors had threatened to expose Menendez if he helped Hans Dietrich in the struggle with his unknown enemies. They'd said nothing about placing soldiers in or near Colonia Victoria, to nab those enemies as they were fleeing from the crime scene.

It was perfect.

Outside of Colonia Victoria, no one except Menendez knew that Dietrich had requested armed assistance from the DAS. Therefore, no one in Bogotá would blame Menendez if he failed to stop the raid that Dietrich seemed to be expecting. He was not a mind reader, for heaven's sake!

Yet, on the other hand, it was entirely possible that one of his informants might have dropped a hint concerning trouble at the compound. If the information seemed trustworthy, it was only common sense that Menendez would take some action to investigate and apprehend the criminals responsible, if any violence occurred. More to the point, it was his sworn duty.

He might even be a hero when the gunsmoke cleared.

Menendez checked the large clock on his office wall. Arturo Obregon would not be pleased to have his orders altered once again, but he would do as he was told without complaint.

How much time would it take to reassemble Obregon's strike force? An hour? Two? No more than that, Menendez was convinced, if they began at once.

There was no time to waste.

Now that his course was set, his mind made up, Menendez did not hesitate. He placed two calls—one to the officer in charge of readying the helicopters and the other to Inspector Obregon. There was a moment's puzzled silence on the line with Obregon before he answered with a brisk, "Yes, sir! As you wish, at once!"

Menendez cradled the receiver, smiling to himself. The deed was done, and everyone should now be pleased.

Well, everyone, that was, except Hans Dietrich.

If there had to be a sacrifice, why not the aging Nazi and his clique of crazy sycophants? The world, Menendez thought, would get along quite nicely without any of them. It would be a happier, more peaceful place for him, without the

Germans, even if he missed their regular deposits to his secret bank account.

No matter.

In Colombia, the bribes were never hard to come by. Menendez had money enough for two lifetimes already, and more would be coming his way before long. He was sure of it.

Colombia's drug dealers, robber barons and corrupt politicians would see to that. All of them needed a policeman they could trust to overlook their dirty dealings, for a price.

Joaquin Menendez was their man, and once he'd reinforced his reputation as a fearless enemy of terrorists, the price tag for his services would certainly increase.

And why not?

It was the very definition of free enterprise.

Colonia Victoria

BOLAN HAD DONE HIS BEST with Naldo Aznar, on the sat phone. Now, as afternoon wore down toward evening and the gift of darkness, all that he could do was wait—and hope he'd done enough.

In Bolan's personal experience, drug runners stayed alive and out of jail by being paranoid, suspecting everyone around them of conspiring toward their downfall. At the top of the illicit food chain, where weekly income figures had at least six zeros, paranoia reigned supreme. Death awaited any man who looked the wrong way at a topflight dealer, anyone whose conversation left a nagging question mark and planted seeds of doubt.

The rule was simple: when in doubt, take 'em out.

Now, even though Aznar had no idea who'd called him on his private line, he would be thinking about Bolan's words, his warning against Dietrich and the Arabs. It would seem to be a trick, of course, too obvious for words. But how could he ignore it?

Bolan had been lucky when Aznar mentioned his lost men. Until that moment, Bolan hadn't known whose troops the fifteen ill-dressed shooters were, but he'd been quick enough to jump on it, taking a chance.

And he had scored.

It would give Bolan's fabrications about Dietrich and the Sword of Allah credibility in Aznar's mind; that much was obvious. What Aznar chose to do about it was another matter. Bolan couldn't read the future, but he hoped, if nothing else, that Aznar's anger and suspicion drove a wedge between the dealer and his hosts. Perhaps they'd even quarrel, and if quarreling come to blows—or gunshots—better yet.

It would be nice, for once, to have the enemy do Bolan's wet work for him, but he wasn't counting on it. When they reached the compound, sometime after dark, he knew there'd still be bloody work remaining for his team to tackle.

Were they ready for it?

Bolan really couldn't say.

He'd gone along with Guzman's plan to storm one of the guard towers, without truly believing it could work. The upside, for a cynical survivor, was that even if he failed, if he was killed before he set foot on the chosen tower's ladder, Guzman would provide a fair diversion for himself and Cohen as they dealt with their appointed tasks.

They'd flipped a round, flat, coin-size stone to settle it, since neither of them carried any jangling change. She'd won the motor pool, if you could call that winning, and he'd given her two of the four grenades he'd salvaged from their first skirmish with Dietrich's men. She had the larger task—ten vehicles, not counting motorcycles—but he reckoned she would think of something.

Bolan's first target would be the compound's helipad. Two choppers had been present during his reconnaissance, then one had flown away, returning only in the past half hour, since his chat with Naldo Aznar. Now, while he was thinking of the helipad and how he would approach it, Bolan heard another helicopter closing from a distance, on a north-south course.

More guns? Or would it be last-minute party favors for the Führer's birthday bash?

Bolan sat listening, poised on his perch, frowning when the whirlybird appeared to stop well short of Dietrich's forest settlement. Sound could be tricky in the forest, but he would have bet a month's pay—if he got pay—that the chopper had touched down at least a mile north of the compound. When he heard its engines next, perhaps two minutes later, they were dwindling in the distance, going back the way they'd come.

Another mystery. He ran the possibilities that came to mind.

First up, a ploy by Dietrich that involved airlifting reinforcements to a point outside the compound, where they could advance and hopefully catch Bolan in some kind of pincers movement.

An alternative: perhaps Aznar had hit the panic button after their brief conversation, calling up more guns to help his odds. But could a flying squad be mounted and delivered in so short a time? Would Aznar have them dropped so far from where he needed them?

Doubtful.

Other scenarios ran through his mind. A Sword of Allah backup squad was possible, but once again, why drop them off a mile or more from where the action was expected? Brognola had handled the official end of it, apparently, but Bolan made a mental note to watch for uniforms, regardless.

Who else could be dropping in to join the party?

The Mossad? He instantly dismissed it, trusting Cohen to inform him if she'd called for backup, as they came down to the wire.

A mystery, he thought, again. Just what I need.

But what he really needed was the night. And from the shadows creeping in among the trees, he knew that it was almost time to move.

HANS DIETRICH SAW Naldo Aznar and two of his bodyguards approaching from the general direction of their quarters. He was tired of fielding questions from the paranoid Colombian, but their relationship compelled him to be civil, at the very least. Masking his grimace with a smile of welcome, Dietrich turned from his inspection of a large floral display to face his guests.

Aznar's first question took him by surprise.

"What does that say?" the dealer asked, nodding toward the elaborate wreath.

"A simple 'happy birthday,'" Dietrich answered. "Is there something you require, Herr Aznar? Anything at all, within our capability?"

"I'm curious to know how many telephones there are in camp," Aznar replied.

The question, coming out of nowhere, nearly cost Dietrich his smile.

"I'm sure that I have no idea," he said. "If you would care to ask the quartermaster…"

"More specifically, how many satellite phones?"

"My friend, if you have need to place a call, by all means—"

"I already have a telephone," Aznar said, interrupting him. "I need to know how many others are in camp."

Dietrich was frowning now. He couldn't help himself.

"I have one in my quarters for emergencies. We keep another with the shortwave sets and two-way portables, in the communications hut. Aside from that, our Middle Eastern guests have one that I have personally seen. If I may ask the purpose of your questions—"

"Señor Dietrich, I've received a most disturbing call by way of satellite. The caller is unknown to me. I did not recognize his voice. His comments led me to believe he might be calling from within this camp."

"This person threatened you?"

"I won't say that," Aznar replied. "It was more in the nature of a warning."

"Against what?"

Aznar dodged the question, saying, "He should not have had my private number. He should not have known that I am here, with you. He should not know about the fifteen men I lost this afternoon."

"The number was precise?" Dietrich asked.

Aznar nodded. "And I never mentioned it."

"The only thing I can suggest… I mean, it seems so obvious," Dietrich replied.

"Explain."

"Your private line, your movements, and the disposition of your men. Who else would know all that, except someone within your own cartel? An aide, perhaps or—"

"No! I told you that I did not recognize the voice!"

"My friend, with all respect, I doubt that you have heard the voice of every man who works for you, or who has knowledge of your business. Even so, there are devices made to alter vocal tones."

"I know that!" Aznar snapped. "But it was someone in or

near the camp, I tell you! How else would he know about the bonfire you've prepared?"

"The bonfire?"

"He referred to it," Aznar said.

"In what context, may I ask?"

Something dark and dangerous flickered behind the narcodealer's eyes.

"It's not important what he said. My point is that he's seen that pile of lumber. How long has it been there?"

Dietrich stiffened to suppress a shudder.

"We began construction of the pyre this morning," he replied.

"Which means he's seen the camp today!"

"And you believe this person is responsible for the attack upon your men?"

"He didn't say that. I suppose it's possible."

"In which case, he could hardly be here in the compound," Dietrich said.

"Outside, then! Watching us!"

"But when he threatened you—"

"Not threatened. Warned!"

"And again I ask you, warned against what?"

Aznar glanced at his bodyguards, frowning. Their cold eyes shifted toward Dietrich.

"Against betrayal," Aznar said. "Specifically, the Arabs."

Dietrich was certain that he left something unsaid, but he was not inclined to press the matter.

"They are…different…I grant you, but we share a common cause, united in—"

"I am a businessman, *señor*. As you well know, my politics are strictly limited to dealing with the people who can help my business. Those who threaten injury are either paid to change their attitude, or else they are eliminated."

"Once again, we are in full accord," Dietrich replied, ignoring Aznar's not-so-subtle threat, when he could cheerfully have slapped the man or had him shot.

Not yet.

Nothing could be allowed to spoil the celebration of Hitler's birthday. Afterward, perhaps, if Aznar still persisted in his attitude. Despite what Aznar might believe, he was not irreplaceable, by any means.

Much less invincible.

As Aznar turned to go, he said, "Someone is watching us! I tell you this!"

"Fear not," Dietrich replied. "We shall maintain surveillance through the night."

"I have more people coming," Aznar told him. "They should be here soon."

"And always welcome."

Dietrich forced another smile. Watching Aznar retreat with bodyguards in tow, he wondered how many more bodies they could fit inside the compound's morgue.

Caquetá Department

"I was only following orders. Only following orders."

Inspector Arturo Obregon repeated the phrase in his mind, trying it on for size, and wondered whether it would be enough to save him if his latest job went bad.

Obregon was confused and troubled by the latest orders from Joaquin Menendez, which had placed him back aboard the Bell 412 helicopter, clutching his M-16 assault rifle and facing eleven armed men dressed in camouflage fatigues. The second helicopter, bearing twelve more troops, flew in tandem behind them, like one giant insect pursuing another.

They were returning to Colonia Victoria, but on a different mission, as Menendez had explained. Not to protect Hans Dietrich and his Nazis, but to capture or eliminate any guerrillas who might harm the compound's residents. The major difference, as far as Obregon could tell, was that they would be landing in a forest clearing northwest of the settlement, rather than using Dietrich's helipad and watching from inside the compound.

Arturo Obregon was no historian, but he had finished high school and completed one year at university in Cali. He grasped the irony of his defense, and understood that it had failed the Nazi criminals at Nuremberg.

Nor would it help him if the job went wrong, should Menendez use him as a scapegoat. Only Menendez and Obregon knew what orders had been issued. At a trial, it could be argued that he—Obregon—had overstepped his authority, or even acted without official sanction.

Who would the judges believe, himself or the director of the mighty DAS, who probably had damning dossiers on all of them, prepared for just such an eventuality?

His best bet, Obregon had instantly decided, was to carry out his orders to the best of his ability and hope that nothing blew up in his face. If he gave Menendez no cause to criticize him, there should be no problem.

He would therefore do exactly what he had been told to do: observe Hans Dietrich's compound from a distance and intervene "in timely fashion" if the German's were attacked.

The first part—observation from a distance, in the forest— had confused him until Obregon decided that Menendez didn't really want him to protect Dietrich's compound. He could dispatch a scout to watch the place and radio if anything happened, but his men would be a mile or more away from the immediate action. Even if they double-timed, ignoring danger, it would take them twenty minutes, easily, to reach the scene.

He had explained that to Menendez, making certain it was crystal clear. The director had responded, "Do your best."

So, that was it. He was supposed to kill or capture Dietrich's enemies, without preventing them from staging their attack in the first place. It was too much for Obregon to fathom, without understanding all the crafty politics behind it, and he didn't really care. He had already seen and done enough bizarre things as a DAS inspector to believe that his career had anything to do with honest law enforcement.

Someone, somewhere, had decided that Hans Dietrich should be punished, possibly eliminated. At the same time, his attackers had to be seen to feel the full weight of the law—after their private mission was completed.

Sitting in the helicopter jumpseat, Obregon wondered if drugs were mixed up in this business somehow, as they seemed to be in everything else, from government to religion and sports. Maybe the rumors were correct, that Dietrich was involved with one of the cocaine cartels, and now he had offended them, resulting in a contract on his life.

Or was it something else?

No matter. Obregon's concern was with himself, his men and the apparent success of his mission, in that precise order.

If something happened at the compound but he missed Dietrich's assailants—lost them in the forest, say, or never even caught a glimpse of them—at least he could score some points by returning with his squad intact. To lose men in pursuit of nothing might be more than he could bear.

Or maybe not.

Each day Arturo Obregon learned more about himself, his strengths and failings. The majority of what he learned was neither pleasant nor a source of pride. So far, he had accommodated those lessons and learned to live with them.

And living was the key.

He would be no good to himself or anybody else if he was dead.

Another lesson. When the action started, *if* it started, in Colonia Victoria, Arturo Obregon would shoot first and reserve his questions for some other time.

Following orders all the way.

WHEN LONG SHADOWS OBSCURED the forest floor, Bolan descended from his tree. He climbed down slowly, cautiously, convinced there were no searchers crouched in the vicinity, but still taking no chances as he left his perch.

On solid ground once more, he took a moment to survey the woods as far as he could see, confirming his initial sense that there was no trap waiting on the ground. When he was satisfied on that score, Bolan crossed the six or seven yards to Cohen's tree and whistled softly, two notes with a quick rising inflection at the end.

Another moment and he heard her scrabbling down to meet him, Guzman shifting in the branches somewhere above and behind her. Cohen's boots and legs appeared before the rest of her, as if the tree was giving birth to her feetfirst. At last, she dangled from a limb six feet above the ground, released her hold and dropped into a crouch.

Guzman was slower, slipping once in such a way that Bolan thought he was about to plummet, but he got the job done after all. After hours in the tree, he seemed a little shaky with his feet on terra firma, and the first thing he requested was a bladder break. That sparked a need in Cohen, so they all took care of business, then regrouped where they had started.

"It's dark enough for Dietrich's party to be starting," Bolan said. "So we'll move in now, but carefully. He may still have patrols out, and he'll certainly have sentries at the compound.

Nice and easy does it, going in. We don't want to spook anyone before it's time to rock and roll."

"I have decided on the eastern tower," Guzman said. "It is
the nearest to us, now, and from the top I can see both the cars
and helicopters."

Bolan nodded, saying, "That's good thinking. We should
synchronize our watches."

It was a moment's work, no more. When that was done, he
had them double-check their weapons: fully loaded magazines and live rounds in the chambers, safeties off for speed's
sake, fingers well outside the trigger guards.

The rest of it was automatic, when the action started and
they were fighting for their lives. He couldn't tell them how
to move or what to use for cover, how to choose a target, when
to fire or watch and wait. In combat, bottom line, it was every
man or women for him- or herself.

They were a team, of course, each member with a job to
do. But in the present circumstances, with the odds so heavily against them, no one could assume that any individual
would even make it to his jumping-off point, much less carry
out his full objective and survive to talk about it afterward.
And when that was the case—a team so small, against an
enemy so strong—each individual could only do his best to
carry out the master plan.

To stay alive.

He led them through the deepening shadows toward their
target. At a hundred yards, they heard the strains of martial
music wafting through the forest. Bolan couldn't tell if it was
live or a recording, but he hoped for live, since soldiers playing tubas, drums and trumpets were unlikely to be armed.

At forty yards, his ears caught snatches of a marching
song, but Bolan couldn't pick out any words. He finally decided that they were singing in German, likely some battle

hymn from the thirties. Unconsciously, even against his will, Bolan found himself marching in time to the beat.

"What is that?" Guzman asked.

"*Das Lied der Deutschen*," Cohen answered. "It was Hitler's anthem."

"So, the party's started," Bolan told them. "Let's hope no one asks us for our invitations."

CHAPTER SIXTEEN

Hans Dietrich raised his voice at the conclusion of his nation's wartime anthem, belting out the verses with a power that belied his everyday appearance.

His heart swelled with pride as the cheers and applause followed after the song he'd first learned in his early teens as a member of the Hitler Youth. Its message had propelled him through the war years and beyond, across the decades when the outside world believed that the Third Reich had truly been defeated in the spring of 1945.

What fools they were!

To think that anyone, much less the lowly Jews and Communists, could ever crush the Master Race! They had to be mad. And their insanity, the arrogance it spawned, would serve him well.

Already, he was making strides against the enemies of his embattled Fatherland. The Zionists had felt his sting, and through collaboration with the Sword of Allah, Tel Aviv would suffer even more.

Dietrich saw Muhunnad Qadir, Nasser Khalil, and the others away to his left, faces bathed in the light of the bonfire.

They would not sing, of course—likely considered it some violation of their grand Islamic principles—but Dietrich didn't care. What mattered was their presence in the compound, their agreement to continue on a course of action that would gravely damage Israel and its allies.

They were fools to trust him, had apparently learned nothing from the hard lessons of history, but they were useful for the moment. Inferiors made good cannon fodder and distracted the Israelis from pursuing those who pulled the puppet's strings.

Each time an Arab youth strapped on a load of Semtex and committed suicide somewhere in Israel, killing ten or twenty Jews in the process, Dietrich was doubly pleased. Let one Semitic people kill another, then eliminate themselves. It would save Dietrich time and bullets, in the end.

He regarded the Middle East as a self-cleaning oven. Turn up the heat sufficiently, and it consumed whatever was inside, eliminating waste products of all kinds and eradicating human stains. His only true regret was that the Arabs had no nuclear warheads.

It was a problem Dietrich hoped to solve in the new year, through contacts on the Russian front. Another miracle, the way some former Communists now saw the error of their ways and fell in line with members of the Aryan movement.

Not that the mercenary shift would save them when the final purge began.

Hans Dietrich knew he might not live to see the world completely cleansed of inferior scum, but he had made a start. Perhaps, if he was fortunate, he might follow the movement's global progress from a box seat in Valhalla.

But not yet.

He was not ready to release the reins of power.

Not today, of all days, when Der Führer's spirit filled him, making him feel young and strong again.

He turned from the bonfire, checking his soldiers in the nearest tower first, then scanning the perimeter as far as he could see by firelight. His appointed sentries were on guard, no doubt regretting that they could not join the party, drink their share of beer, but every son and daughter of Colonia Victoria was raised to honor duty first.

They would not fail him now.

Somewhere beyond the fire's light, lurking in the forest, Dietrich knew his enemies were drawing closer, waiting for a chance to strike. He wished that they would hurry, make themselves available for slaughter without any more delays.

Dietrich had scores to settle, answers to extract from any who survived the battle. He would crush them absolutely, revel in their suffering, as in the glory days of old.

He had forgotten nothing from the camps, when it came to obtaining information, milking every bit of knowledge from a tortured mind and body. He would lead the younger generation by example, and instruct them in the art of stealing souls.

But first, he needed enemies to practice on.

Where are you? Dietrich thought. What are you waiting for?

The band struck up another song, the anthem of the brownshirts, cherished even after they were purged in 1934, on the Night of the Long Knives. Again, Dietrich lifted his voice with pride.

All that he needed now, to toast his happiness, was beer—and blood.

BOLAN HUDDLED with his two companions at the northeast corner of the settlement, concealed by trees and shadows well beyond the reach of firelight. They were now as ready as they'd ever be to penetrate the compound, facing odds of more than a hundred to one.

Bolan watched sentries pacing off the settlement's perimeter, most carrying their rifles slung, eyes peering into darkness from beneath the brims of classic German helmets. He could see the polish glisten on their belts and jackboots, on the silver pommels of their sheathed daggers. From time to time, an officer in SS black would make the rounds, addressing certain lookouts in their native tongue and snubbing others.

There were thirty men on the perimeter, by Bolan's count, excluding tower guards. Each walking guard patrolled a section ranging from one hundred fifty to two hundred feet in length, parading back and forth. But they could only face in one direction at a time.

Guzman had an advantage for the penetration, since his camouflage fatigues and his complexion matched the other native mercenaries visible inside the compound. He spoke Spanish, as they did, and carried an assault rifle identical to theirs. Bolan surmised that in the semidarkness, with most of the camp's inhabitants distracted by the bonfire festival, Guzman should have no major problem reaching his selected guard tower.

Beyond that, it was anybody's guess as to what happened next.

The plan was not—had never been—to level Dietrich's compound or to annihilate its several hundred tenants. Bolan had not come equipped for scorched-earth demolition, and he couldn't call an air strike down upon Colonia Victoria. His goal was the elimination of Hans Dietrich, any chief lieutenants he was able to identify, and any special visitors—including Naldo Aznar, Nasser Khalil and any other ranking members of the Sword of Allah who might cross his path.

The first phase of that plan was to ensure that no one flew or drove away once Bolan and his team had crashed the party. Taking out the choppers and the compound's motor pool restricted any fugitives to fleeing through the woods on foot, where they were vulnerable to attack or simply getting lost.

Beyond that, it was basic hunting, complicated by the mob scene and the fact that many of the camp's inhabitants were armed and trained for combat. Bolan counted on his two allies, confusion and surprise, to help him balance the intimidating odds.

Civilians were another problem, but he wasn't sure how many of the compound's tenants qualified, given their training and life-long indoctrination in the Nazi mind-set. Bolan had a sense that any one of them would kill him to protect their leader—or if they were simply ordered to, by someone in authority.

As if attuned to Bolan's thoughts, Cohen whispered, "Show no special treatment to the women. They're as bad, or worse, than any of the men."

"How do you know that?" Guzman asked.

"Remember Ilse Koch and all her tattooed lampshades," Cohen said. "Don't let any of these Nazi bitches get the drop on you. Treat them as human, and you'll soon be dead."

Guzman blinked back at her and said, "You sound just like them."

"Suit yourself, then," she retorted, "if you want to die."

"Time out!" Bolan said. "If we're going, put the argument on hold."

The others lapsed into uneasy silence, watching him to keep from staring one another down. The last thing either of them needed at the moment was a personal distraction, but it might not hurt to have their nerves on edge, to keep them both alert.

"We've got our jobs," he said, "and nine o'clock remains the cutoff time. Whatever isn't done by then, assume it won't get done at all. Agreed?"

Two sullen nods.

Nine o'clock gave them an hour to raise hell inside the

compound and regroup, if they were able, at a rally point a hundred yards south of the settlement. Assuming any of them made it, they would push on through the night, due west, toward San José del Curillo and their hidden vehicle. Bolan carried the only keys, but if he didn't make it out, he trusted Cohen to hot-wire the Mazda.

"All right, then," he told them. "Let's do it."

NALDO AZNAR STOOD among his bodyguards and watched the Germans dance around their bonfire. They had formed two concentric rings, boy-girl-boy-girl and holding hands, the inner ring rotating clockwise while the outer kept pace in the opposite direction. From the air, Aznar supposed, it must look well rehearsed and rather clever.

It reminded him of what the Indians might do. Some kind of harvest festival, perhaps, or else a pagan celebration of fertility. He did not understand a word that any of them sang, but from their beaming faces he supposed it was a happy tune.

Which puzzled him, considering the men Dietrich had lost that afternoon. He understood that only two of them were "Aryans," but still, in Aznar's world such losses would provoke anger, perhaps fear—at the very least, a feeling of anxiety.

Instead the Germans danced and sang as if they had no cares in the world, cavorting like the victors of triumphant battle. Aznar wondered whether they were all too drunk to comprehend their situation, or if they simply had lost touch with reality.

He guessed that it was possible, existing in a time warp that preserved the culture and the doctrines of a madman's government, eradicated from the outside world by devastating war. Inside the bubble, children were conceived, born, raised and educated as if Nazi Germany had never crumbled in defeat, but rather had retained its strength and pride throughout successive decades.

Sixty years meant…what? Three generations, if the fugitives had started breeding right away. Their females could conceive as adolescents, if the insular society permitted it—and from the rumors Aznar heard, Dietrich encouraged procreation of the so-called Master Race without regard to race, familial relationships or any other strictures of mainland society.

Aznar conceded that the children he had seen seemed bright enough, and healthy. There had been no slack-jawed idiots roaming about the compound, but he also understood enough about the Nazi scripture on eugenics to suspect that children born with handicaps might not survive.

Aznar could only marvel at the evil of the world, and that forced him to smile, considering the journalists and politicians in America who called *him* evil, singling out his business as the root of every problem in their decadent society.

So far, there'd been no sign of Dietrich's enemies, although the bonfire had been blazing for a quarter of an hour and the party atmosphere should have encouraged any watchers in the dark forest to make their move. Aznar's forty-three gunmen were on full alert, prohibited from drinking even one glass of the beer their hosts were swilling as if there was no tomorrow.

Happy songs and leaping flames aside, Aznar could not escape a feeling of impending danger. Maybe it was simple paranoia, but the longer he stood watching the frenetic festival, the more he longed to get away.

At last, when he could bear the strain no longer, he told one of his lieutenants, "Go find Dietrich. Tell him there's been an emergency at home. We have to go. Don't offer any details. If he argues, send him over here to me."

"Yes, sir. But…the helicopter only carries half of us."

"Which means," Aznar responded, "that the sooner I get back to San José del Guaviare, the quicker I can send it back for you. Now, go and do as you are told!"

JORGE GUZMAN FELT NUMB as he approached the guard tower he had selected, putting one foot down before the other like a zombie, almost as if someone else controlled his mind, the very muscles of his body.

It had been his choice, though, when Matt Cooper told him he was free to leave. Now he would have to live or die with his decision.

Entering the compound proper had been terrifying. He had waited for the sentry on his sector to pass by, reaching the farthest point from Guzman, then rushed across the unmarked line before the German turned to catch him at it. Cooper had discovered that the guards were not coordinated on their beats, did not maintain a steady pace or synchronize their movements so, for instance, that the guard on Sector A was not prepared to cover Sector B when Sector B's patrolman reached the far end of his beat.

A sharp commander would have seen the flaw and fixed it, but the present system had loopholes. Guzman had slipped through one of them.

He reached the base of the guard tower without being challenged. Standing at the foot of its tall ladder, Guzman scanned the firelit night around him for a witness who might notice him, sound the alarm when he began to climb. He saw no one except the roving sentries. All the other Germans and their native hired help were distracted by the band, the dancers and the blazing fire.

The band would help, he thought. If he could time it properly, the drums and brass might muffle Guzman's pistol shots.

He slung the Czech assault rifle over his shoulder, took a moment to adjust the IMBEL pistols tucked beneath his belt—the .45 on his right side, 9 mm on the left—then gripped the wooden ladder and began to climb.

He estimated that the gun platform was twenty feet above

ground. It was roofed and shielded from inclement weather by a waist-high wooden railing all the way around. Access was through a trapdoor in the middle of the platform's floor. A person entering the guards' enclosure therefore had to rise up in plain view of both, unless their backs were turned and something on the ground below distracted them.

Guzman did not believe in miracles.

He had a plan sketched in his head. Instead of trying to force the trapdoor and put the two guards on alert, maybe prompt them to shoot him on sight, he planned to knock and call to them in Spanish. Make it something plausible, in case one of them actually spoke the language—food or drink, perhaps, sent up to them by Dietrich. When the hatch was opened, he would have his pistol cocked and ready.

It would be cold-blooded killing, unlike anything he'd done so far, since meeting the American and Gabriella Cohen, but it was his only chance.

If he froze, pistol in hand, he was as good as dead. The Nazis would not hesitate to kill him if he threatened them and failed to follow through. Or, worse, they might disarm and capture him, deliver him to Dietrich's other soldiers for interrogation. If the raid failed, thanks to Guzman's weakness, it could mean a long, slow death by torture, rather than a bullet's mercy.

He would fire.

Of course, he would.

The ladder swayed a bit under his weight, but Guzman kept on climbing. At the top, he leaned against it, freeing both hands, raising one to rap against the trapdoor while his other drew the IMBEL .45.

"¡Hola! Le traigo cerveza y bocadillos."

Whether they understood his offering of beer and sandwiches or not, the guards were moving, jackboots clumping on the platform over Guzman's head. He waited, heard a latch thrown on the trapdoor and was ready when it rose.

He aimed his pistol at a pale Teutonic face framed in the opening, used his left hand to shove the trapdoor back and fired at point-blank range.

TWO SENTRIES WERE ASSIGNED to guard the compound's helipad, a concrete slab spanning roughly half the square footage of a standard soccer field. Depending on their size, Bolan supposed the pad could accommodate four or five choppers at once, but only two were present as he crouched in shadow, waiting for his chance to move.

The same Agusta A109 Hirundo sat where it had on his first pass, in daylight. An Aérospatiale Super Puma also sat idle on the pad, but in a different position than it or its twin had occupied hours earlier. That made it the chopper Bolan had heard flying out and returning.

But why?

Forget it.

Whatever the larger aircraft had removed or delivered, its work was already done. If it had carried passengers away from Dietrich's compound, they were now beyond his reach. If it had ferried reinforcements to Colonia Victoria, Bolan and his two comrades simply had to deal with them.

As Bolan had to deal with sentries now.

Two choppers on the pad, two soldiers set to watch them. One was stationed at the west end of the pad, not far from Bolan, while the other was positioned at the farther, eastern end, presumably so that the two of them could cover every angle of the helipad.

It worked in theory, but in fact, it placed both choppers in between the sentries, cutting off their view of one another. Making each one vulnerable on his own.

There was no point in wasting time while Guzman scaled his tower and attempted to eliminate the two machine gunners. Drawing his knife, Bolan crept to the farthest edge of midnight shadow cast across the helipad by looming trees and waited for the guard to make a slip.

Like turning from the steady forest breeze to light a cigarette.

Tobacco killed, but rarely in the way it did this time. While Juan Doe lit his smoke, Bolan came up behind him in a nearly silent rush, clapped his left hand over the target's mouth and chin, wrenched his head around and drove the blade into his brain stem from the right.

Instead of fighting for his life, the guard collapsed into unconsciousness and death, resembling a giant puppet with its strings cut as he slumped in Bolan's grasp. The rifle slung across his shoulder made a faint metallic sound on contact with the pavement, but the sound lacked decibels enough to travel far.

One down. The other also had to die before he could destroy the helicopters and proceed.

Counting the seconds in his mind, half listening for gunfire from the compound proper, Bolan slipped around the nose of the Agusta A109 Hirundo, keeping the larger bulk of the Super Puma between himself and the surviving sentry on the helipad. Some sixty feet of empty concrete lay between the choppers, leaving either free to lift off without fear of damaging the other's rotor blades.

During his transit from one chopper to the other, Bolan was exposed to anyone inside the compound who might glance in his direction and observe him. For that reason, he avoided slinking, shunned the hasty movements that would attract attention, mark him as a stranger in a hurry. All he had to do was to stroll across the pad, taking his time, holding the knife well down beside his thigh. Its dark blade, streaked with blood, reflected no moonbeams.

He reached the Super Puma, risked a quick glance at the second sentry through its cockpit window. The guard's back was turned, but any slight sound from Bolan as he made his way around the chopper might alert him, bring the rifle off his shoulder for a close-range killing shot.

Just wait.

Concealed from the surviving sentry's view, Bolan checked his watch. Guzman should have subdued the tower guards by now, unless he had been spotted during his approach. And even then, Bolan anticipated gunfire from the compound, signaling his failure. If he heard nothing within—

Pop! Pop!

Were those gunshots? The background noise of drums and tubas, voices straining to their limit on another Nazi marching song, obscured the sound.

Bolan stretched for another quick glimpse of the sentry, who apparently had missed the sounds or else chose to ignore them. When no shouts or screams arose within the compound, Bolan thought perhaps his ears were playing tricks on him.

Then a machine gun opened fire, raking the crowd around the bonfire, muzzle-flashes winking from the tower Guzman had selected as his goal.

Bolan was moving as the sentry turned in that direction, cursing softly, grappling with his rifle. The young German had already taken three steps toward the battleground when Bolan clutched him from behind and drove the eight-inch blade between his ribs, through muscle and lung tissue, clipping the aorta with its razor edge.

The second sentry took a little longer dying, bleeding out inside, but time was relative. It may have felt like nothing to the dying man, a candle flickering before it was extinguished, but it seemed like hours to the Executioner. At last, the young man shuddered in his grasp and died.

Wiping the knife with two quick strokes across his second victim's tunic, Bolan sheathed it, palmed a frag grenade and turned back toward the Super Puma's cockpit.

It was time to raise some hell.

NASSER KHALIL HEARD THE FIRST gunshots, stiffened slightly, half turned toward Muhunnad Qadir at his left side, then told himself that one of Dietrich's Nazis had to have fired a pistol in the general excitement of the celebration.

It was Khalil's first birthday party for a long-dead German dictator. For all he knew, gunfire directed at the moon and stars might be routine. For all he knew, the dancing Germans might rip off their clothes and leap into the bonfire.

No such luck, he thought, and nearly smiled.

Until the next shots suddenly exploded overhead.

This time there could be no mistaking the machine gun, or the fact that it was firing toward the party crowd. In the split second prior to grabbing Muhunnad Qadir and covering him with Khalil's own body, Nasser saw the muzzle-flashes from a tower on the far side of the compound, winking at him like a semaphore message of death.

"Stay down!" he warned the man who struggled underneath him. "They are shooting at us!"

But from what Khalil could see, that was not strictly true. If anything, the German lookout in the tower seemed intent on taking down his own people, rather than singling out Hans Dietrich's non-Teutonic visitors. As Khalil watched, the bullets gutted half a dozen startled dancers, pitching one of them into the fire, dropping the others close enough beside it that they had to have felt the heat, if they were still alive.

"We need cover!" Khalil shouted to his companions and the men who had accompanied Qadir. "We need our weapons!"

Roughly half of them broke from the little clutch they'd

formed instinctively at the first sound of shots. Those sprinted for their quarters, where a closet bristled with Kalashnikov assault rifles. Khalil produced a compact autoloading pistol from beneath his baggy shirt, considered firing at the guard tower, but then decided it would be a waste of energy and ammunition.

Suddenly two more machine guns opened up, blazing away above the screaming, panicked crowd. Khalil cringed for a moment, then discovered that the tardy guns were firing on the first guard tower, spraying slugs in the direction of their erstwhile comrades.

What in God's name was happening?

Khalil knew only that he had to move, and quickly, before someone's gunfire pinned him to the earth for good.

"Get up, sir!" he hissed at Muhunnad Qadir. "We must go now!"

Qadir struggled to rise, Khalil assisting him, and ran with shoulders hunched in the direction of their bungalow. Behind them, sentries from the settlement's perimeter had joined the other tower guards, firing at the maniacal machine gunner on high. Their bullets did not seem to faze him, but Khalil knew it was only a matter of time before someone got lucky and dropped the shooter.

"He must be deranged," Qadir said as they reached the shelter of the small house next to theirs. "No wonder that we find a madman here, among so many."

But Khalil was not so sure.

Suppose this shooter—if he was alone, in fact—was part of the invading team Hans Dietrich feared, which had already killed more than two dozen at Colonia Victoria. What, then? Were others lurking in the forest, creeping forward to attack the compound at that very moment?

As if triggered by his very thoughts, a flash of light and sound erupted from the helipad, perhaps a hundred yards distant. Almost at the same instant, yet another blast sounded from the direction of the compound's motor pool, echoed by more explosions like a string of giant firecrackers.

"Quickly!" Khalil told Muhunnad Qadir. "We must retrieve our weapons and get out of there!"

JORGE GUZMAN COULD NOT have named the weapon he was firing if his life depended on it. It was, in fact, a Belgian MAG—for Maitrailleuse d'Appui Général, or general-purpose machine gun—adopted for use by more than seventy-five nations worldwide. Belt-fed and chambered for the standard 7.62 mm NATO round, the weapon weighed twenty-four pounds with its bipod attached, and fired at an adjustable cyclic rate of 650 to 1,000 rounds per minute.

Guzman had no idea of the current setting, but he had quickly mastered the MAG's simple reloading procedure, inspired by the German MG42 so widely used in World War II. When one belt was exhausted, all he had to do was lift the trap on top of the receiver, place the first round of another belt in place, then close the trap and fire.

Simple.

The real trick, as he'd quickly learned, was ducking bullets from the other guard towers and from the crowd below him.

But Hans Dietrich had been clever. When the towers were erected, each of the three snipers' nests was armored against gunfire from the sides, and from below. Even the trapdoor had a sheet of steel layering its inner surface, clanking when Guzman stepped on it, shifting back and forth in search of targets.

And there was no shortage of those in the firelight, ducking and leaping as Guzman swung the MAG's muzzle in wide arcs, spraying death into the Nazi ranks below his lofty perch. None of the revelers had visibly reacted when he'd shot the tower guards, one lucky bullet each, but there was no ignoring Guzman when he cut loose with the MAG, firing directly at the bonfire dancers and their band.

What strange and mournful sounds the tuba players made when bullets struck their bodies and their instruments at 2,730 feet per second. Some of them sounded like moaning dinosaurs as they fell, while others simply screamed like dying men.

Guzman felt as if he was in a trance, like someone hypnotized and ordered to perform some action that was alien to him. And yet, the throbbing weapon in his hands felt right. It did not torment him to see the advocates of global genocide fall thrashing to the ground with gaping, bloody wounds.

He was in full command of the compound, until the gunners in the other towers started firing at him. Even though their bullets could not penetrate the waist-high walls of Guzman's aerie, he was forced to duck and crawl below their line of fire, rising to duel with them from corners where they least expected him. Fire from the ground was less important, passing by at angles that made hits unlikely, but he knew he was surrounded now.

That he was never getting down.

The small crate of grenades surprised him, but he guessed that Dietrich had prepared for any possible emergency. They weren't the old "potato masher" model used by Wehrmacht troops in World War II, resembling tin cans fastened onto wooden handles. These looked more like small green apples, with a ring and detonator mounted where the stem should be. Guzman had never used a hand grenade before, but he had seen enough movies to grasp the concept.

Pull the pin and throw.

He lobbed one toward the bonfire without looking, heard the solid crump of its explosion seconds later, and was satisfied. He tossed two more over the side, one toward the band, one in the general direction of the ground fire that was peppering his roost.

More screams below, some of them sounding like death rattles to his ringing ears.

And it was time to duel the tower gunners once again.

Which tower first?

He chose one, on a whim, and braced the MAG against his shoulder, rising to his knees and hammering a long burst toward the enemies he couldn't even see.

DESTROYING VEHICLES WAS EASY, although Cohen lacked sufficient hand grenades to blow them all at once. Instead, she waited until Guzman started firing from his tower, then approached the first Hummer in line, smashed in a window with her rifle's stock, and dropped one of her two grenades into the driver's seat.

She was already moving when it blew, triggering 2- and 3-round bursts into the fuel tanks of each vehicle she passed in turn, laying a trail of gasoline behind her as the first Hummer erupted into roiling flames. It only took a heartbeat for the fumes to catch, and then the line of trucks and cars was swallowed by a chain of secondary blasts that left her ears humming.

The off-road bikes were last in line, and Cohen sprayed them with a full half-magazine, stitching their gas tanks and their fat tires full of holes. Across the compound, she saw fireballs rising from the heliport and knew that anyone who fled the compound would be traveling on foot.

Retreating from the sudden heat of burning vehicles, Cohen dropped the empty magazine from her rifle and snapped in a fresh one. More grenade blasts from the center of the compound drew her gaze in that direction, but she could not peg their source. Cooper had clearly used his two grenades to wreck the helicopters, and it made no sense that Dietrich's soldiers would be lobbing hand grenades among their own people.

What, then?

Had Guzman's tower been equipped with more than a machine gun? If it had, she reckoned that the squat Colombian would prove more difficult to kill than she had first imagined.

Or a lucky round might take him down before he had a chance to fire another shot.

That fear, at least, was laid to rest as Guzman started dueling with the Nazis in the other two guard towers, matching their incoming gunfire nearly burst for burst. He strafed one tower, then the other, moving back and forth with an agility that came as some surprise to the Mossad agent.

She had clearly underestimated him, in terms of skill, courage and ruthlessness.

Around the bonfire, sprawling corpses testified that he had listened to her last-minute advice, playing no favorites among the Nazis based on sex. She could not count the fallen, and it hardly mattered, unless Hans Dietrich was one of them.

Time to find out.

Cohen circled away from the line of burning vehicles, jogging to her left, watching for sentries as she made her way into the settlement. Most of the guards on the perimeter had been distracted at first by the fire from Guzman's tower, but now some were returning to the helipad and motor pool, in search of enemies who weren't secure inside an armor-plated sniper's post some twenty feet above their heads.

Two of the sentries came toward Cohen with the bonfire's light behind them, double-timing toward the shattered vehicles that once had been their lifeline to the outside world. She could not tell if either one of them had seen her yet, and waiting to find out was tantamount to suicide.

Kneeling, she shot the nearer of the runners in the chest and dropped him, swung her weapon's muzzle slightly to the right and found the second dodging, looking frantically for cover.

Her second short burst spun the second target through a clumsy pirouette and dropped him facedown in the dirt. His fingers scrabbled briefly at the soil, as if trying to dig a foxhole for himself, then he lay still.

Young men, from what she'd seen of them, in classic Wehrmacht uniforms.

Not Dietrich, then.

She rose and moved on, searching for the one man in Colonia Victoria who absolutely, positively, had to die.

CHAPTER SEVENTEEN

Bolan was off and running, even as the shock waves from the second helicopter's detonation rocked the compound. He moved rapidly, with shoulders hunched, hearing the shrapnel hiss and whicker overhead. In front of him, on the far side of the compound, he could see the motor pool engulfed by roiling flames. The bonfire in the compound's midst now seemed like a reflection of the other, larger fires.

Around it, all was chaos.

Jorge Guzman, in his high nest, had a raging duel in progress with the gunners in the other guard towers. Bolan could see his shadow duck and weave, firing in one direction, then another. Every time incoming bullets drove him under cover, frag grenades came arching from the platform where he sheltered, wreaking havoc on the Nazis and their native mercenaries down below.

Bolan left Guzman to it, homing on the bungalow he'd marked as Dietrich's home during his first reconnaissance of the compound. The leader's bungalow was larger than the others set aside for families, presumably denoting Dietrich's status as the heir to Adolf Hitler's bloody throne. A flagpole, offset slightly from the leader's bungalow's front porch, displayed a large swastika banner flapping in the fire-whipped breeze.

Where were the guards Bolan had been expecting? He supposed that some of them had joined the skirmish line firing at Guzman's tower. Others should be watching over Dietrich, though, assuming that their lord and master had retreated to his quarters when the feces hit the fan. Their absence told him Dietrich wasn't in the bungalow, but Bolan had to check it out, regardless.

He had one foot on the porch steps when someone behind him shouted a command in German. Bolan understood the tone, if not the words. He was the only white man in the compound dressed in camouflage fatigues instead of SS black or Wehrmacht gray, and that made him the enemy.

He spun and dropped into a crouch, raising his Steyr AUG before he had a clear fix on the target. Twenty feet in front of him, and slightly to his left, a lean man in a uniform that had gone out of style in 1945 stood, aiming a pistol at Bolan's face.

Or rather, at the place where Bolan's face had been before he hit his crouching pose.

The pistol bucked and sent a bullet whistling over Bolan's head. It drilled Dietrich's front door, as Bolan's rifle spit a 3-round burst, the 5.56 mm manglers ripping through his target's chest, making the ex-live Nazi part of history.

Before another member of the tribe could spot him, Bolan turned and rushed the bungalow's front door. A kick proved that it wasn't built to keep determined enemies outside. Bolan swept through the six rooms, probing closets, ducking for a look beneath Hans Dietrich's king-size bed, and found no one. On his way out, he swung the Steyr's butt to smash the glass covering Hitler's stern-faced portrait in the living room. It toppled to the floor and shattered as he cleared the front door, hesitating on the porch.

Guzman was still alive and fighting, lobbing hand grenades and spraying bullets as if he had all the ammo in the world at his disposal. When he emptied the machine gun, Guzman still would have his rifle and two pistols, but it would become a very different game.

He was already fighting for his life, but if he lingered in the tower too much longer, it would simply be a matter of postponing certain death.

Unless, that is, he got some help from allies on the ground.

Bolan was still seeking his top-priority targets—Hans Dietrich, Naldo Aznar, anybody from the Sword of Allah—but he would accomplish nothing by a mad dash through the furious, chaotic crowd, killing and checking faces afterward.

That kind of frantic action was a ticket to disaster. It was far better to have a plan, and Bolan hatched one on the spot.

Instead of trying to read Dietrich's mind—or Aznar's or Khalil's—he set off toward the building that he'd marked as the repository of Colonia Victoria's spare arms and ammunition. He could raise hell there and possibly help Guzman in the bargain.

All he had to do was get there in one piece, find what he sought and blow the rest, then take the other tower gunners by surprise.

Simple.

Except that he'd be jogging sixty yards or so across the open compound, with armed Nazis milling all around him, while Guzman fired random automatic bursts into the crowd. He didn't have a clue where Gabriella Cohen was, but he wished her well.

Another forty-seven minutes remained before the cut-off time they had agreed to in advance, and so far Bolan hadn't seen one of his major targets in the flesh.

But they were out there, somewhere, waiting for him.

He could feel it in his gut.

Without a backward glance at Dietrich's cut-rate palace, Bolan launched himself in the direction of the compound's armory. He ran as if his life depended on it.

Which it did.

"HURRY!" Naldo Aznar snapped at his men. "Let's go!" When half of them stood rooted in their places, Aznar shouted at them once again. "Come on! We're getting out of here!"

They moved at last, some of them seeming to emerge from shock by slow degrees. Perhaps they'd never seen killing on this scale in their lives, but that was no excuse for freezing up at the first gunshot or glimpse of blood.

"How will we go, boss?" one of them asked.

"The helicopter's gone," another said. "It's burning, like the cars."

"We all have legs," Aznar replied, "unless you want to wait around and have them blown off at the hip."

Another hand grenade exploded at that moment, twenty-five or thirty yards away, as if the enemy had planned to emphasize Aznar's comment. There was no further hesitation when he left the sheltered space between two bungalows, where he had huddled with his men after the shooting started.

"This way. Follow me."

They obeyed, falling into line behind him, forming a rough column of twos as Aznar led them away from the heart of the compound, toward the tree line and the stygian darkness beyond.

"We go in there, boss?" one of the gunmen closest to him asked.

"Shut up!" he snapped, then paused long enough to tell them all, over the sounds of automatic gunfire from the compound, "Where else can we go? Where else is safe?"

One of them raised a hand, childlike. "If we get lost—"

"Then we shall wait for dawn, stupid," he answered. "Even here, the sun still rises in the east and travels toward the west."

"Yes, sir."

"Can we leave now?" Aznar challenged them. "Or shall we waste more precious time with foolish questions, until all of us are dead?"

Grim silence answered him. When he was satisfied, Aznar turned toward the forest once again and set off at a loping run. His men could either keep up with him or be left behind to die.

In fact, Aznar knew that the course of action he'd chosen was hardly ideal. He assumed they would be lost before they'd traveled half a mile into the forest, but so what? The light and noise behind them would prevent them doubling back toward Dietrich's compound and the worst danger. Beyond that, they were all well armed and Aznar had his sat phone.

How lost could they get?

The woods were dark, but they were not in a steaming rain forest. There were no jaguars, crocodiles or anacondas waiting to devour him and his men. If they were forced to cross a stream and get their feet wet, they would simply buy new shoes and slacks when they returned to town. If some idiot fell down and broke his leg, they could decide whether to carry him or to leave him with a bullet in the head to seal his lips.

But Naldo Aznar would survive the trek, in any case.

It was his destiny.

And Hans Dietrich would suffer for the hell to which his guests had been subjected. The decrepit Nazi already owed Aznar for the deaths of fifteen soldiers. Now the sheer indignity of fleeing through the forest in the middle of the night was being added to his tab.

When Aznar was relaxing, safe at home, he would consider Dietrich's punishment. The simple answer was to kill him, but perhaps Aznar should hit the bastard in his pocketbook, instead.

How many kilos of cocaine, delivered free of charge, would it require to make amends for fifteen lives? For Aznar's helicopter? For his personal humiliation?

As he thrashed and stumbled through the forest undergrowth, it suddenly occurred to Aznar that Hans Dietrich might be dead already—or, if still alive, that he might not survive the night. And while his life meant less than nothing to Aznar, per se, the prospect caused Aznar to curse Dietrich once more, for making enemies who jeopardized their partnership and who might put a painful crimp in Aznar's yearly profits.

Goddamned crazy bastard. So obsessed with killing Jews he'd never even met that he would sacrifice a fortune to his personal insanity.

Aznar made up his mind while he was tugging to release his left pant leg from clinging thorns. If Dietrich managed to defeat the enemies hell-bent on killing him this night, Aznar would put the old man out of his misery, scatter his lunatic Nazis and claim Colonia Victoria for himself. Once certain palms were greased, Aznar was confident the government would not complain. Some politicians, he supposed, might be relieved. Even the faraway Israelis should be pleased.

It wasn't often that Naldo Aznar devised a plan that would please nearly everyone—excluding, always, the persistent drug-enforcement agents from America. If they had known what Aznar had in mind for Dietrich's coca crop, the DEA might have sent troops to help defend the Nazi and his followers.

Too late.

Whichever way the present battle went, Dietrich was finished. He just didn't know it, yet.

JORGE GUZMAN HAD TWO BELTS of machine-gun ammunition left, coiled neatly into metal boxes, but he didn't know that meant that he was down to his last 440 rounds. He also didn't know that the MAG's manual recommended switching barrels after every second belt on sustained fire, but it would have made no difference.

Guzman had no replacement barrel, and would not have known how to install one if there'd been a knee-high stack of them available. He *did* know that the weapon's barrel had become uncomfortably warm, but that was understandable. As far as he could tell, it had not spoiled his aim, although he'd had no luck eliminating his opponents in the other two guard towers.

They would kill him soon, Guzman supposed. Either a lucky shot would strike him as he rose to fire his weapon, or some Nazi on the ground would lob a hand grenade into his nest while he was busy ducking bullets, dueling with the other tower gunmen.

One way or another, Guzman knew his time was running out. So be it.

He had not really expected to survive the fight, after he volunteered to storm the tower and provide the cover fire for his companions. Guzman had not understood the impulse when it seized him, and he certainly could not explain it now, not even to himself.

He wasn't suicidal, although a casual observer might conclude the opposite. When he'd decided on his task, insisted on performing it despite the best advice from Cooper and from Cohen, it had simply filled a need to do something. It was his contribution to the cause.

And now, it was about to end his life.

Two belts of ammunition left, and three more hand grenades. When all of that was gone, he had his rifle, half a dozen extra magazines and the two pistols wedged under his belt.

Not much, against so many enemies, but it would have to do.

At least, for the time he had left.

Guzman was rising to fire another burst toward the western guard tower, when a massive explosion erupted behind it, sending flames into the air some twenty feet above the nearest tower. Guzman saw his human targets turning, cringing from the heat and shock wave of the blast, but something on the ground caused him to miss the providential moment.

What was it?

Matt Cooper! He was running from the site of the explosion, firing short bursts from his automatic rifle at the nearest Nazis and their native troops. As Guzman watched, he dropped three men then ducked beneath the western tower, sheltering beside one of its vertical supports.

What was he doing now? By firelight, it appeared that he was stooping, taking something from a satchel slung across his shoulder, reaching down to—

Bullets rattled from the armor of Guzman's platform, forcing him to duck and lose his view of Cooper. The Colombian turned and duck-walked toward the south side of his platform, angling his MAG in that direction, ready to respond.

Before he rose and fired, though, something made him glance back toward the western tower. He was just in time to feel another blast and see its flames rise toward the platform where his enemies were crouching, safe from Guzman's bullets. Now they rose, their faces twisted with the cries of alarm, as their guard tower dipped, leaned crazily and then collapsed away from Guzman, toward the blazing furnace of the compound's armory.

He understood, now. Cooper was assisting him, trying to save his life. It might be wasted effort, but at least Guzman could cover the American if Cooper tried to reach the southern tower.

Rising with a fierce smile on his lips, Guzman leveled his MAG and held its trigger down, pouring a storm of bullets toward his enemies.

GABRIELLA COHEN SAW THE FAR GUARD tower fall, its structure shattering on impact with the ground, spilling its occupants like broken mannequins and crushing several stragglers with its weight. A man who might have been Matt Cooper, dressed in camouflage fatigues and taller than the average Colombian, ran from the flaming ruin toward the southern tower, while Jorge Guzman distracted the opposing gunners with another long burst from his MAG.

Teamwork.

She could have joined them, made it three against the tower, but she had already used up her grenades, and she had other prey in mind.

If Hans Dietrich was still alive, she meant to remedy that situation. And if he was dead…then, what? How would she ever know?

He might be cooking in the shattered armory right now or lying shot somewhere amid the chaos that consumed Colonia Victoria. How would she ever know, unless she stumbled over him by accident?

Keep looking! the small voice inside her head demanded. *If you don't find Dietrich, there's still Nasser, still Qadir, still terrorists and Nazis all around you.*

In another heartbeat, she was moving, seeking faces that she recognized from memory. In the confusion, no one seemed to notice her at first. Around her, other women carried weapons, but she was the only one decked out in jungle-fighting garb, and that eventually registered with two young blondes—twins in their twenties, from the look of them—who called to her in German.

"Halt, Jude!"

Cohen faced them squarely, saw the pistols that they held helped them on their way to hell with two bursts from her mini-Uzi, muffled by its sound suppressor and by the chaos in the compound.

The young women fell together, trembling through their death throes as they once had snuggled in the womb. It seemed a waste of precious life to Cohen, but the choice was theirs, and once they'd made it there could be no turning back. No second chance.

She let the mini-Uzi dangle on its sling and clutched her rifle as she moved deeper into the madness of the camp. A short Colombian in cammo clothes that matched her own ran toward her, empty handed, babbling in rapid-fire Spanish, but she tuned him out and dropped him with a buttstroke to the face. He might survive, if he was very lucky, and she didn't feel like gunning down an unarmed man.

Not that one, anyway.

It was a different story when a pseudo-SS officer lurched into Cohen's path. He'd lost his cap somehow, with its impressive silver death's-head, and a ragged scalp wound veiled the left side of his face in crimson. He was wobbly on his feet, his hands empty, but she couldn't tell about the black flap-holster on his belt.

Blue eyes swam in and out of focus in the firelight as he spotted her and registered her difference. "Who are you?" he demanded.

Cohen remained silent, squeezing off a 3-round burst that splashed his black tunic with red to match his face.

The Nazi sat, hard, then raised one arm as if to reach for her, perhaps to clutch her throat. She thought about her grandparents in Auschwitz, and her next shot was a reflex action, drilling the Nazi above his left eye.

She stepped around him and kept going, pausing only when another echo of machine-gun fire from the opposing towers suddenly demanded her attention. Cohen ducked into the shadow of a nearby bungalow, found no one hiding there and paused a moment to survey the battleground.

Guzman was firing at the Nazis in the other elevated sniper's nest, ducking as they returned fire. Sudden movement at the base of Guzman's tower drew her eyes to ground level, and she saw a group of soldiers, three or four, huddled around the ladder that would take them up to challenge him.

Cursing, she brought the rifle to her shoulder, sighting at the targets who were sixty yards or more distant from her position. Other people ran between her and the soldiers grouped beneath the tower, spoiling Cohen's aim.

She felt an urge to rush across the open ground and take them by surprise, but two of them were climbing now, and the Mossad agent knew she'd be too late. Instead, she held the rifle steady, set for 3-round bursts, and closed her mind to any suicidal runners who might pass in front of its muzzle as she fired.

Her first burst seemed to miss, although the top man on the ladder turned his head in her general direction, pressing closer to the upright ladder, as if it could somehow shelter him.

She made a small adjustment in her aim, then fired a second burst. This time the lead climber lurched sideways, off the ladder, tumbling headfirst to the ground among his comrades.

Number two was fumbling with a weapon when she shot him off the ladder, maybe hoping that he could defend himself against an unseen long-range enemy. Although the firelight made it difficult to say, his head seemed to explode before he toppled backward, scattering the soldiers crouched around his fallen friend.

The other two returned fire, in a vague and aimless way that never sent their slugs within ten yards of Cohen. One of them was turning, just about to run, when she shot him in the back. The other stood his ground and died firing his weapon from the hip, an empty gesture of defiance that accomplished nothing.

She had lost count of those she'd killed, not much for keeping score, but none of them were those she'd come to find. Alive or dead, Dietrich, Qadir and Khalil were still waiting for her, somewhere in the compound.

Cohen checked the magazines on both her rifle and the mini-Uzi, then went out to find them.

OTTO JAEGER FOUND Hans Dietrich crawling on all fours behind the compound's mess hall. Even coming up behind him that way, Jaeger recognized the custom-tailored suit.

"Mr. Dietrich!" Jaeger called, jogging to overtake the crawling man. "Are you all right? Here, let me help you."

Dietrich gaped at Jaeger for a moment, as if staring at a stranger's face, then cautiously accepted Jaeger's hand and struggled to his feet. His clothes were soiled, one knee exposed by torn trousers, but he seemed otherwise unharmed.

"My leader, are you wounded?"

"No," Dietrich said. "There were explosions. I—I don't… Otto, what's happening? What's happening?"

"Our enemies have found us. Many of our people have been killed or wounded," Jaeger said. "Sir, I'm not sure if we can hold. The best thing for you now is to escape."

"Flee?" Dietrich echoed him. "I am not a coward!"

"No, sir. I do not suggest it. But perhaps the wise thing is to find another place and start again. In 1945—"

"This isn't 1945!" Dietrich snapped, his voice raised loud enough that Jaeger feared it would betray them to their prowling enemies. "I'm not a teenager, for God's sake! Do you suppose that I can start again, at my age, and create another haven for our people?"

"Sir, I only mean—"

"That I should run away. I heard you perfectly, Otto."

"To save yourself! Who else can lead us?"

"Who is left to lead?" Dietrich asked. "Who remains, after this night?"

"My leader—"

"I lead nothing!" Dietrich shouted at him, wild-eyed. "Listen to my followers, my children, dying as we speak!"

Jaeger could hear the shots, the screams, the gunfire and the crackling of flames. They echoed in his head like the sound track for hell on Earth.

"How many are there?" Dietrich asked him.

"Sir?"

"How many enemies inside the compound, idiot?"

Jaeger could only flinch and take it, so conditioned was he to obedience, but even without knowing it, his knuckles whitened as he clutched his IMBEL MD-A1 submachine gun.

"I don't know, sir."

"Perhaps only the three reported from the village, earlier? Could that be true, Otto?"

"Sir," Jaeger answered stiffly, "it has been impossible to count them."

"When you're busy running, I suppose it's difficult," Dietrich replied. "Give me your weapon."

"Sir?"

"Give me your weapon!"

Jaeger did as he was told, then quickly drew his pistol from its holster, half convinced that Dietrich meant to kill him. If the old man tried—

"Now, come with me!"

"What are you doing, sir?"

"You want a leader, Otto? Then you follow me, goddamn it!"

Without another word or backward glance, Dietrich turned toward the sounds of battle on the far side of the mess hall, moving with determined strides to join the fight. Jaeger went after him, uncertain as to what else he could do.

You can get out, he thought. Get out and save yourself.

But there would be no coming back, in that case, if Dietrich somehow managed to defeat the still-unknown invaders. He could not come crawling back in that event, would only face a firing squad if he attempted it. Dietrich would certainly remember Jaeger's shame.

Unless…

The back of Dietrich's head and neck were close enough for Jaeger to reach out and touch. It would be simple, just a heartbeat's work, to raise his pistol, aim and fire into the leader's brain. Whatever happened next, whether his Aryans were slaughtered or emerged victorious, no one would link Dietrich's death to Otto Jaeger.

Never, in a million years.

It was a grave temptation, but he could not follow through. Jaeger owed everything—his personality, ideals, his very life itself—to Hans Dietrich. Born in Colonia Victoria and nurtured there, brought up to serve the Master Race, he could not yield to cowardice and sacrifice the only leader he had ever known to save himself.

It was unthinkable. Better to turn the pistol on himself and die immediately, than to live with such oppressive shame.

Like every other soldier in the colony, Jaeger had sworn a solemn oath to follow Dietrich into hell itself, if need be.

Now, he swallowed back his fear and did just that.

ARTURO OBREGON KNEW he was getting closer to the battle when he saw firelight glowing through distant trees. He was not close enough to smell the smoke yet—or the gunsmoke, for that matter—but the crack and pop of small-arms fire was growing louder by the moment, punctuated by explosions great and small.

And from the sound of it, his men were both outnumbered and outgunned.

There was a good chance that before he reached the compound, most of the hostiles would kill one another. If they had not managed it by then, he could hang back and give them more time to complete the job, waiting and watching to select his targets for the grand finale.

It was not exactly by-the-book police work, but the DAS was known for cutting corners, bending rules, ignoring certain statutes altogether when it suited Director Menendez and the wealthy men who pulled his strings. In fact, the plan hatching in Obregon's uneasy mind would suit Menendez perfectly.

But first, they had to reach the compound to find out exactly what in holy hell was going on.

Before they'd started east from their insertion point, when the first sounds of battle echoed from the distant settlement, Obregon had picked a scout to lead the way. That officer was fifty yards or so in front of Obregon, just barely visible by moonlight as he flitted through the trees. If he'd been any faster on his feet—

Dammit! Why had he stopped?

Before the scout could offer any verbal warning, Obregon himself heard men approaching through the forest, taking no great care to keep their voices down or to move with anything resembling stealth. He recognized the sounds of Spanish, even though his ears could not pick out the words.

Not Germans, then.

But who?

Obregon hissed and signaled to the troops behind him, fanning them into a skirmish line. Their gear and weapons rattled as they jogged into position, making too much noise to suit him, but the faceless men advancing toward them did not seem to notice.

Obregon's lone scout fell back to join his comrades, whispering, "Two dozen, boss. Maybe more. Not German."

"No. We'll stop them here," Obregon said, hoping he sounded calm and confident.

Another moment passed before he saw the first man-shadows moving toward him. Moonlight glinted here and there, on gun barrels.

"Stop where you are!" Obregon called to them. "Drop your weapons!"

The shadow figures partially obeyed him. They stopped where they stood, but did not drop their weapons.

"Who is that?" one of the faceless gunmen demanded.

Obregon identified himself, repeating his command for the strangers to lay down their weapons. None complied, but one of them called back to him, "Don't worry. We're friends."

"Tell me your name, friend!" Obregon demanded, scowling at the night.

After a moment's hesitation the apparent leader of the group replied, "Naldo Aznar. You recognize the name, I think?"

Obregon swallowed a bitter surge of bile and clutched his M-16 more tightly. "Lay your weapons down," he ordered once again. "Come forward with your empty hands raised and be recognized."

Another hesitation before someone in the shadows opposite replied, "Fuck this.

When the shooting started, Obregon was braced and ready for it, crouched beside a tree that offered cover from at least some of the hostile shooters on the firing line directly opposite. He ducked, squirmed lower, as the first rounds whistled overhead, and heard one of them strike the scout beside him, the young man cursing as he fell.

"Fire!" he shouted. But the command was drowned out, blown away by smoky thunder, as his men returned fire, pouring rounds into the ducking, weaving figures on the other side of no-man's land.

Now that the worst had happened, now that battle had been joined, Obregon was startled to discover that he wasn't petrified with fear. Instead his rage took over, steadying his hands as he took aim and fired a short burst toward a human shape some twenty yards in front of him.

The figure lurched, rocked on its unseen heels and fell.

One down, out of two dozen, maybe more.

And as he chose another target, Obregon knew something else.

At this rate, he might never reach Colonia Victoria at all. The battle raging there, much larger than his own, was someone else's problem. He was focused solely on survival and the swift eradication of his enemies.

Naldo Aznar.

One of Colombia's "most wanted" men, though no one in authority made any effort to arrest him. Bringing Aznar's carcass back to Bogotá would either make or break Arturo Obregon's career.

And at the moment, as he dropped another shadow man into the weeds, it didn't seem to matter which.

COHEN NEVER FOUND Hans Dietrich, but she met the Arabs quite by accident—or was it Fate? They were emerging from a bungalow, or possibly from behind the bungalow, and moving in the general direction of the helipad. She counted ten in all, and recognized the two leaders.

It was a moment when she simply could have cut them down with her assault rifle, empty the magazine into their bursting flesh and follow with the mini-Uzi if she thought that any of them still survived,

She could have.

But she didn't.

Knowing it was foolish, even as she raised her voice to make it heard above the sounds of combat all around them, Cohen called to the retreating group in Arabic, "Khalil! Qadir! Where are you going?"

Whether it was hearing names, their native tongue or just an unfamiliar female voice, the small Sword of Allah party hesitated. Heads turned, seeking the woman. When they saw her, every man looked surprised.

Why not?

A strikingly attractive woman stood in front of them, obviously neither German nor Colombian, dressed as a soldier, with an automatic rifle in her hands and other weapons dangling from her hip and shoulder.

Before any of the assembled terrorists could speak, she asked, "Where did you think you could hide from the Mossad?"

As they began to scatter, raising weapons, Cohen held down her rifle's trigger and raked the clutch of ten from right to left, then back again. She saw half of them fall, the others stumble, staggering to find some cover, fleeing the line of fire.

She couldn't tell if those still on their feet were wounded or if those who'd hit the ground were dead. Khalil and one or two of his assassins were returning fire, forcing her to retreat, still firing, toward the shelter of a nearby bungalow.

Once under cover, the Mossad agent switched out magazines, waited a moment, risked a glance around the corner and withdrew before a storm of bullets flayed her face.

She'd seen one of the standing soldiers grappling with Qadir, trying to lift him from the ground, and it had seemed that Muhunnad Qadir was awkwardly assisting in his own rescue.

Wounded, she thought, or he would not have fallen.

Which way would they go?

Not toward her, obviously, and she didn't think they would lurch into the middle of the compound, which had turned into a slaughterhouse. Those narrowed options meant they had to continue southward, toward the wreckage-littered helipad, or turn hard-right between the nearest bungalows and strike out for the camp's western perimeter, the woods beyond.

In either case, she could retreat and intercept them, put the line of bungalows between them as she ran, then either meet them as they suddenly appeared in front of her, heading westward, or pop out behind them once again, surprise them on their dead-end expedition to the helipad.

Whatever happened then, she knew this much: Khalil, Qadir and their companions would not find a helicopter waiting to evacuate them from Colonia Victoria.

She turned and ran, ignoring a stitch in her side. She turned another corner, running parallel to the Arab survivors, slowing to check the space between successive bungalows as she proceeded.

Nothing.

Cohen didn't know why anyone would risk death trekking to the helipad, when it was so clearly out of commission, but the strange choice made her work a little easier. Glancing behind her as she ran, confirming that none of the terrorists had raced around behind her once she left them, the woman kept pace with her enemies.

At last, she saw that only two more bungalows remained before she found herself on open ground, facing the former helipad. Dietrich had placed it thirty yards or so beyond the nearest structures, to reduce the disruption of takeoffs and landings. Now, the firelit space was just another killing ground.

She paused, peered down an empty passageway between the last two bungalows, then crept along it, rifle shouldered, ready to unleash more killing fire at the first sight of living enemies. Arriving at the other end, she listened first, heard no voices speaking in Arabic, and steeled herself to take one final look in each direction.

Had they pulled ahead of her? Were they behind her, just approaching, so that they would see her when she poked her head around the corner? If they'd passed, had they left someone covering their backs?

She held her breath and took the chance, a quick look to the left, then to the right.

They were beyond her, four men moving closer to the helipad, with two of them supporting Muhunnad Qadir between them. Walking on his own, Nasser Khalil was carrying some kind of automatic weapon, checking out the shadows at the far end of the final bungalow in line.

Almost exultant, Cohen stepped into the open, sighted on her targets from a range of twenty feet or less and took them down. No warning call, this time. No fancy footwork. The Israeli simply shot them in the back, then moved in closer, firing two rounds more into the heads of Muhunnad Qadir and Nasser Khalil.

When it was done, she felt the sharp stitch in her side again and raised a hand to ease the muscle spasm. Instantly, her palm was smeared with warm, fresh blood.

One of the Arabs had been lucky.

Cohen cursed, retreating into cover, setting down her rifle as she fumbled through the contents of her small first-aid kit.

Opening her shirt, she pressed a wad of gauze over the throbbing wound, and taped it to her blood-slick flesh as firmly as she could.

It was the best that she could manage, but it wouldn't last for long. If she remained to fight, she was as good as dead, with no prospect of finding Dietrich.

With determined strides, she put the slaughterhouse behind her, moving toward the rendezvous with Cooper and Guzman. She wondered whether either of them would arrive on time. If they would come at all.

And if they did, whether they would find Gabriella Cohen still alive.

BOLAN RECOGNIZED Hans Dietrich as he came around a corner of the compound's spacious mess hall, carrying an automatic rifle, followed by a bandaged man who clutched a pistol in his fist. Wherever he'd been hiding, it was clear to Bolan that the Führer of Colonia Victoria had found his nerve and was prepared for battle, even if it meant his death.

Which pleased the Executioner no end.

He raised the Steyr, sighted first on Dietrich's companion and slammed a bullet through his bandage-swaddled skull.

Despite the general cacophony around them, Bolan's shot made Dietrich flinch and turn, first glancing at the sprawled form of his sidekick, then facing in Bolan's general direction. Dietrich peered into the shadows, mouthed a German curse and raised his submachine gun.

Bolan squeezed off two more semiauto rounds and saw them strike Dietrich more-or-less dead center in the chest.

The impact staggered him, then dropped him to his knees. The SMG slipped from his fingers and he fell across it as he slumped facedown into the dust. Bolan could easily have fired again, into his cranium, but he was satisfied that Dietrich wouldn't feel it, didn't need an extra shove toward his reward, his punishment or pure oblivion.

Whatever waited for him on the other side, Dietrich was on his way.

And Bolan had about run out of time.

Firing had ceased from Guzman's tower, but he didn't know if that was good or bad. He didn't know where Naldo Aznar was, or any of the Arabs from the Sword of Allah. He could stay and search for them until sunrise, if that was what it took—or until someone gunned him down—but he had made a promise to his comrades.

He would meet them at the designated time and place, if he was able. And if neither of them made it, he would start the long trek back alone.

It wouldn't be the first time he had lost friends or companions on the battlefield. The Special Forces code required that no wounded or dead be left behind, but he was only human, after all. He wouldn't know if Cohen and Guzman were missing until one or both of them had missed the rendezvous. And by that time, it would be too late to return and search for bodies, even if he'd had some way to carry both of them through miles of forest, to their waiting car.

For what?

He focused on the meeting place and hoped that both of them would find it soon. He could afford to wait a little while, if they were late, but life was filled with deadlines that could never be postponed indefinitely.

Bolan left the compound as he'd entered it, a silent shadow gliding into deeper darkness, there and gone.

EPILOGUE

DSA Headquarters, Bogotá

Joaquin Menendez had his heart set on escape. Whatever it required, he needed to escape from the incessant shrilling of his telephone.

It had been ringing off the hook for almost hours now, since midnight on the day Hans Dietrich and so many of his Aryan disciples were annihilated at Colonia Victoria. Worse yet, they had not been alone.

His men were still reporting from the mountain battle-ground, along with a team of "special investigators" named in haste by the attorney general. That, in itself, had been an insult to Menendez, telling him that someone higher up the food chain did not trust him, but he still had confidence that he could ride out the storm.

Meanwhile, people he'd known and served for years, along with some he'd never heard of, were haranguing him with questions day and night. The fact that Menendez had answers for so few of them just made things worse.

Who were the ten Arabs found dead at Dietrich's colony,

armed with illegal weapons and carrying fraudulent passports?

What was Naldo Aznar doing at the compound with twenty-odd men on the night it fell? And why was he off in the woods when he met the DAS patrol led by Inspector Arturo Obregon?

For that matter, why was there a patrol in place at all? And if Menendez felt the need to send men to the colony, why were they air-dropped at a landing zone a mile from Dietrich's compound?

On the latter point, he had an answer already rehearsed, supported by newly promoted Captain Obregon from his hospital bed, where his left leg would be in traction for the next two weeks, repairing bullet-shattered bones.

According to the story, an informant had predicted "trouble" at the colony, but Menendez did not feel justified in troubling Señor Dietrich if there was no actual disturbance. Therefore, he'd dispatched Obregon's squad as a discreet preventive measure, just to be on the safe side. When Obregon heard gunfire, he had rushed toward the compound—and met the felon Naldo Aznar fleeing from the scene. Aznar's men fired the first shots, and it proved impossible to capture even one of them alive.

As for the rest…

Menendez could not say and would not speculate as to the link between Colombia's top cocaine runner and Hans Dietrich. Only full investigation, likely taking weeks or months, would show if they were friends, or if Aznar had played some role in the massacre. None of Colonia Victoria's shell-shocked survivors felt like talking at the moment—which, in fact, suited Menendez to a tee.

Concerning the dead Arabs, he'd had no idea on Earth who they might be, until a courier had left a package with the desk sergeant downstairs, then vanished on a motorcycle before anyone could question him. Inside the butcher's-paper wrapping, Menendez found two fat dossiers, identifying two of the dead as Muhunnad Qadir and Nasser Khalil. Both were officers of a Middle Eastern terrorist group, the Sword of Allah, and the eight men who'd died with them were presumably their bodyguards or soldiers. Skimming through the dossiers, Menendez found apparent evidence of their collusion with Hans Dietrich in a plan to launch a global war against Israel from his stronghold inside Colonia Victoria.

Menendez had concealed the dossier inside his private safe. No one on Earth besides himself possessed its combination, and the safe came fitted with a backup system that would instantly incinerate its contents if the door was forced by any means.

He could not share the story of Han Dietrich's outside terrorist activities with his superiors. It would destroy Menendez to admit that he had missed a group of globally notorious fugitives, not once but many times, as they flew in and out of Bogotá to visit Dietrich at Colonia Victoria. A veritable mob would clamor for his resignation, and Menendez would be lucky to escape with merely being stripped of honor, pay and benefits.

In fact, he might wind up in prison.

Once the bastards started digging, peering into shadowed corners at the DAS and documenting his malfeasance, there would be no end to it. Better to flee the country now, with the nest egg he'd socked away, than to be left with nothing, rotting in a cage.

But he'd suppressed the urge to panic, locked away the damning files and offered up a silent prayer that whoever had sent the dossiers to him would be satisfied with Dietrich's death and the disruption of his power base.

What would become of Dietrich's fellow lunatics, Menendez neither knew nor cared. Some of them were undocumented aliens who'd slipped into the country, one way or another, and attached themselves to Dietrich at his compound.

Those would be deported to their native lands, if such could be identified, or jailed until they felt inclined to talk. Aside from one or two old codgers who'd been living at the settlement since Dietrich set it up, the rest were all Colombian by birth, and therefore subject to the nation's laws, even if they professed undying loyalty to the German Fatherland.

Menendez was inclined to prosecute them on whatever charges seemed appropriate—sedition, gun-running, creating false passports and other ID papers, cocaine trafficking—but it was not his choice. The DAS investigated crimes and made arrests, but the attorney general's office took cases to court.

Which meant more phone calls, this or that attorney nagging him for details about this or that defendant, dragging on for months, perhaps for years. It made his stomach ache, just thinking of it, and Menendez knew he had to get away.

Not permanently. Only for an hour, maybe two. He'd called ahead to warn his mistress, and she was—of course—available at his pleasure. Menendez chose to drive himself, because he didn't want a driver answering the telephone and interrupting him.

No one in the office asked where he was going, and Menendez offered nothing as he left his fifth-floor office, rode the elevator down to the ground floor and walked out to the building's large fenced parking lot. His BMW M3 sedan sat waiting for him, polished to a lustrous sheen.

Menendez slipped into the driver's seat, already feeling better, more relaxed. He took a deep breath and released it slowly as he twisted the ignition key.

Next morning, a front-page report in *El Espectador* declared that the explosion had destroyed five cars, aside from that of its intended victim. Windows had been shattered for a block in all directions by the blast. The DAS was seeking leads in the assassination of its late director, but no one had yet determined how the bomber managed to avoid surveillance cameras in the parking lot. An editorial suggested that the bombing might be linked to the Colonia Victoria disaster, calling on the government to crack down, both on radicals and drug-related crime.

Israeli Embassy, Bogotá

MACK BOLAN AND JORGE GUZMAN presented false ID to armed guards at the gate and waited while a phone call cleared them for admission to the embassy. The same guards scanned them up and down with handheld wands, then frisked them for good measure, before passing them along to an unarmed escort.

These days, you couldn't be too careful with a pair of rugged-looking strangers off the street.

Their escort ushered them inside the embassy, directed them to sign a guest book while he studied their IDs once more, then handed each of them a clip-on plastic tag identifying them as Visitor in English and Hebrew. That ritual completed, he conveyed them to an elevator and rode with them to the third floor, where they moved past numbered doors and stopped at 309.

The escort knocked, received his summons from a female voice and held the door for them until they cleared the threshold. When it clicked behind him, Bolan turned and smiled at Gabriella Cohen.

"You look good," he said.

"Better, at least," she granted. "Please, come in! Sit down!"

She was in bed, but might have run to meet them if they hadn't waved her down, shaking their heads and warning her against undue exertion. As she settled back against a mound of pillows, Bolan saw a grimace steal across her face.

"It takes a while," he said. "The pain. You'll get there."

"So they keep on telling me," she answered. "It's the first time I've been shot, you know? I'm hoping it's the last."

"The second time's no better," Bolan told her.

"I've been warned," she said, then skipped tracks to another subject. "Did you hear about Menendez?"

"Hard to miss," Bolan said.

She raised a fist, index finger extended and made circling motions overhead, then risked a little shrug. Telling her visitors that someone might be eavesdropping, although she wasn't sure.

"It sounds like someone didn't think Menendez should escape his punishment," she said. "I wonder if it might be Naldo Aznar's people settling a score."

Or the Mossad, Bolan thought, dishing out a not-so-subtle warning to the government about collaboration with a gang of Nazi renegades.

"Could be," he said. "Most of the bombings in Colombia trace back to drugs or politics, or both."

"I think so, too," Cohen said, as she winked and shook her head.

So it was silently confirmed, and anyone who might be listening would know that Cohen had performed her duty, feeding her erstwhile companions the prescribed dose of disinformation.

"You will be going home soon, I suppose?" Guzman asked.

"In a few more days," she said. "I'm finished here. Will you be staying?"

"I don't know," Guzman replied. "I have been offered work in Mexico, with documents. It may be time for me to go, as well. I have no family."

"Sounds like a good idea," Cohen said. She asked Bolan, "Did you have a hand in this?"

"It's all Jorge," Bolan replied. "He went so far beyond the call on this job, he impressed some people."

"And came back without a scratch," she said. "I'm jealous."

"I've never been so frightened in my life—or so excited," Guzman said. "I knew I should be dead at any moment, but their aim was bad. They kept on missing me."

"You didn't miss," Bolan told him. "That was some performance, for a novice."

Guzman's smile faltered, his shoulders slumped a little. "When I said I was excited…understand, I did not mean that I—"

"Enjoyed it?" Bolan finished for him. "You were fighting for your life, for *our* lives. You came through it. What you're feeling now is called survivor's guilt. Don't let it get you down. There's nothing wrong with coming out of battle on your own two feet."

"I understand, but this is all still new to me. And with the job in Mexico…"

"I'd be surprised if it was anything like this," Bolan remarked. "I'd be surprised if you saw anything like this, ever again."

"I hope not," Guzman said, "but if it happens, then at least I'm ready for it. Yes?"

"No doubt about it," Bolan said. "You're ready, and then some."

A little moan from Cohen when she shifted on the bed told Bolan it was time to leave. He hadn't planned to stay long, in any case. They could've talked for hours, yet, and not said anything important.

There was nothing left to say.

Paths crossed in Bolan's world, lives intersected, then moved on. Tomorrow was not guaranteed to any man or woman, in the covert killing trade.

"Maybe I'll see you, sometime," Bolan said.

"Maybe," Cohen replied as she squeezed his hand.

Both knowing that it likely wouldn't happen.

"So, we'd better split," he told Guzman. "I've got a flight to catch."

El Dorado International Airport

BOLAN WAS GOING OUT as he'd come in, unarmed and using someone else's name. Guzman had done the driving chore and left his car—another rental—in the airport's short-term parking lot. Inside the terminal, they passed police in uniform, with submachine guns slung over their shoulders, and felt perfectly at ease.

Well, more or less.

There was still a risk of possible arrest, but Bolan wasn't worried. There were far too many people running interference now, from Washington and maybe Tel Aviv. If nothing else, they would be muddying the waters, giving him and Guzman time to slip away unnoticed.

"When's your flight to Mexico?" he asked Guzman as they were idling in the terminal.

"Tonight, at nine o'clock," Guzman replied. "I have my bags already, in the car."

"You'll do all right," Bolan predicted.

"I am not so sure."

"Don't sweat it, anyway. You got the job done. Pulled your weight, and then some. Anything from here on out should be a piece of cake."

Or, maybe not. Still, Bolan thought it couldn't hurt to boost the fledgling operative's confidence a little.

"And for you?" Guzman inquired. "What's next?"

"More of the same, I would imagine."

"It troubles you?"

The question took him by surprise. Bolan considered it and shook his head.

"Not for a long time now."

"I'm sorry," Guzman said.

"For what?"

"There is a great deal more to life, or should be. I hope to find more, one day."

"I take it one day at a time," Bolan replied.

"Ah, yes. Twelve steps."

"Something like that."

But Bolan wasn't looking for a cure, some magical recovery. He'd found his niche, and if it was a place in life most people would have trouble just imagining, much less surviving, it was still *his* niche.

The boarding call for Bolan's flight came over the loudspeakers, first in Spanish, then in English.

"You must go now," Guzman said.

"Looks like."

They shook hands solemnly and Guzman said, "Thank you."

"For what?"

"I'm not sure yet," Guzman replied, and flashed a crooked smile. "Perhaps I'll let you know, if we should meet again."

"Till then," said Bolan.

"Until then. *Vaya con Dios.*"

Go with God.

As Bolan turned away to board his flight, he reckoned that it couldn't hurt.

The Executioner
Don Pendleton's
FACE OF TERROR

America faces an attack from within...

A cadre of violent bank robbers is wreaking havoc in the Midwest. Covered faces, jungle fatigues and foreign accents have everyone thinking an Arab terror cell is to blame. While tracking them, Mack Bolan discovers he is fighting an enemy nobody wants to suspect—American soldiers. Bolan soon realizes the group's ultimate objective is to destroy a major American city. As the deadline approaches, the Executioner decides it's payoff time, handing the traitors the ransom they deserve.

GOLD EAGLE®

Available February 2009 wherever books are sold.

ROOM 59

CLIFF RYDER

BLACK WIDOW

An isolated international incident turns into mass murder....

Young women widowed in Chechnya's bloody conflict with Russia are now willing suicide bombers. Room 59 wants an agent to go undercover as one of the Black Widows—and they recruit MI-6 operative Ajza Manaev. In a world where loyalties and the playing field are often shifting, Ajza is inducted by hellfire into Room 59's hard and fast rule. She's on her own.

Available April 2009
wherever books are sold.

GOLD EAGLE ®

GRM596